When We Were Wolves

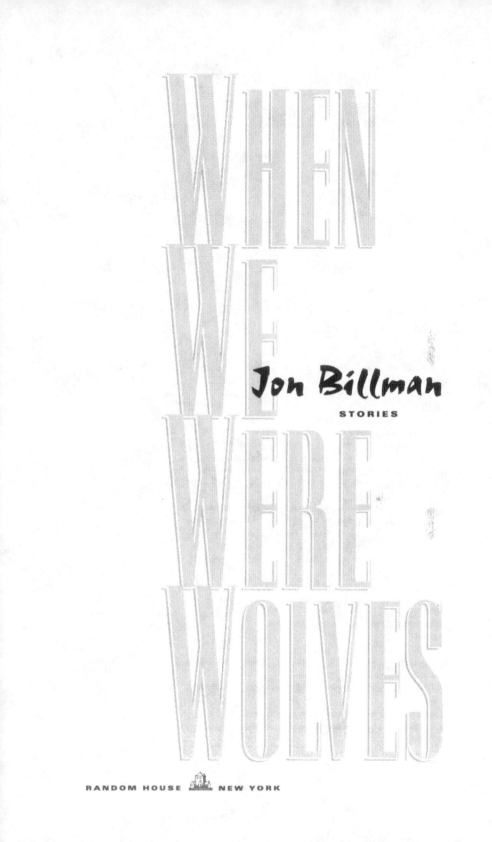

WHEN WE WERE WOLVES

Jon Billman

STORIES

RANDOM HOUSE   NEW YORK

Some of the stories in this work were originally published in
*Ascent, Esquire, High Plains Literary Review, Missouri Review,
Owen Wister Review, Paris Review, Redneck Review, Scribner's
Best of the Fiction Workshops 1997, South Dakota Review,
Zoetrope,* and ZYZZYVA. In addition, "Calcutta" appeared on
the Sam Adams Web Page.

Library of Congress Cataloging-in-Publication Data
Billman, Jon.
When we were wolves : stories / Jon Billman.
p. cm.
ISBN 978-0-812-99231-1
1. Country life—West (U.S.) Fiction.   2. West (U.S.)—Social
life and customs Fiction.   I. Title.
PS3552.I472W48   1999   813'.54—dc21   99-14952

Random House website address: www.atrandom.com

BVG 001

Book design by J. K. Lambert

146484122

FOR HILARY

I was obliged to submit to being helped back to camp, and in the cool of the evening watched the return of the fishers, who were as proud of the strings of ugly little things they carried as if they had been pickerel or bass.

—Elizabeth Bacon Custer, *Boots and Saddles*

Acknowledgments

Cheers to my family, my parents, Duane and Nancy, and especially to my wife, Hilary, for the trainload of patience and the lantern-light reading. Here's to John Keeble, who shared his wine and turkey and gave me the best writing advice I've ever received: Write hard. To Mick and Pam, for a place in Zion to hang my hat. To everyone on the fire crew in Lead, South Dakota—you showed me how to identify my escape routes. Here's to Ham and Kim, Kristin Lang, and the Wyoming Arts Council. Here's to the magazine editors, to Leigh Feldman, my agent, and Courtney Hodell, my editor, for the jalopy tour of downtown Faith. To all the philosophers and liars in Kemmerer, Wyoming. And for the hand with the branding iron, here's to Annie Proulx, my friend on the other side of the Divide. May you always have tight lines, dry powder, and a shot of whiskey in your coffee cup.

Contents

When We Were Wolves

Indians

ike all prolonged natural disasters, the Dakota dust bowl bred superstition. Real estate changed hands by the bushel. The government and railroad boosters had told dirt-poor eastern farmers that if they moved into the Great American Desert and plowed, the rains would come. But unlike the chinch bugs, rain had not followed the plow here. After the buffalo were gone, the cattle ate the buffalo grass down to nothing. Then came the barbed-wire fences that only wind and soil and grasshoppers could pass through. After a few good wet years the droughts came. Then more mice and rabbits and winds. Without asking, folks in the Dakotas got parts of Texas and Oklahoma, and Canada landed good Dakota bottomland for a whistle. Townships, counties, entire states began to hold collective days of prayer to try to coax God into ending the suffering. It was a form of spiritual cloud-seeding as well as a one-ring circus. Preachers wrung their hands, looked at their shoes, then at the sky. People's new hope was that beating the socks off an Indian ball team might change the medicine.

We spent most of the Depression as barnstormers, living like the hoboes who packed the boxcars thick as blackbirds and playing other Indian League reservation teams, civic all-stars, semi-pro teams, barnstorming colored squads, CCC teams, Rotarians, and prison teams for whatever beans, chickens, Grain Belt beer, and gasoline we could get.

We drove around the Dakotas with the windows open, our mouths shut against the dirt that would settle on our teeth. Sometimes the dust would be so bad we had to keep wet handkerchiefs over our faces to breathe. When we were playing well and did have the money, we weren't allowed in most hotels or motor lodges. We stayed in the colored motels, but those were rare in the plains. Usually we stopped the car and slept with fleas and chiggers on wool blankets under the stars. Never rained anyway.

Our pitcher, Job Looks Twice, could tell the weather in his sleeve. "Hot today," he'd say in the relative cool of the morning when we set out in the old Model T for another town. Waves of heat would rise from the hood of the car. Dust rolled in the open windows and stuck to our faces. "Very hot." It was in the last of the wet years that Job, drunk as nine Indians, had fallen asleep on the tracks in downtown Sioux City, giving his right arm to a loaded eastbound grain train.

They could not reattach his arm because they never found it. For a time, just after the accident, Job cursed God and prayed that he might die. But the stump healed without infection, and unlike the rest of the country, Job's personal depression was short-lived. He cropped his hair, bought a new black traveling suit and straw fedora, and—good thing he pitched from the port side—went on to keep us well above 500. This in 1931, when it wouldn't rain any real amount on the plains for another ten years. Ever since the accident, Job could forecast the weather in his sleeve, from some feeling, or nonfeeling, where his arm used to be. We knew it wouldn't rain, for Job's barometric arm told us so. Dust was a part of our lives.

Job was a second-generation product of the missionaries and, after the accident, became obsessed with repentance. The loss of the limb had thrown the big lefty off-balance just enough to make his curve ball dance and his slider tail slick and hard. With the stump, which began just above where his elbow had been before Sioux City, he cradled his left-handed, three-fingered glove against his chest. He released the ball, followed through with his good arm, and capped the glove onto his good hand before the pitch reached the strike zone.

Job could field bunts as well as shots rifled at the mound, but he didn't need to have much range as a fielder: the other Indians—Asa Red Owl, Carp Whitehorse, Baptist Thundergrass, Walter and Jacob Elk, Jeremiah "Big Chief" Montgomery, Otis Downwind, and myself—covered the field like a trade blanket. At the plate Job learned to bunt one-handed and usually beat the throw to first.

In those days farmers and bankers would search the dawn sky for signs of rain, but the only clouds were clouds of dust, the only storms the soil-and-wind rollers that blew out of the south and west. "We cannot expect to understand the mysteries of God's weather," Job would say. He believed everything happened for a reason, God's reason. And unlike the rest of the team, Job never tried to question the logic behind it.

Besides his beloved spitball, Job was partial to another illegal gem he called his needleball. At any general store you could buy 78-rpm phonograph needles fifty for a dime. Job kept a few of the needles stuck in the seams of his trousers and a dozen or so more behind the mound under his rosin bag. With a motion that looked like he was simply wiping his only hand, he would unquiver a nee-

dle and finger it into the threads of the ball. The weight of the needle put rising zip onto his fastball and a ten-inch break in his nickel
curve. Umpires would examine the ball but never find anything because the impact with the mitt or bat knocked the needle from the
seams and into the dirt.

Before his accident Job's needleball had nearly killed a white
man over to Woonsocket. The guy had used his spikes on Baptist
Thundergrass at second base in the first inning, and Job had been
brushing him back all afternoon with a salvo of knockdowns at the
chest. Job would get the batter nervous and deep in the box, then
paint the outside corner for strikes. A fastball in the eighth got
away and he caught the batter in the temple. The man appeared
dead, but as it turned out, Job only blinded him.

The Woonsocket players, too stunned to charge the mound,
hovered around their downed comrade, fanning dust away from
his nostrils. A minister climbed out of the stands and stood over
the body, saying a prayer for his soul. Big Chief Montgomery
walked out of a dirt devil in right field and started the car while the
newly blind man held everyone's attention. The Indians lit out of
town under cover of a dust storm. Blind man couldn't do more
than snap beans for a living. Ever after the Indians steered clear of
Woonsocket.

When Job lost his arm to the grain train he had thought it was
retribution for the blinding. Arm for an eye. Job believed that if he
lived a good life his de-railed arm would be waiting for him when
he died.

"Sometimes," he said, "I'll reach for something with the arm
that's not there. A tin cup. A baseball. I can feel the thing but can't
pick it up. Then I'm aware that it will not be raining anytime soon."
Job was sure weather came from heaven. "If my good outweighs
the not-good and I make it there, I'll get my arm back. And the
blind man from Woonsocket will get his eyes."

As boys, we had an old horsehide ball my father, a missionary from Sioux Falls, had given us. Though I was white and Presbyterian as hell, I had hair black as a crow. I wore it long and braided. I tanned like a buffalo hide under the sun. My father's life work was to save the heathen from the fires of damnation. When the Indians took to barnstorming, I chose baseball over Jesus, packed my Sunday suit in a canvas satchel, and set out for the open prairie with the Everywhere Spirit.

We had all grown up together in Porcupine, playing prairie ball on a sand-and-rock field in the cool of early evening. As kids, when the Cubs and White Sox games were on and the weather allowed for good reception, we would sit cross-legged in the mercantile owned by Asa's mother and listen through the static on a storage-battery neutrodyne set to the Chicago teams on WLS. The nine of us, shiny black hair, no shirts, dirty bare feet, stared at the radio among the canned goods. The radio put the idea of professional baseball into our heads. We would play ball, passing around our one and only glove, taking turns spitting Red Man chaw into the sweet spot and working it in with our fists. We learned to field bad hops bare-handed, bad hops being the rule.

Job stayed out past dark every night, throwing at a red strike zone painted on an outhouse behind the store. Throw, walk, pick up the ball, back to the makeshift mound, throw again at the target he could no longer see. Job's pitching made a slow, metered thump against the weathered wood, like the beating of a drum at sunset.

I began to stay behind with him to catch, where the whistling sound of his pitches became so familiar that soon I could catch Job in the dark. Though I was small and skinny, I grew to realize that my purpose in life would be to wear the secondhand tools of ignorance in the dirt behind home plate.

"How's the arm tonight?" I'd yell to Job as I squatted to catch a fastball, knowing he wouldn't answer. His mind was too busy listening to the electric hum of his pitches.

We got the red-and-gray wool-flannel uniforms, patched and stained, but free, from a women's relief circle over in Mud Butte. The uniforms were at least ten years old, having belonged to a team of white ranch hands. The team name came easy—the felt letters across the chest already scripted: MUD BUTTE INDIANS.

—

The Indians' play had much in common with the colored teams of the time. We were hustlers. We liked to bunt. We loved to steal third and home. We utilized the squeeze play and the hit-and-run. We knew about sacrificing.

Sometimes our aggressiveness cost us runs. But often, against the better teams—colored teams and semi-pro squads out of Aberdeen or Jamestown or Dickinson or Mobridge or Chadron or Stillwater—we made up the difference between losing and winning through hustle alone. This with only an hour or two of bad sleep in the car and just nine players—no one on the pine. Job Looks Twice had to pitch the entire game, and even doubleheaders some Sundays. The winning was so easy we sometimes put one of the Elk brothers on the mound and rested Job's arm. Some days we played our hearts out and won. Other days a different luck would pick up a bat and knock us into the next county.

Close calls always went to the other team. Called strikes were unheard-of. Job never argued with umpires, because he knew it was fruitless. The umps had the support of the fans, who sometimes resembled angry mobs. The other teams had to either go down swinging or hit the ball into play so we could glove it.

Our vested interest in winning games went well beyond pride. When we didn't win we didn't get paid. We were in high demand.

Our name was hoodoo. Many people believed that beating the Indians would bring a break from the dust. As well as being the catcher, I also arranged the Indians' schedule, which usually meant wiping the layers of dust from my face, tucking my braid down the back of my collar and hustling into town while the rest of the Indians scrounged up supper by the river. Except for Job. We'd find the local watering hole and speak with the mayor, the sheriff, barkeeps, the undertaker, the men who planned the games. They ran ads in the local newspapers, cartoons of feathered savages with big teeth and tomahawks running bases. Word of our winning preceded us, and opposing teams shot beanballs at our heads in the early innings. Sometimes it was a hard sell to get the men interested in playing us at all. "Beat us and maybe it will rain," I told them, their eyes on Job and the arm that wasn't there. *Hell,* their faces would say, *if we can't beat a one-armed Indian baseball team, we don't deserve rain.*

"You shouldn't sell us on rain," Job said to me once on the way back to the river camp. "It will come back to hurt us."

"Sometimes it's the only way I can sell us," I said. The more I sold the Indians as rainmakers, the less Job accompanied me to town, until finally he stopped altogether.

———

Just before the Indians lost Job to the weather for good, we'd played an honest-to-God rainmaking in Custer and won under a hot, cloudless sky. The pinewoods around Custer were terribly dry and infected with beetles, and fire threatened to flatten the entire town. Heavy woodsmoke from the lumber kilns hung in the brown trees like a premonition. The mill boss let his employees off on a Wednesday afternoon for the game and townsfolk took a desperation holiday. Custer also had gotten word that beating the Indians would bring rain. The Indians beat the Colonels 7 to 0. We were glad for the victory and downright thankful to make it out of town with our hides. They were too mad that we took away their rain to bother paying us. These white towns took their water rights seriously. It was a long time thereafter before Custer got rain.

We kept winning games and it kept not raining. Sometimes we got paid, but most often not. Job began believing in the pattern of winning and no rain, no matter how hard we tried to talk him out of it.

"Maybe it is true," Job said to me after the Custer win. "You say it when you go to town."

"I only say it so they'll want to play us. It's business," I tried to reason.

"We won the game and I know the weather," he said, gripping his empty sleeve. "There is no rain."

"Times are hard," Otis Downwind said. "Back in Winner I saw a porcupine behind the roadhouse eating on a onion."

"So what?"

Otis looked at Job and paused. "Times are hard when a porcupine's gotta eat a onion."

After a few more nonpaying, no-rain wins, when things were looking especially hungry for the Indians, I managed to set up a rainmaking game in Faith, with a couple of other games along the way. We spent the next few days in the car, heading into the setting sun, to Faith, at a bone-jarring thirty miles per hour.

———

The car wasn't a thing to rely on. The best Model Ts lasted about thirty-five thousand miles. Ours had over fifty thousand miles when Asa bought it from an old man in Mitchell. The car handled the rutted dirt roads like a cattle car. The wind and dirt had sandblasted the paint off and the body was rusted nearly through. Now and then it would backfire—Kaboom!—loud as a field gun. For relief from the heat we hung canvas water bags from the door hinges.

Condensation formed and made the air blowing over the bags less hot. When the radiator boiled over—which happened every fifty or so miles with the load of us—the bags came in handy. Some days the T started. Other days it didn't.

Tumbleweeds collected along the fencerows and dirt drifted against the tumbleweeds until it almost covered the fences. What grass was left burned. Smoke filled the sky and we never truly did see it blue. Some days, through the haze, a dirt roller would birth out of the horizon. It looked like a thunderstorm, but blacker, angrier. Sometimes it would strike while the Indians would be on a ball field, sometimes we'd be in the middle of nowhere in the Ford. The sun would disappear altogether and there'd be midnight at noon.

———

On the way to Faith we stopped to wash our uniforms and feet with rocks and powdered soap in a shallow, muddy slew of the Bad River. Job loved to fish for catfish. He would bait his hook with a grasshopper at the end of a braided line on an old cane pole he carried strapped to the car like an antenna. Some folks who had already lost everything lived along the rivers in Hoover camps. They fished for food and when the carp and catfish weren't biting there was no dinner. Out of canned hams and beets, our guys hadn't eaten since early the day before, when we caught a few bluegills and Job beaned a rain crow with a fastball. We roasted the pigeon-tasting bird over the campfire and ate it with coffee.

The next day Job landed a channel cat that must have gone fifteen pounds. He picked up the fish by the lip and walked to a little camp of tents that met with the river and the highway. He gave the cat to a family of sharecroppers with eight or ten young kids.

"What in hell," said Carp Whitehorse. "You gave them our dinner for nothing?"

"Not for nothing," Job said, shaking his stump at the third baseman. "Nothing is for nothing."

Our uniforms dried flapping in the wind on the long drive to Faith.

—

The Indians blew into town from the east. I slowed the car and idled down Main Street to the ball field at the west end of town, near the sun-bleached Lutheran church. Folks on the square pointed and stared. A brass band warmed up with scales in a weathered gazebo.

The outfield in Faith was dirt, cracked and hard, just like the in-field. Barbed wire separated center from the scrabbled wheat field, where brown-and-yellow shoots of Russian wheat gasped for water and fought to stay upright. This wheat held hope. As Job threw me some lifeless pitches and the rest of the Indians played pepper and stretched, the bleachers slowly filled with baseball fans, the con-victed, and the simply curious.

"How's the arm tonight?" I yelled to Job.

"Which one?" Job said.

There was at the time a white barnstorming team from a reli-gious settlement up in Michigan called the House of David. They let their hair and beards grow long and God-like and kept Bibles with them in the dugout. We had met the Whiskers on the road be-fore, at chautauquas and county fairs, and respected them be-cause, yes, they preached humbly to the fans before the games, but after the first pitch their spirits were real. Their fervor for God turned into a fervor for baseball and winning. They cursed like Philistines in their blue-and-gray uniforms and threw at batters' heads. A Whisker—pitcher named Benson—eventually made it to the Bigs. The games were as intense as firefights. It was like facing Jesus at every position.

This game would be our first-ever night game. Crude portable lights were trucked in along with generators. The steel stanchions were short and the lights yellow and not very bright, creating shadows behind everything. It made possible an incandescent noon at midnight. To folks in those parts, and even to us, a night baseball game was a miracle.

Farmers and the CCC crews were all off from work and gathered in town at dinnertime to eat and talk about baseball and the possibility of weather. Horses and mules pulled wagonloads of children. A Methodist church had set up an old army tent and a choir practiced and sipped iced tea. Faith had the feel of the chautauqua.

Drunk on a dram of humidity that some of the old-timers sensed, the crowd watched us take infield practice. Hope and desperation played on their faces—babies crying, mothers crying, fathers cursing and praying in the same breaths. They cheered our mistakes while grasshoppers danced in the dusky light that filtered through the dust. Ministers and deacons in dark suits and straw hats passed walnut collection plates.

———

From the tin lean-to visitors' dugout, we watched the Whiskers take infield. "I have felt weather in my arm all day," Job said while fishing the June bugs from the water bucket with the drinking gourd. "Tonight there will be weather." The air was heavy with humidity. Heat lightning flashed to the west. "We will be rewarded with God's prosperity."

In the hazy twilight both teams racked up errors involving lack of sight. As it got darker we played blind to the balls that were hit over the lights, which were many. Line drives hid in the lights and the outfielders had to react to directions from their infielders. We communicated with whistles, growls, and shrieks only the Indians understood. Even Job's breaking balls were hard to pick up in the shadows, and I had to track them by sound through the batter's grunts of frustration.

The Indians hit the ball hard and put runners on base all evening. Except for Job, who seemed to have lost a step in beating the throw to first. But we did score runs, even driving two long balls into the wheat, one with two aboard.

The umpiring had been stacked against the Indians from the very beginning. The umps were Faith Rotarians who didn't see any benefit in another Indian coup. Job couldn't get a called strike, and most of his pitches lacked snap and heat and the Whiskers spent the evening whacking breadbasket strikes into the outfield and sometimes beyond. I knew Job was convinced that throwing the game would be an offering of something more important than the purse money we would never see, a tithe of weather that would bring the Indians something more. Losing would mean rain, a final truce. Job believed he could control the hellish dry spell and its curse on all the land. He was now willing to lose on purpose, a personal sacrifice that he believed with all his soul would bring a saving rain. The other eight of us weren't convinced and wanted to beat the Whiskers like a drum.

Job kept shaking off the pitches I called, hurling instead easy fastballs, sliders that didn't slide, and change-ups that weren't much of a change. In the fourth I started to the mound to talk some sense into him, but how do you avoid a sermon at a time like that? Our eyes met. He pointed at the storm cell that was building over the Black Hills to the west. I realized I had nothing to say to him that would matter and walked back to my crouch behind the plate. More slow fastballs.

But the Indians battled hard at the plate as well. A pitching duel this wasn't. Both teams batted around two innings in a row.

———

Indians were up one at the bottom of the ninth, 13 to 12, Whiskers on first and second, two out. From his one-armed stretch Job checked the runners. Then again. He shook off my signs until we agreed on a fastball. His eyes were yellow and sorry, like the chiefs on old tobacco cans. He hadn't licked his fingers or gone to the rosin bag or the seam of his pants for a phonograph needle all game.

Then Job put a dull fastball into the wheelhouse of Joe Garner, the Whiskers' cleanup man. Garner stepped into the bucket, swung through, and massacred the easy mushball. A rainmaker. Otis Downwind in left ran underneath it just to say goodbye. The stitched horsehide that Job had always said possessed the spirit of the horse was still traveling skyward into the humidity when the wind came fast and quiet, ambushing the ball, pulling it down into the surprised glove of Otis Downwind, and ending the game.

From my knees in the dirt—the knees I can feel the big storms with now—I could hear the wall of wind coming toward the diamond like a night train.

Loud claps of thunder boomed just west of center field. Lightning struck the prairie with a dozen electric arrows. "Smell the rain!" the crowd yelled. "The miracle! Do you smell the rain! At last, thank God, the rain!"

The crowd stood, noses skyward, mouths open, like baby birds. For a moment, the Indians, too, were transfixed by the rush of wheat under the black umbrella of clouds. Then, silently, eight of us ran off the field to the car, Otis desperately throwing himself into the crank, trying to turn the engine over.

"Job, come on!" I yelled over the wind, but he didn't move, didn't even turn to look at us. By now, everyone but Otis and me were piled in the car.

The crowd reached to touch the weather, and Job, still on the mound, face to the sky, waved his gloved hand and stump in the air in exaltation. Thunder cracked as the engine fired up and the crowd yelled louder. The car sputtered slowly away from the field, picking up speed toward the dirt highway, as Otis and I ran beside it, still calling for Job.

The storm rolled eastward across the prairie, onto Faith, with the sound of a thousand horses racing to the river, and the wheat was beaten with hailstones the size of baseballs.

Kerr's Fault

e're on top of my aluminum trailer in Hams Fork, adjusting my satellite dish because the earthquake jounced it cock-eyed and instead of the French porn channel Wayne showed me I could get, I now have snow. "I got a dad in Preston, Idaho," says Wayne, pointing to the northwest with a socket wrench, says it like he's got another in Denver and maybe one in the garage, says it like he's holding on to this dad because he might come in handy someday and you just never know. "He just bought a new compressor, a real portable job. I'm gonna hook it onto this big brush I got ordered and we'll be in business." Wayne's already in business so I know this new business is recreation, sport, diversion, and maybe he'll count me in. I am glad his talk is of art. It is late afternoon and the high desert snow is starting to turn purple, like a bruise.

"What sort of business?" I ask.

"You'll see," he says. And I know he's right.

This is the Renaissance man, the Wayne Kerr I used to know, who, when I first came to Hams Fork two years ago, reached out his hand and was the only one to offer me a beer; my friend Wayne Kerr who is passed around here in conversation like so many Bible stories of miscreants and ne'er-do-wells. Wayne believes every creature on land has a counterpart at sea. He's becoming an artist again since he met Copper, his new model and his new girlfriend.

It's colder than billyhell up here, but I've got a vista. My trailer sits on the windy east scarp over Hams Fork, so that standing on the roof I am even with the water tower across town behind the school where I teach history. I can sight along U.S. 30 just this side of one of the Mormon ward houses and the port of entry where over-the-road drivers idle their rigs and secure trip permits before driving through Wyoming. Westbound, the cable of asphalt leaves the valley and turns into Utah.

I can look out over the shiny tops of trailer after trailer set in awkward rows on gritty Old Testament gray, sage and sooty snow lapping at rusty snow machines and four-wheel-drives as if someday the land, with a swarm of locusts and a hurricane wind, might muster up enough force to take back this godforsaken desert. No one wants to live up here. You are exposed and can see too much; I can look right down into the sewage-treatment plant. I see the smokestacks from the coal-burning power plant that lights half of Salt Lake City. There are mine shafts all underneath my trailer and they are on fire from an explosion fifty years ago. You can smell the smoke. It's March, the temperature doesn't get above thirty in the daytime, the regional suicide rates rise, and I still have flies.

If you are not Mormon in Hams Fork, you have a past. I was married. It pushes a man against the wall to come home from work and find everything he owns in the front yard in the rain. I have lived in a car that didn't run. Slept in libraries.

My wife was pretty, but now she lives in Illinois. Right now I am content to stand up here and watch.

—

The water tower stands like a phallus—Be fruitful!—and is our skyline. It is white and inviting: WELCOME TO HAMS FORK. Without it Hams Fork couldn't flush. The caged ladder doesn't begin until twenty feet up a leg, I guess to keep crazies or a dizzy kid from scaling the thing to paint his girlfriend's name in Day-Glo letters, or hanging himself from a rope halfway down and really giving this town something to see when the sun comes up. I teach U.S. and Wyoming history mostly, where white men put their names on everything, shot rifles at Indians and got their pictures in the textbooks and their surnames on maps. I know it by heart and it bores the hell out of me. The aluminum skin of the roof is thin—no insulation—and under the wind I can hear the faint buzz of the TV that keeps me company. I never turn it off. We don't have a town square, we have a triangle. Elevation at the triangle is 6,923 feet above sea level. Hams Fork is proud of its elevation, above most, closer to God level. The Mormon ward houses stand guard at both entrances to the valley like Monopoly hotels. They are the size of aircraft carriers and have no crucifixes, just thin steeples, antennae. I'm fighting like king-hell to keep my job and, to tell you the truth, I'm getting my teeth kicked in.

—

VACANCY flashes over the Antler Motel, just behind the empty-parked Union Pacific coal train from west of here, which sat too long in civilization and now tells a spray-paint story of Vegas or L.A.: *Westside Bombsquad, Gabriel,* city fish, black cartoon people, *Roman, Jessie,* girlfriend hearts. The big brown building southeast of the cemetery is the Afghan Apartments, where a lot of Texas and

California swampers live because they don't have to sign a lease. I lived there when I first moved to Hams Fork two years ago, and you can hear people fighting and throwing things and crying and dreaming and screwing and laughing at all hours through the thin Sheetrock walls. A lot of babies get made there. It is also where a few heads get blown off with self-inflicted shotgun blasts.

I learned this seven years ago, when I was twenty-two: nothing is easy. Once from up here on my trailer I saw a couple of gray hoboes go by below me. They weren't doing anything, just drumming through on a noisy coal train. I wonder how I'd do being a hobo, or how the hoboes would do teaching history. I'm watching Wayne work on my antennae because he knows what he is doing. The wind whips our hair like flags.

From here I've seen dogs committing intimacy. People in town below are only maybe two millimeters high. You can see the top of Wayne's house, a not-so-nice older home over on that side of the switchyard, where most of the community pillars and bishops live in very nice newer homes. All of them, actually. His house used to be a hospital when Hams Fork was just a coal camp without a name. Wayne needs to put a new roof on the place this summer—his shingles are spongy—though he probably won't; but if he asked me, I would help him do it. I would stand shirtless on Wayne Kerr's roof in our brief summer and not be ashamed. Wayne's house is close enough to mine that he could hoof it up here, but he doesn't. It's got a widow's walk and a laundry chute.

You cannot see Abraham Lincoln's head from here. But we've got it, down on I-80, a ways east. Just his big traffic-stopping head, like a huge Victorian gazing ball in the world's biggest rock garden. There are toilets and a gift shop where his boots would be. Abe himself was never west of Missouri, but he gets his head in Wyoming. He looks sort of confused.

A hawk is riding a thermal above the water tower, above the little brown birds whose names I don't know, up, around, up, up, over. I came here because in the atlas this seemed the cleanest of slates and it read like starting over. Tens of thousands of years ago, way before the coal was a sulfurous swamp, Hams Fork used to be the bottom of a deep ocean. Now, even in winter, dust covers everything.

"Ouch," says Wayne. The wrench slipped and he has scraped his knuckle against the rotor bracket, drawing slow blood in the cold. It hurts my hand just to look at it.

"Bet that hurts," I say. Wayne just looks at me, bent over at the waist. He sorta grunts. I go back to watching, waiting.

"Let's see if that does it," says sweaty Wayne. But with my ear to the aluminum, I still hear fuzz from below.

———

Today, this is what I told my first-hour Wyoming history class: Prairie women, from the East, went crazy out here because they papered their walls with white flour sacks, the snow glared white, the sun was bright, no sunglasses. No perspective. Nothing to keep them grounded. While their husbands were out hunting jackrabbits, they went crazy in a white hell. This happened mostly in Kansas and Nebraska and the Dakotas, but it adds drama to an otherwise damnright boring class.

———

Just before dark I stand up here with this monocular I ordered from a catalogue. You have to hold the thing very still because even the slightest movement distorts everything and it's more like looking through a cheap beer glass, but I watch wildlife: moose, deer, antelope, stray dogs, elk, Robin. After work I peer around and think until my stomach hurts or my face gets too numb to feel or both. When lights go on I can see people doing warm things through the windows of the Afghans.

I'm on the Black List right after Wayne, and the commandments of town life don't pertain to me anymore. They are just holding their breath until my contract runs out in May. I'm a little earwig in their hair, nothing like what Wayne is. A white moon is rising in the east. I wish the monocular was a telescope. No French satellite. It's getting dark and lights are coming on. I go for beer.

—

The earthquake caused a lot of reverberations in Hams Fork. "A five-point-five on the old Rectum Scale!" yells Wayne, letting off steam, daring God to do better, a bigger earthquake. Still no Galaxy 4, Channel 17, but I reach Wayne another can of beer, which I guess I shook up on the climb back up the ladder. Half of it runs down his arm as foam and he swallows the other half in two gulps. I tell him I read in the paper even the oil geologists didn't know about the fault and it doesn't even have a name yet and Wayne says he's not surprised and they ought to call it something profound like Kerr's Fault and I agree that that sounds as good as anything. The surprise quake cracked a hatchery pool up above Lake Viva Naughton, near the epicenter, and knocked a few dishes off shelves, sheared off some rivets on the water tower, cracked the pavement in the IGA parking lot, but did little more than give everyone something to talk about at the Busy Bee Cafe. And see to it that I'm not watching any French huff and puff while I grade bad Civil War term papers tonight. The mountains keep the vibrations in check.

Wayne says he's not sure just what is the matter. He drops a nut, which bounces once on the roof and lands silently in a scrub pine below. "You'll never find it in the snow in the dark. I'll grab one at home and drive it over later," he says.

"No hurry, I can wait," which is difficult to say. Wayne leaves. I stay to enjoy the view for a few more minutes. Robin hikes by but Wayne does not see her. She does not see me as I stand up here, stiff as the water tower, watching. I must look two millimeters tall.

I need to tell you about Robin.

—

Crazy Wayne Kerr, the used-to-be-artist, he'd tell you. His last passion left with the itinerancy of a former model, a traveling nurse; no one beautiful or vital ever stays in Hams Fork long. "The smallness of this town has beaten me into painting goddamn landscapes for goddamn tourists," he'd say with indifference in his tar-and-nicotine voice, though he makes quite a little cash from these paintings he churns out by the dozens and sells out of the office at the Antler Motel. "Now I just do crafts." Wayne says "crafts" like a filthy word, coughing it out of the back of his throat and spitting it into the wind. Wayne makes enough to keep imported green bottles of beer with foil over the caps in the old refrigerator in his studio and to pick up a dime bag of Mexican hash whenever he wants, which is quite frequently. He'll sometimes spend all night in the studio drinking, smoking, chewing, spitting, churning out twenty-minute landscapes with cheap Prang watercolors and a fanbrush, listening to that sixties and seventies music of his: old Stones, Doors, Creedence, Janis Joplin. He works three easels at a time: rock, rock, rock. Cloud, cloud, cloud. No trees. Lots of perspective.

Robin is the wife Wayne's got. She used to model for Wayne's paintings before she got to be "hippy," as he calls it. Now she just teaches math at the junior high and makes little geometrical wind chimes out of monofilament and aluminum conduit that she hangs all over their back porch and eaves. Wayne sometimes takes some to the Antler with a load of landscapes and elbows his friends into buying one here and there to keep her happy, to keep her feeling useful. Angel music, she calls the tinny pings and dings that fill the air. Music for angels and the ghosts of dead Shoshone, she says. Yes, right, make sure you write this down, Wayne's wink says.

Sometimes a tourist will want one of Robin's chimes and the guys will be sitting around drinking coffee or Cokes with morning rum and they'll look at each other from the corners of their eyes and grin and look outside to check the license plates on the tourist's car. The tourists always ask How far is it to Jackson Hole from here? Never do they buy anything on a return trip; they've already spent their wad, are tired of the excitement of it all, the raree show, don't need a fish-line wind chime. She was a nurse in Vietnam. We have in common that we both teach and are friends of Wayne Kerr, but that is about it. Robin is pretty in the way wood smoke smells nice.

I asked how far to Jackson Hole too, when I came here from the tired Midwest, because on the atlas it's only an inch, maybe an inch and a quarter, away, but this place is far from anywhere. TV tourism spots for Wyoming do not show Hams Fork. They show natty fly fishermen and chesty cowgirls grilling steaks and dinosaur eggs, Devils Tower, snowy peaks, never the desert. Never a local throwing chunks of sucker meat on a treble hook at a rainbow trout choking in runoff, never a strip mine or a PTA meeting. On TV this place looks like starting over.

Robin's hair is the color of new motor oil and she smells like apples when she walks by at a crowded district meeting. She is also on the List because of what Wayne did, because of what Wayne does. In their forties, no kids. The wind doesn't quit blowing in Hams Fork and you can hear the Kerr place all over town.

———

The administration was not impressed with my lesson about Benjamin Franklin, an artist, and I was called on the rug. Again. My lecture in question included his rendezvous with concubines, illegitimate children, painting, voyeuristic tendencies. The history books fail to mention those elements that make a man real. The Mormons pretend they never existed.

"What will you tell them in your next Ben Franklin lecture?" they wanted to know.

I answered, "He was a man with poor vision who is engraved forever in the history books but did not get his face put on a rock in South Dakota?"

"Yes," said the Mormons.

I asked Wayne once how come he doesn't just fly this place and move to Jackson or Park City and open a real gallery. "Because the tourists there tend to have more taste," said Wayne Kerr the realist. "Because our tourists are bait fishermen's wives from Ohio. Besides, I haven't finished a real painting in twenty years."

Do the Mormons want truth? "Hell no," says Wayne.

———

Through the window I have seen Wayne fly off the handle and just start throwing and kicking maybe three hundred dollars' worth of landscapes around the studio until he's so winded and shaky and coughy he can hardly stand, which doesn't take long. He's careful, though, careful not to hit the figures, the beautiful almost-finished oil figures he's kept hanging in gold no-glass frames next to the oil figure studies on cheap gessoed paint-board scraps that form a collage in the studio as a reminder: a reminder of what he used to do, what he has done, will do again.

I could feel for Robin.

———

I wait an hour and call Wayne but he isn't home yet. It is dinnertime for most people here. Robin checks and says, Yes, their satel-

lite dish is fine and sure enough their French porn channel—
Galaxy 4, Channel 17—is coming in clear as sunshine, but I know
she doesn't watch it and Wayne doesn't need it, so wouldn't you
know, they're getting it loud and clear now. She adds that there's a
new crack in the foundation along the side of the garage where the
studio is, and wasn't that quake something. She'll send Wayne over
when he gets in. That is, if he gets in, because Wayne is probably
seeing Copper over whiskey sours at the Number 9. This is the
most we have ever talked and I don't say this to Robin, don't wish
to make her sad. But Robin knows Copper will leave and take with
her Wayne's new passion, and passion, she knows, Wayne needs
like oxygen, vitamin D, and fat in winter; she tells herself she married an artist and can't bear a passionless Wayne. We talk about
California weather and school. Since the quake I pick up garbled
AM radio over the telephone. It's not real clear but the Jazz game
is on and for a minute I listen to the fantasy of professional bas-
ketball and Robin's voice.

—

He is painting real paintings again. "Pictures," Copper calls them
in her nasal red-haired Montana accent. "Beautiful pictures," she
says in a way that allows for the fact that she's in them. He's even
growing his beard back, though this time it is streaked with gray.
Copper is from Billings, an explosives engineer fresh out of School
of Mines where, Wayne tells me, she switched from electrical en-
gineering when she found she had a penchant for blowing things
up. She's with the Wyoming branch of some outfit out of Houston
that puts out derrick fires with dynamite. Word of mouth had it
that Wayne Kerr used to do figures, nudes, and she approached
him at a junior high faculty party where she was a date of one of
the assistant football coaches who spent the better part of the
party overshaking everyone's hand and drawing plays on damp

cocktail napkins. "I hear you're into oils," she said to Wayne, making a little "o" with her lips on "oils" and sucking the rest of the word in like good cigar smoke. They talked for an hour and a half while Robin ate celery. Copper rides a vintage motorcycle and Wayne says she's good and wild and narcissistic and that that ain't easy to please. I see here in the Casper *Star-Tribune* that geologists still can't pinpoint the fault.

—

Okay.

So the superintendent and principal are on me. I am a good teacher and that is a problem for them. They make unannounced visits and just sit in my classroom, taking notes and trying to get to me, write me up on trifles they find in dusty policy books, then put the pink slips in my permanent file. It doesn't matter that I can lecture the hell out of Thomas Jefferson, the Gettysburg Address, or women's suffrage (Wyoming was the first). They are frustrated because they cannot write *Is a friend of Wayne Kerr* in my file. I buy beer. I like blue movies. They know because they watch. They see. Things are harder for Robin; she has tenure and they must ride her harder, search a little deeper, raise their voices a little more. They just won't hand me a new contract in May, they'll have a fat file of why's, and I'll be starting up again in another middle of nowhere somewhere else. Though those places are becoming fewer. It isn't easy, but there is a point you have to hit where you quit sweating. With each move I travel a little lighter. I'm just not quite sure which side of that point I'm on.

—

It is March and not nearly spring, not nearly warm, not nearly the May or June recess we get from winter. But Copper is out there in the night, a whiskey shadow on her old piston-knocking Indian

Chief motorcycle, though it still snows hard and the north winds from Canada and Montana still blow and howl like hell and find every bad rivet and seam on this trailer; out there in her leather jacket and faded jeans with holes and grease and tears all up and down her legs and nothing underneath, long red mane flying behind her. Up and down Main Street, Antelope Street, U.S. 30 and 189; all over Carmel County, miles of black snowdrift backdrop. She leaves a trail in the cold from the bike's hot exhaust and the breath that comes from deep inside her. I hear the Indian—the Indian!—as I climb onto the roof, and watch her streak through the warm fog of streetlights.

People get a little anxious this time of year. Mormons have turned to coffee. I've seen Copper open a beer bottle with her eye socket. The fire of that Indian is rhythmic and steady, something heartening. I hope Wayne will be by soon.

———

Mormons populate more than half of this town—almost three quarters. They're on the school board and the town council, and they own the grocery store and all of the gas stations. The Mormon priesthood have visions and see things against their eyelids. What I am going to tell you next is in my file. They know I helped Wayne one night when he airbrushed Revelation 22:18 and left his mark on thirty-two cars of a Union Pacific coal train that took half an hour to lumber through the switchyard at the center of town that next morning: "I warn every one who hears the words of the prophecy of this book: if any one adds to them, God will add to him the plagues described in this book." On the last car, the one right after "book," Wayne sprayed this cartoon Joseph Smith hammering away on a laptop computer and the Book of Mormon spitting out of a laser printer. Cartoon Joe had a little name tag above his pocket, just like the guys at the Chevron station: *Joe*. I just carried the big carbon dioxide tanks and paint—Wayne's got a bad back—but they knew. Copper kept watch, though it was okay because the train was parked out in the middle of Pratt Canyon, real nowhere. It started getting light and Wayne didn't get the "Book of Mormon" quite finished, so that it read "Book of Mor," but everyone got the idea. This made the paper in Cheyenne when the Revelation rolled through on its way to Omaha and power plants farther east. It was the first time I had felt alive and useful since the idea of being married stopped sounding like a good one. I don't feel that alive now. Wayne's an atheist, but he knows his Bible.

The Hams Fork *Gazette* front page called it "Juvenile Graffiti," but Wayne just called it something for the boys at the bar. "In this place you've got to make your own fun," he says. This is true and I'm glad to see it, and with Copper, Wayne makes much more of his own fun more often. Every once in a while now you'll see one of Wayne's words roll through town: plagues, words, if, one, book, God. His new paintings are impressive.

It's all right to go to the bar more often now that I'm new history, a lame duck soon to be extinct like so many dinosaur birds buried in the high-desert sand. I go with Wayne because he has never bought in to living with someone else's standards and his attitude gives me a lift. He writes editorials to the *Gazette* (the *Gazoo*, he calls it) under the pen name Stephen Hero, Star Route, Hams Fork, Wyoming. He harangues the mayor, the town council, the school board, the Carmel County sheriff, the bishops, the superintendent, the chief of police. All for fun, he says, all for fun. I don't really give a shit about any of that, Wayne claims after really throwing the dictionary—sometimes the Bible—at them. All for fun. The thing is, though, he is always dead-on and the written replies in next week's paper never touch him. But they are keeping score for sure, bet everything they are, a running count. Wayne's new word, I think he coined it, is "Custerian."

—

I don't sleep well anymore. The alcohol helps. I get recurring nightmares. It's evening in the dream, summer and green. I'm at the drive-in with friends and peers and most times they have dates. We laugh and drink and make fun of the movies. Between features all the other cars leave but ours. Then the big gray speaker in the window quits working and we only can see the movie, not hear it, but we don't mind and sometimes don't even notice. Then the picture gets fuzzy and I guess I must fall asleep. When I wake up in the dream I am alone. It's cold and the windows are iced over from the inside. I try to start the car from the back seat and the starter just grinds. I get out of the back seat in just my underwear and run around in the snow. No one is here at this boarded-up theater in the middle of nowhere. The marquee out front reads CLOSED FOR SEASON. I look back toward the car and my footprints are blown over. I didn't bring a shovel. I have jumper cables but I'm alone in the world. Every dream it's a different drive-in.

—

A while back we worked out a deal. I'm learning to sketch, a first step. Wayne lets me sit in the studio for twenty minutes or half an hour now and then and I sketch from what he has already done, his work with Copper and the unfinished figures and parts on the walls: arms, legs, breasts, hips, faces, sex, and shadows. In exchange for lessons and studio time, I change his oil and wash, sometimes vacuum, his truck. I'm going to run the idea by him of maybe sketching Robin sometime, maybe paint her. If I make it that far. For some Polaroids of Copper I gave Wayne two racks of Heineken.

—

"Persistence of the New West" he will call his next exhibit, and when he says this he looks a little younger, a little thinner, a little taller. He's even making his own paints with lead and cadmium, toxins from deep in the ground that Wayne says are truer in color and tell a more accurate story. Copper has been posing in cowboy boots and nothing else, Stetsons, lariats; she has posed with little mini-cigars, a fringed leather jacket over naked skin, a buffalo hide, skis, branding irons, whiskey bottles, Susan B. Anthony dollars, a rawhide whip, nothing, fly-fishing vest, chaps.

I have seen them work when Robin says they're in the studio and I walk out, not wanting to disturb them, and look through the curtain crack in the little foundation window. There is an energy that fills the air and ground of the studio; art and sex, yes, but also, somehow, magic. The mad, naked nude painter, Wayne Kerr. Copper, like art-history-book prints of Titian's Mary Magdalene looking to the sky in ecstasy, wraps her long hair around naked shoulders, breasts, sex. He puts his Rockies cap on backwards and a thick black-handled brush crossways in his teeth and bites down on it as color rushes and swirls for minutes at a time until the session is over, until he's slick with sweat, the pain is gone, the egg is out, the painting is begun; until the mouth brush is splintered, wet with tobacco spit, used. I've seen it more than once. Then he'll take her, most always from behind like a dog, and they'll scratch and howl and bite and curse, Copper's white breasts turning red with heat, Wayne's hairy waist and gut heaving with in-rut, mythical lust, really driving his back into it. He plays a lot of Mozart now. It's been a long time since Wayne has had one of his landscape-kicking fits.

———

The UPS driver is a Mormon. Wayne and I are convinced our packages ride around town for a few extra days but what can you do? I'm opening a package of new paints, safe paints, wash-with-water acrylics, and glance out my front window and see Robin walking. I often see her walking, hiking out her frustrations at having her name uttered in the same sentences as mine when the microphones are turned off at school board meetings and in the lounge before the 8:15 bell rings, where a clique of teachers are taking last hits on their Monday-morning herb tea. She is frustrated from being looked at by housewives when she's searching—maybe humming a hymn or a folk song—through the cereal aisle, looking for Honeycombs for Wayne.

She takes long, strong strides and stares straight ahead, inhaling, exhaling hard, sweating, her breath trailing behind her, misting her long brown hair until it vaporizes and another puff of breath takes its place. She walks down a stretch of fenced-in yard where a young elkhound is thrilled to be running beside her until the end of his fence, where Robin looks at him like she could be party to every dog wish if only that were in the design of things, and for twenty yards or so it is. She walks past the stockyards and rodeo grounds, up the BLM road that leads to the radio towers and relay station on top of Sarpy Ridge. The snow is deep and less sooty up there, well above me. Through my monocular I'll see her trudging through thigh-deep drifts, kicking, slapping at the white with her fists, throwing it, daring the earth to move. The snow dampens her screams of anger—anger because she is under fire for what her husband did and anger because she is not an Indian-riding redhead with big tits and shit for morals—until she gradually disappears into the blackening winter sky. By daylight the wind has wiped clean her tracks, footprints that from down here are only sixteenths of an inch, millimeters apart. Wayne says her mind deals in the concrete and they are concretely married and he still comes home most nights and still puts his dishes in the dishwasher.

Up there maybe there's less chance her prayers get trapped in the inversion of wood and coal smoke that sometimes hangs over the valley. But maybe those prayers blow to Utah. She copes. Robin is from California, where they have real earthquakes.

———

I'm grading some horrid red-pen term papers and watching aerobics, which I can still get on ESPN, and drinking a beer. It's ten o'clock or so now, but I'll skip the news. Women. The knock at the door is Wayne in overalls. Before I answer he mounts the ladder with the new fifteen-millimeter nut he promised me this afternoon and I'm in my living room with the remote control and the window open. I set the control box to Galaxy 4, Channel 17. Fuzz, snow, snow, okay! "That's it!" Three French women have cuffed a no-clothes policeman to the radiator and are smearing him with ice cream and licking it off to some kind of psychedelic Wagnerian fugue, *dow dow dowww, whokaneeow, whokaneeow.* Wayne tightens up the nut on the antennae, pounds across the metal roof and back down the ladder. I go outside to meet him, to thank him. He's breathing hard and looking through the window at the TV. "You know," he says, "what does this tell you about the state of our nation?"

"This is France," I say.

"That's right. Use your phone?"

Wayne checks in with Robin. I can feel the weight of her disappointment on the other end, Wayne's excitement on this end.

"You still with me here, man?" asks Wayne.

"I thought you were going to get some new equipment. From your dad?" I'm stalling for myself, but I know I'm in. Wayne doesn't even hear me. The dogs are running tonight.

This is a problem I seem to always have had: How do I know how much I have? And how do I know when I am losing it? I get up and pull my coveralls on, go out to the truck, and we're off. "Hey," says Wayne. "You can hear those UFO freaks from that Albuquerque station on your phone."

We park in the sage on the other side of U.S. 30. The only traffic is an occasional semi, so there is no real effort involved in keeping unseen. It's clear and the moon makes it possible to pick up outlines well without being seen from a distance.

"Look at that honey moon," says Wayne. "Magical." It creates a shadow over everything we do. A bolt cutter makes short work of the lock on the cyclone and barbed-wire gate. I muscle the ladder off the truck and drag it to the base of the tower. Wayne fixes a bandanna over his face like a nineteenth-century highwayman, turns his cap around, throws a climbing rope over his shoulder, and nods at many quarts of paint, the pressure regulator and tanks—twenty pounds of gas in heavy steel cylinders, three of them—in the rusty truck bed, nothing lightweight from the Idaho dad. I just get the ladder telescoped and steady and, like a kid on a beer buzz hell-bent to spray his girlfriend's name on the tank, bad-back Wayne scoots a quarter of the way up, to where the caged ladder starts, before I get to the bottom with the clumsy tanks. Over my breathing I can hear soft pings like hail on aluminum as Wayne takes to the top like a house spider. I look up and can barely make out the WELCOME I've seen a hundred times. It's Wayne's canvas tonight. He drops me the rope.

My face and fingertips go numb in the sharp midnight cold. The air is thin—another hundred and fifty feet above sea level—and I'm shaky when I get to the top and get the godawful-heavy CO_2 tanks hoisted up with us. Heights are not as intimidating in the softness of moonlight. I look down. Who has not thought about what jumping into shadow would be like, before you have to be pushed, knowing from cold memory what is there in the daylight? Would you pass out in the air from fear? Would you still be alive after landing? Without the conviction to pull it off, these thoughts are pretty harmless. I lock the couplings in, adjust the regulator, and Wayne is in business at fifty psi. "I'm cold," he says. "What took you so long?" But he's been busy painting in his mind, preparing, sweat beading on his high forehead and breath freezing on his beard in the stinging wind, an athlete. His eyes are dark and intent, pen-and-ink Zeus eyes from junior high textbooks.

I can see the dim reflection on my trailer, across the valley. From here it looks cold and empty, like a beer can in a field, looks like it will blow away and keep blowing and not stop for barbed wire or Nebraska in the western wind. Two windows are lit at the Afghans, yellow and warm like cabin lanterns. Wayne's drafty house. Lights are on, Robin is awake, grading papers, pacing, worrying. Coyotes are singing.

The heavy, old, and leaky Paasche airbrush hisses, a high-pressure serpent in Wayne's hands. His strokes are swift and graceful. He turns his head only to spit over the edge. I watch for police cars and hit him on the back when I see the lights below. We freeze for a moment until the headlights turn away—a bread truck, a mine truck—then he starts in again, blending densities with overspray, caressing with pressure. His painting becomes a mating dance, which has been rehearsed hundreds of times in his mind. I am cold. Wayne gradually strips as he sweats and soon he's down to only dark, holey polypropylene underwear and backwards Rockies cap. He pauses, wheezing, only to switch the airbrush tips I retrieve from the rucksack of tools on my back, dump the paint cup, and for me to change colors: True Blue, Grass Green, Spectrum Yellow, Ruby Red. I clean tips and hand the fresh brushes to Wayne like a caddy. It's hard for me to make out the painting completely. Wayne slows to work in detail. The half hours grow into hours, history.

"You'll see it when it's light and it's finished," Wayne tells me when I disturb him once to ask what it is. "To tell you now would be to drain my creative energy, to change what I have, risk killing fruition."

"Okay," I say. It is all I say for the next few hours. The painting is coming alive.

The moon has moved across the sky. It's getting lighter out. The hills go from midnight moonlit blue to morning lark. I see deep concern in his face—not panic, but he picks up his pace. I trust in Wayne, though cheating time is something even Wayne Kerr cannot do.

"That's it," he says, putting his overalls back on. With the finest brush tip I pulled up here, this is what he signs in black letters too small to see from below: *w. kerr.* I let out the deep part of my breath that I've been holding all night. We double-check everything, drop the tanks on the rope, descend the ladder, Wayne first, and hustle to the truck. Wayne gets there before me, cranks the old V-8 over while I collapse the ladder, strap it to the truck, lift the tanks and rucksack in. The cab is warm by the time I open the door, the radio is on, Wayne is whistling.

———

At my trailer we open beers, unfold lawn recliners in the snow that is my front yard, and wait for sunrise to unveil the night's work. "Apollo, get your dead ass over Sarpy Ridge!" yells Wayne so that the town below might hear. It's still cold but anticipation is warming, so I forget about it. It's like ice fishing, snow and cold up to my own lounging ass. Waiting for the picture show. Wayne slips inside for more beer and some old doughnuts.

I use my cordless phone to call in sick from my lawn chair so Wayne cannot hear me apologize. The phone rings in my hand like the last straw before I hit the call button. "Hello?" It is the urgent Mormon accent of my principal. "Sorry, I'm sick today," I say. "I can't come in early to meet with you." Over the phone I hear radio interference in the background; they're having hot dogs and green beans at the high school, church bake sale tonight, cattle prices are steady. "I realize it may be important. Put it on a big pink slip. I'll need a sub." A guy over in Farson took his head off with a snow machine and a barbed-wire fence. "Yes, lesson plans are on my desk." Game and Fish will limit deer and elk tags next fall. I fake a cough and hang up. U.S. 30 to Jackson is slick in spots. Geologists found the fault, hooked their equipment up, and named it something I couldn't make out because of the fuzzy AM reception on this cheap telephone. It sounded like "Bring 'em asphalt," but that isn't it.

The first real daylight to come over the ridge is softened with clouds and light snow. The legs of the tower reach up into the fog and support an ethereal redhead mermaid, an enormous half-trout, tuna-can Copper. Shaking with tired and cold I raise my monocular to her to see the detail. I take a deep breath to steady myself, my vision clears. She is art. Slender, asexual amphibian hips and stiff traffic-pylon nipples. Her fluent hair is the same color as the stripe down her speckled side that makes her a *rainbow* troutwoman.

She is sitting on a rock just underneath WELCOME TO HAMS FORK. Below the rock, in flowing cursive letters: *Gateway to Zion and the* GRAND TETONS. She is holding a trident and smoking a mini-cigar. She is complete.

Hams Fork is waking up. Wives and moms are beating pancake mix, scrambling eggs, not making coffee. An occasional orange mine truck rattles along Antelope Street. A four-wheel-drive with whip antennae and a light bar is spinning up the lane, my front yard. It's Frank Grant, chief of police. Wayne waves with his beer-less wedding-band hand. Frank gets out not smiling and adjusts the equipment belt under his belly. "Let's see the hands, Hero," he says. Wayne smiles a doughnutty grin, sets his beer in the snow, swallows, and lays his palms over like a magician. His hands are enameled black, green, Copper-red. My hands are mostly clean and I hold them up like a child counting to ten.

"I'm an artist, Chief," says Wayne, voice full of possibility.

———

In a couple of days photographs of "Wayne's Rainbow" will hang in both bars in town, next to bowling trophies and framed black-and-white photos of rodeo cowboys on bucking horses. Pictures will be shown to me at my contract meeting. On Sunday morning, in both Mormon wards, they will talk about us: me, Copper, Joseph Smith, Robin, Jesus Christ, and Wayne Kerr. Next fall's school calendar is already printed. Copper will apply for a transfer to the city in Texas. She'll get it. She has ridden Hams Fork to exhaustion. Just up and leaving is acceptable, expected in the West.

Robin will keep walking, sweating, and making wind chimes for angels. Looking after Wayne. Loving him despite of, and because of, his passion for art and wildlife.

I'll get out the atlas I keep in the bathroom with back issues of *Wild West* magazine and a Gideon Bible, though I'm beginning to see that opportunity here runs only so far that way until it turns into California. Tomorrow I will take a Big Chief tablet and a dull number two pencil into my principal's office, shove them under his gray nose like a divorce, and say, "Excuse me. Put my recommendation here, you no-balls, Diet Coke–drinking, blacklisting, goddamned son of a bitch." And he'll do it.

The Mormons will talk prophetically of select revelations, earthquakes, and visions. And I will be as alone as I have ever felt.

———

But if you could have been around Hams Fork a hundred and fifty years ago, and passed through the landscape as a beaver-trapping tough with Jim Bridger or Jedediah Smith, before coal barons, before Mormons, soda ash, and oil, before you could stand outside and watch satellites pass through the night sky or silhouettes kissing in warm apartment windows, when this history was wild and new, you could have just pointed and named something of permanence, a mountain, a river—at least a creek—after yourself. Or they would have named it for you, a permanent mark, just for being here.

Wayne Kerr will continue to shake this little town like a ball bearing in a paint can.

Custer Complex

Kurt Strain was being sent to a ghost fire. The Monday before Thanksgiving he received orders from the National Inter-agency Fire Center in Boise to act as Incident Commander on a large project fire in the Sioux Ranger District of the Custer National Forest, Camp Crook, South Dakota. He had just returned home to Wyoming from a controlled burn to manage chaparral in central California, thinking his season over. Global warming, he thought. A swamp fire in the South maybe, but South Dakota? Custer Complex, the fire the computer was sending him to now, had burned two years before. Now the Custer Complex was cold as a file cabinet: sixty thousand acres of charred snags, ash, and snow.

They sent resources anyway; the computer had the final word. Logistical arrangements had already been made before the situation could be confirmed by a staff or committee of human beings in the brass echelons of Forest Service management, several of whom were halfway through double Johnnie Walker Reds and a tray of stuffed mushrooms at the Occidental Grill in Washington, D.C., when the order went out. Strain was a computer ghost himself now because the computer was the only commander that kept track of his whereabouts. But he was a good firefighter and he had experience. The season should have been over for him, but instead he was being called to an old fire that had burned out two years ago; he didn't know this, but it wouldn't have surprised him. Strain wondered how much longer he would be able to put up with the bureaucracy. He repacked his fire gear, including the six-weight Orvis Western Traveler fly rod and box of nymphs and drys; he planned on digging in.

———

The season had started in April, southern Arizona, when two nine-year-old boys soaked a Gila monster in gasoline and lit it on fire. The lizard skittered into the juniper, and nine thousand acres later Kurt Strain, the saw boss, found himself supervising four sawyers— out-of-work loggers who knew a great deal about power saws and dropping large trees, and very little about fire behavior. Strain's objective there had been simple: make sure the sawyers don't get burned over.

In the desert short-pine savannas of the Southwest they had worked at night, by headlamp and moonlight. The humidity would rise however slightly, the temperature would drop, and the fire would lie down until midmorning. Strain loved night duty, fishing at night with the scorpions and bats. He spoke to himself in the darkness, "Kurt Strain, common tree shrew, learns to fly like the Mexican fishing bat."

Forest Service records showed that Strain had been officially reprimanded for, among other acts of insubordination, fishing on the job. He lined his crew out on a detail, then rigged up the fly rod he kept in a map tube in his fire pack. The Fire Safety Officer and Division Group Supervisor were not impressed by the rumors, though Strain was somewhat of a cult hero to the firefighters, the ground pounders. He rarely ate MREs, the Forest Service's surplus military rations: Strain ate fish grilled over the coals of whatever conflagration he happened to be on. In Arizona he had caught endangered Gila trout and Apache trout, a threatened species. These fish he released unharmed, opting to eat the more prevalent rainbows and cutthroats.

An old regulation, still on the Forest Service books, allowed for one bottle of beer with lunch. This didn't include fire duty, though it wasn't unusual for beer to get packed into Strain's spike camp with the water, saw gas, fusees, and bar oil; this was the West, the Forest Service, and drinking beer was not drinking.

—

Strain's insubordination started after a campaign on a series of high-desert fires in western Colorado. A unit of hotshots was sent to a mountain to control a fire in heavy piñon juniper and bur oak—nothing salable. Their safety had been sacrificed for a public-relations stunt. Residents of a small subdivision five miles away were watching operations with binoculars from their patios. The prudent thing would have been to let the fire burn up the ridge, then over and down to a Cat line on the other side. It was all desert and didn't need to be saved. The order went through to stop the fire's run before it torched out at the ridge. Strain's crew had been choppered in to help retrieve the fourteen bodies, most of them college kids.

At thirty-six, Strain now realized that the Forest Service was less an overevolved branch of the Boy Scouts than a branch of the military. Catch 22. Once you started questioning logic, nothing on a project fire made sense, and it became very difficult to work sixteen-hour days and nights, taking inane orders, accomplishing little other than comforting a public raised on Smokey Bear. He began fishing. Carrying a concealed fly rod was not legal grounds for dismissal; his supervisors never caught him blatantly fishing on a shift. They knew he did, but couldn't prove it, so they busted him down to a seasonal firefighter from his full-time position as a timber sale manager. They were sure this would cause him to quit. Instead each fire season got a little longer and he readily made enough money to do nothing other than hunt, ski, and fish all winter long. His true life's work. Let some Fucking New Guy or lifer charge hell with a bucket of water.

An unprecedented buildup of forest fuels, a severe drought, and consistently dry storm systems that contained much ground-to-cloud lightning had resulted in five million acres burning left of the ninety-eighth meridian by mid-July. Strain was convinced of global warming and he planned to adjust by spending more time fishing. The geographical frontiers gone, he believed the next frontier would be weather: hurricanes, blizzards, monsoons, infernos. The flap of a butterfly's wings in Argentina *does* cause a tornado in Texas; we wouldn't win the war against the elements. When things got bad enough, he would drive to Baja, live off the gutted peso, and take up marlin on the fly.

According to the Forest Service, the world would end in fire. The flammable buildup came on the skids of years of successful fire suppression. Now the fires—most ignited by lightning—burned hotter and faster than ever before. A thick haze hung in the sky over two time zones, and the eastern vacationers stayed on their side of the river and attended ball games and theme parks, played golf, and motored through Civil War battlefields with the windows up. The western smoke reached even the easterners, intensifying their sunsets, turning them a deep salmon, the color of steak closest to the bone.

In August Strain worked as a crew rep, a liaison between three twenty-man Bureau of Indian Affairs handline crews and the fires' Incident Command teams. Crew reps were minor administrators, glorified baby-sitters, politicians. They made sure the Montagnards carried their fire shelters, washed their feet, and didn't suck a bottle. Strain slowly led the Indian crew, following lightning fires up western Colorado and back into Wyoming, where they'd started. The Indians, who were often aloof and laid-back to a point of being dangerous to themselves and others, quickly tried his patience, and for Strain the assignment became a painful endurance event. *The next time I'm mobilized as a crew rep,* he wrote in his post-incident evaluation, *I'd better be in charge of real firefighters or a company of sorority pledges from Michigan.*

The all-white crews he led approached forest fires as if in war. It had occurred to Strain years before that the white people would never live with the West the way natives could before the advent of the reservations. They would always be battling droughts, floods, snow, cold, heat, infestations, wildfire. He realized he was more like the Indians, in it for different reasons than saving the West's precious timber resources for Boise Cascade and Georgia Pacific shareholders to get richer. Given the choice between summer camp and all-out war, he'd be roasting marshmallows. Call it selfish.

———

The government policy of suppressing Indians like they suppressed fire was simple on paper, but it went against every natural law, and in turn cost the taxpayers billions. But fire is fire and Strain was indispensable in a tight spot; the men who worked with him knew it.

By October things had cooled considerably and he began a series of controlled burns, pyratory exercises that burned tracts of heavy fuels to improve vegetation and lessen the chances of an uncontrolled, unpredictable fire later. It was doing God's work in hasty catch-up fashion. The Forest Service had dipped into Smokey Bear funds to run a multimillion-dollar ad campaign to inform the public about the need for these controlled fires. As he sorted beadhead nymphs and stoneflies and tucked the aluminum fly box into his redpack, Strain remembered thinking a good idea would be to wait for an easterly wind, run a hot line from southern Oregon to Mexico, and burn out the entire state of California. In November his mucus turned from black back to clear. He flew back to Dubois, where he thought he'd have a winter season of fly tying and reading.

—

A man in a Stetson rancher, jeans, and green Forest Service shirt arrived for Strain in a mint-green pickup. They were headed to the blue-and-orange Bell Jet Ranger on the grass tarmac in a pasture at the edge of town. The chopper was taking Strain to South Dakota to the ghost fire.

In the pickup, Strain studied the faxed incident report. The driver briefed Strain as they drove.

"Where are my resources?" asked Strain.

"Right now? My guess is the casino bar. Initial resources have been ordered. Looks like you're getting reservation handline crews from Pine Ridge, Rosebud, and Standing Rock. They'll be there as soon as they can sober up and get on the bus, I guess. The pilot's name is Sherman Two Crows. We call him Mayday. He's been flying fire all summer. Knows what he's doing."

The tail of the chopper read: TOMAHAWK CHARTERS AND HELI-SKI. Mayday was a mercenary. The belly of the craft was smoked black. The Forest Service cowboy walked up to the bubbled window and banged on it with his fist. Mayday started awake. "Yeah, okay," he said. He had long, oil-black hair and a sparse goatee of long, threadlike whiskers, like a catfish. He wore his headset over a

Spokane Indians baseball cap, a Nomex jumpsuit, bright orange like a prisoner's, and logging boots. Mayday gestured for Strain to throw his redpack in the back and get in the other side.

"Good luck," said the cowboy.

The big turbine whined and struggled to take. Mayday smelled of garlic and Jet-A fuel. Mud-caked floor panels. Strain had seen cleaner bulldozer cabs. The windows were scarred and the insides covered with the hulls of sunflower seeds. Between the front seats stuck the battered, oily twenty-eight-inch bar of a Stihl 044 chain saw, stained red with slurry or blood. A couple of grasshoppers caromed off the insides of the windows. "What's the chain saw for?"

"To cut trees with," Mayday said.

"Why do you have it beside you?"

"Sometimes you gotta cut your way down."

Good Lord, Strain thought.

The rotors took and beat the stiff wind. Mayday pulled on the collective with his left hand. The ship rose five feet in the air. He twisted the cyclic between his legs as if it were the handle on an antique coffee grinder. Seams creaked.

"What year is this thing?" asked Strain. Untrimmed, the ship spun 180 degrees on an axis of cold, dry air, rose, and nosed east, with the wind.

" 'Seventy-six," Mayday said. A brown grasshopper landed and stuck against his forearm. "Eighteen seventy-six. Custer wishes he would have had this son of a bitch at the river."

After a turbulent jump over the Shoshone and Bighorn ranges they flew in silence over the Powder River and the sage country of eastern Montana, dusted white with what little snow could cling to the prairie in the cold late-autumn wind. The bird flew over the Seventh Cavalry's route to the Little Bighorn from Fort Abraham Lincoln in North Dakota.

Mayday looked bored and hungover. He sipped from a plastic Mini Mart coffee mug and chewed sunflower seeds from a big bag stuffed into a slot on the instrument panel that once housed something electronic.

Another fifty minutes of 110-mile-an-hour Montana between his legs, steady turbine whine, rotor thrum, and vibrations, and the Jet Ranger began descending toward a cluster of cottonwoods and willows along the Little Missouri River. Camp Crook.

Strain expected to see convection columns coming off the complex of wildfires. To the west lay a chaste range of low mountains. Burned snags stuck through the skiff of snow like gray hairs on an old white dog. On the north end of the town were the rusted, corrugated remains of a sawmill. A dirt main street consisted of a tavern with a bug light above the painted letters BAR. A weathered gazebo leaned, nearly toppling over, in a weedy city park. There was a service station and two abandoned Victorian houses. From the air Strain could see at least two dozen dogs running the dirt streets. No smoke.

The town had been founded as a cavalry camp. Brigadier General George Crook, who, unlike Custer, was famous for his restraint and rode a mule instead of a horse, spent the long summer of 1876 chasing hostiles around the prairie with little success. The Sioux set prairie fires that plagued the troopers on the days the elements of heat and drought didn't do the job. The soldiers had to clear firebreaks at every camp. Crook's outfit ran out of water several times, and out of food on one mission, which caused the men to resort to eating their horses. They didn't kill many Indians, but the fishing was good. Crook was supposed to back up Custer at the Little Bighorn campaign, but was pushed southward at the upper reaches of Rosebud Creek and spent the battle trout fishing in the Bighorns. The Sioux torched half a million acres in an unsuccessful attempt to burn them out, but Crook's supply wagons made it through. The afternoon Custer took his beating, General Crook caught seventy cutthroat.

The most prominent building was the saltbox that housed the Sioux Ranger District headquarters. A tattered and faded American flag stretched toward the northeast like a guidon and served as a windsock. Mayday nosed the Ranger down in a slow, controlled auger. "Duck on your way out," he said. "I wouldn't want ya to get scalped."

—

Strain had always thought of South Dakota as a buffer state between Minnesota and the West: white-tailed deer, Indian reservations, and Republicans. The Sioux Ranger Station at Camp Crook was the Forest Service Region Two's last outpost to the east. Dogs had the run of the few dirt streets and sagebrush trailer lots that made up the town. The dirt Main Street was sided with a few old and rundown frame buildings. Underneath the words HELLO FOLKS, OUR FIRE DANGER TODAY IS, a plywood Smokey Bear pointed to where a giant plywood thermometer had been. No need for Smokey now.

A bearded man in a ratty pickle suit limped out onto the makeshift helipad, a dog on his heels. His gray hair waved in the rotor blast like frosted cheatgrass as he shielded his eyes with his forearm. With his left hand he waved Strain to the building. Mayday gave the ranger a mock salute, pitched the ship to the west, and throttled back over Montana.

Strain walked upright away from the ship. He had logged several thousand hours of flight time—riding shotgun. The bearded ranger yelled over the turbine whine and rotor slap, hunched over as they walked to the building. "Before you ask I'll tell ya!" A few hearty late-November grasshoppers fastened to their pantlegs. The man's breath smelled like herbicide. "After the Nam I became a hydrologist on the Trinity National Forest. Veteran's preference. My family loved northern California and I did too. Rained like the jungle. I got mixed up in the details of a dirty timber sale and they busted me out here in the name of a promotion. I'm now head ranger of this hellhole. No more family except Festus." He pointed to the Border collie–blue healer mix at his feet. "Name's Horton Wynn and I bet you could use a drink with all this clusterfuck fire-in-winter business. I sure could. At ease, son."

The Sioux Ranger Station had been a schoolhouse built in the forties to strict utilitarian specs. Saltbox frame, shake shingles, peeling cream paint, government babyshit-brown trim. Routered into the shutters and the heavy oak door were the silhouettes of cookie-cutter evergreen trees, a wintertime project for the forest's first ranger. Storm windows covered all the windows, their frames so rusty that they appeared not to have been taken down in years. A stone chimney stood along the south side.

The interior was dimly lit. Dust floated in the wedges of sunlight at the windows. Yellowed posters of 1950s-era Smokey Bear and crumpled boxes lined the hallway. Newspapers covered Wynn's desk, the floor, and every chair in the office. Behind him, smoked hard hats, Nomex web gear, and a framed photo of Ronald Reagan on horseback. Wynn opened a file drawer and pulled out a bottle of Lord Calvert. His hand shook as he poured the whiskey into Only You! coffee mugs. "How about a little dose of the Lord this afternoon, Strain?"

"It's eleven o'clock in the morning, Mr. Wynn."

"Never too early for religion. Name's Horton. You're on Camp Crook time now. The absence of the Burger King is pure demographics. Don't drink the water here; we're battling a bombproof coliform bacteria. Might as well be Mexico. Would you like some coffee in yours?" Strain shook his head. "Don't worry, there's more for this afternoon."

Strain took a sip. "Boise tells me your forest's on fire."

"Not my forest—belongs to Washington, D.C. And yeah, it's on fire because computers in Boise say it's on fire, but the flames went out two years ago. Now I listen to the AM, wave to ranchers, and scratch my tired old ass. Once a month I make the drive into Ekalaka or Buffalo for groceries. See, there are certain assignments that folks are afraid to even mention, afraid their name might get noted with the locale and next they know they're calling Atlas Van Lines to see if they go to Hell. The brass doubts there are worse places than this they could send me. This is the Forest Service equivalent of the Foreign Legion. I don't want any more promotions." He took a long sip. "I gassed-up a truck to take up there in the morning. We'll get a look at this fire then. You want to phone in your arrival time to Boise?"

"Suppose I should. So there isn't a fire at all?"

"Nope."

"I could choose to get angry," Strain said. "Instead I'll choose to fish. Hell, I'm on the clock."

Outside, a pair of black Percheron draft horses grazed, picketed in a pasture of browning hound's-tongue, shooing the last of the fall's bottle flies with their tails.

"Bottle flies in November," Strain said. "What do you make of grasshoppers and bottle flies in November?"

"What do you make of being humped to a fire that isn't a fire? Look." Horton paused and lit his cherrywood pipe with a series of sucks and blows. Captain Black pipe smoke filled the room. "That NIFC Data General computer is ahead of the times. Sometime, soon enough, fire season is really gonna last all year long. The aquifer'll be long dry, so we'll desalinate ocean water, irrigate, and grow oranges. Best not take the change of seasons for granted. Anyway, it's cold enough for me. My blood don't have the circulation it used to."

They played cards, Omaha and stud, in front of a bare electric heater. Strain hadn't seen a heater like this one in years, since he'd last visited his grandmother who lived on a farm in Missouri. He stared at the glowing filaments as he remembered staring at a blue bug light at someone's drunken lawn wedding. "Why not the wood-stove?"

"Gotta cut wood," Horton said, without looking up from the hand he studied.

The shadows in the room slowly changed corners, and an occasional grasshopper sprang down the hallway. Outside, two curs ran reconnaissance circles around an old turquoise Apache pickup truck.

"In 1966 or '67 Uncle Sam sent Forest Service fire pros to the Nam to supervise firestorm experiments. Broadcast fire. Burn 'em out over there, put 'em out back here." He relit his pipe and blew a convection column of sweet smoke. "Your reputation precedes you, son. I understand you're quite a fisherman. See, Strain, you're like me. One of those guys who never quite grew up. You began in the woods summertimes as a college kid and never wanted to leave. I used to love trees. Now I can't remember what a live tree looks like. Guys like you, Strain, are out there, living down a haunt that has very little to do with putting out trees on fire."

Strain shuffled the deck of Bicycle cards. "Nothing to do with it, in fact."

Horton dealt. "Looks like you'll be here for Thanksgiving."

"I'll pick up a bottle of Wild Turkey at the tavern."

"A soldier needs his ration of spirits, now."

"That and whatever else you like. I'm billing everything to this fire. Think I'll call up Cabela's and order some new fly line."

"Ah"—Horton grinned like a raccoon—"but you're going out with such style." Then, as if to say "I fold," he said, "Dinnertime." He reached in a desk drawer and pulled out two brown plastic bags the size of full IVs. He tossed one to Strain, which landed thickly on his throwaway hand. An MRE: Meal Ready to Eat. Desert Storm surplus rations. "I live on these things." Horton took a Swiss Army knife from his pocket and sliced the top from his bag, then handed the knife to Strain. "I've ordered the house special, SPAGHETTI WITH MEAT SAUCE. What's yours?"

"Says OMELET WITH HAM." Strain searched through his meal: cocoa beverage powder, applesauce, oatmeal cookie bar, instant coffee, waterproof matches, chewing gum, toilet paper. All packaged to last past Armageddon. At the bottom of the bag he found the tiny bottle of Tabasco sauce.

Horton looked up with just his eyes, still chewing. "This stuff is a far cry better than what we had in the Nam. Could be they're riding you out and leaving you hanging. Just like Tom Horn. When the Association has no more need for your services, you're on your own. Watch the trees for snipers."

"I'll do that."

Horton refilled their coffee cups. Strain fell asleep on an army cot with the taste of whiskey and ten-year-old eggs in his mouth, the space heater clicking like a cheap alarm clock.

—

Strain awoke with a hangover at 0900. "I've got another omelet for breakfast," Horton said. He was fumbling with a Forest Service rec. map, slurping his whiskey coffee. "Here's your fire. It's easy to find. Just look for the black trees." Strain shaved and dressed in his Nomex fireline clothes: yellow long-sleeved shirt, green pants, logging boots. Horton had boiled water and handed him a cup and a packet of MRE instant coffee.

Horton dropped the tailgate, clicked his tongue, and Festus jumped in. Town dogs ran over to sniff him as he bent over to lock the front hubs. They crossed a cattle guard that separated private prairie from the Forest Service. Dirty snowdrifts capped the north sides of the rolling hills. The blackened pine covered the small mountains like so much Smokey Bear propaganda. He came to the fork. The road became steep and rutted in mud and snow. He levered the transfer case into four-low. In Strain's rearview mirror, just wind and grasshoppers.

"Why didn't they salvage-log this?" Strain asked. "There was a lot of good timber left."

"Just not cost effective. The mill in Crook closed years ago. Here's your fire." They passed a deserted campground. The wind kicked up ash and snow, salt and pepper, so that he kept the windows rolled up and had to use the windshield washer periodically. Grasshoppers hugged the wiper blades for the duration of the arcing. Picnic tables were charred and splintered. A blackened latrine. I like it here, Strain thought. Now browning and dormant, the Indian grasses had sprung up, fertilized by the rich ash. Mule deer grazed on the bluestem, poa, beargrass, and snowberry. "You're just two years too late," Horton said.

This is the way it ought to be, Strain wrote on the situation report.

They kept driving westward into Montana, the small prairie town of Ekalaka you could drive all the way to on the two-track, to lay in the Thanksgiving supplies. "What do you think of rib-eye for Thanksgiving?" Strain asked. "Holidays stopped meaning much to me just before my second divorce. I'm not one for farm turkey when I can have a good steak."

"You bet. Let's get a box of stuffing though. I love my Thanksgiving stuffing. And a pie. We'll get a frozen pum'kin pie."

They bought all the amenities they could find in the Ekalaka IGA, which weren't many, but they did get the Wild Turkey and the range-fed rib-eyes. "Cash or charge?" asked the lady in horn-rim glasses at the grocery.

"Government voucher," Strain said. The lady looked up over her glasses when she saw who the voucher belonged to. You guys look like bait fishermen, she was thinking, where did you steal this from?

"Hello, Horton," a man in a bloody apron said. The counter lady seemed relieved. Horton greeted the butcher shortly and they stepped onto Main Street to the jingle of the doorbells.

At the truck Horton squinted toward him. "Now, I'm cynical, Strain, read too many of these espionage novels, but maybe they want you out for good."

"That's real possible," Strain said and climbed in. They drove into a stiff headwind. Pronghorn and cattle. "Unless a man's got oil wells mixed in with his cattle, he'd need a ranch the size of Delaware to scratch out a living on these scablands," Horton said. The soil had been beaten by a hundred and twenty years of overgrazing and drought. "Rain never followed the plow to Harding County. It's cursed. Rains down in the Black Hills. Even up to the North Dakota prairie. Won't rain here because we're cursed. And they send me, a hydrologist, out here on the taxpayer's dollar. When I kick the bucket, throw me in the river." The next twenty miles were silent save for the wind and tires on asphalt.

Horton spoke as they dropped out of the burn and neared the cottonwoods that signaled the river that saved Crook's cavalry from dehydration a hundred and twenty years ago. "Maybe this is some sort of suicide mission. They're trying by wrecking your home life. Make you choose. Fight fire and make your wife crazy, or love your wife. I made the wrong goddamned choice. At least the world will freeze over before the realtors get out here." They were back in Camp Crook. The sky hung heavy with rain or snow, give or take a degree or two. "The thing about General Crook. After the Indian Wars on the Northern Plains, he retired to Arizona to chase Geronimo around the desert. Goddamn government sunbird."

"I'm gonna throw some bugs at some fish before the drinking begins. What's in the river?"

"Carp, catfish mostly. Some perch and maybe a sauger or two. Ain't trouty."

"Smallmouth make it this far up?"

"Don't believe. Want to borrow a baitcaster?"

"No, thanks."

"Remember, Strain, whichever way you're headed is north, east is to your right."

—

Dark came early now. Dusk had begun to settle in. Strain didn't wear a watch, another point of contention between him and his supervisors, so he didn't know, didn't care, what time it was. Maybe 1700. Like Horton said, Camp Crook time. Time to fish.

The Little Missouri ran muddy and shoaled from the summer of drought and fire. Strain needed the hike. He reached the closest bank, then walked upstream to find a hole to start with. He walked in ankle-deep water in his fire boots, to a sandbar, and began rigging up. Though grasshoppers still plagued the landscape, a bullet-head grasshopper pattern hadn't yielded anything. Hoping for a sauger, maybe a perch, he chose a number ten renegade his father had sent him. His father spent his long retirement days tying bugs, the lion's share of which he sent to his son in Wyoming. Strain clicked-in his floating-line spool, looped a twelve-foot 4x leader to the line, tied the renegade on with an improved clinch knot, and painted the fly with floatant. The renegade didn't resemble anything in particular, but fish saw something in it. Strain thought of it as the bastard calf of the fly world, and if forced to have only one fly in his cache, he'd think long and hard about making it the renegade. He made several false casts, stripped line from the spool, and let the fly drop in the current and drift over the dark pools. He fished the renegade on top, drying it with false casts, then let the bug soak up river water and slowly sink.

A weak front passed and the evening cooled. Strain was used to the fall-like temperatures from summer night duty at altitude. He fished in his shirtsleeves.

Nothing worked the topwater. He covered the green-black area around him with the thoroughness of a room painter. The fluorescent chartreuse line cut through the dusk like a tracer round.

He felt the line go heavy on the back-cast and he missed the throw. Must have caught a limb, he thought. He retrieved the slack out of the line. A high screech, the pitch of a dog whistle filled the night behind him. Struggling on top of the eddy, at the end of his leader, a bird of some kind. He carefully pulled the slack line and stepped into the water to retrieve what he could tell now was a Little Brown bat. With his left hand he cupped the wings, to keep the tiny mammal from hurting itself before he could cut the barb free. The bat was all of three inches long, rounded ears, face like a tiny bear cub's. He unclipped his Leatherman tool from his belt and unfolded the wire cutters against his pantleg. The number ten barb protruded through the bat's lower mandible, below the tiny triangle of soft pink bat-mouth. "You like my renegade, eh," Strain said in a calming voice. "Fish here don't think much of 'em, but I fooled a pretty stealthy little exterminator anyway."

He deftly clipped the barb and slipped the fly from the bat's mouth, and in the same movement set the tool down and made a cave of both hands. "It'll sting for a bit, but you'll be back to eating your mosquitoes in no time."

Gently, he blew warm breath on the wings and body, then placed the bat on the sand to finish drying. He stepped away backward, carefully, to let the bat dry in peace with a minimum of humiliation. The bat looked more human than birdlike, as if someday man would evolve winged hands and a tail rudder. What seemed odd were so many grasshoppers in November; it didn't seem at all odd for the Incident Commander, no incident in sight, to be talking to a maimed Little Brown bat.

He switched to a hare's ear nymph and made a few more consolation casts before wiping his line clean with a Smokey Bear 50th Anniversary bandanna and wading to the bank for the long walk back to the ranger station, where whiskey and a card game would await him. He tried not to let the politics of his job enter his mind. "Yeah," Horton could be telling them on the phone right now, "he knows it was a computer mistake. He's out fishing on the clock right now. Tomorrow morning we're gonna cook a big turkey." Fuck 'em. He had what was important. He hoped that by now the NIFC Data General computer had disemboweled itself.

The walk back to the ranger station cleared his mind. He smelled wood smoke. It was cold enough so he could see his breath. Horton was messy, having dipped into the Wild Turkey, drinking it neat. Strain fried some potatoes and a couple of the rib-eyes. They ate, leaving the dishes on the counter, and played cards to KVOO-AM out of Tulsa. Horton hummed to the old bluegrass song "Atomic Power"; then came Merle Haggard's "Workin' Man Blues." "Aw, keep workin'," Horton sang as he dealt. Festus nosed his leg.

Two hours later Horton was asleep on an army cot in his office. Strain turned the heater to low and read some of the back editions of the *Rapid City Journal* and *Rocky Mountain News*. A good deal had happened without his noticing. At least the comics weren't dated.

—

Waking, he could hear the unsteady ticking of the electric heater. After a candy bar and instant coffee, he stepped toward the door to walk back to the river. "Take Festus with you, will ya," Horton said.

"He does love to fish. I'll be drunk as ten Indians time you get back."

—

From his fly box Strain selected a two-and-a-half-inch black egg-sucking leach. He fished heavy, using a sinking-tip line and a 2x leader. He liked the heavier six-weight line, even on trout, because he could fire the bigger flies he favored through most any wind. Guys who fished midges tended to be anal-retentive flatlanders. Bigger bugs, bigger fish.

He reached into his pack, pulled out a small bulb of garlic, and broke off a clove. With his jackknife he cut off the stem and peeled it. Then he cut the meat of the garlic against his thumb, letting the thin discs of meat fall into his palm. He placed the garlic on an MRE cracker and started working on the PROCESSED CHEESE SPREAD—"KNEAD WELL BEFORE OPENING," it said on the camo-green package. This was lunch; it would get him through to Thanksgiving dinner. With the garlic oil strong on his hands he balmed the maribou leach and first few feet of leader until it no longer smelled to a fish of epoxy and human glands.

He cast upstream and let the leach soak up the muddy water and sink slowly. The light current swept the rig downstream, past him, and into a hole along the cut bank. He stripped line out until the current took up the slack a hundred or so feet below him. He reeled in and cast upstream again, then again.

Fishing for catfish held the same import for him as casting for Wind River rainbows or blue marlin off Tampico. Technically, he was at work, getting paid. He could see the Custer National Forest to the northwest; his fire was cold. He felt the line slacken, then go taut. He set the hook hard, then dealt out slack line until he could play the fish with the drag on the reel. The pawl drag on the Ross reel buzzed like a chain saw. The catfish went as deep as she could, into the hole, trying desperately to find a sunken tree or barbed-wire fence. Strain could see the water muddy on top of the wallowing cat. Slowly he played the fish out, bringing it to the gravel at the edge of the sandbar. Four pounds, he guessed. He wet his hand and reached under her barbed whiskers, and with his hemostat, pulled the hook free and pushed her back into the current.

Though catching them now still held the same excitement as when he was a kid, Strain had never really liked eating catfish, especially since he knew what they ate, those old goats of the river, their fat full of DDT. Once he had suffered through a sermon by a Bible literalist on Old Testament foods—what was okay to eat, what wasn't. Catfish, skin fish, weren't okay, just like pork. Couldn't eat oysters or shrimp. Ostrich. Crows. Was tuna in a can a skin fish? Bats, too. He remembered it wasn't okay to eat bat, which had been just fine with him at the time. They went home after the sermon and his grandmother fixed a ham.

Anyway, today was Thanksgiving.

Now two or so miles north of town he heard the old civil defense siren. He looked back toward Crook and saw a thick column of black smoke. A trailer house, perhaps. But there weren't many structures in the entire town. He cut the leach from the tippet and reeled in. It had started to snow lightly. "Let's go, Festus." He shouldered his pack and walked south, slowly, thinking about irony and responsibility. Strain knew the fire came from the ranger station.

A short in the ancient wiring. A cigarette on flannel. Or Horton might have kicked a section of newspaper into the heater. The paper would have caught another paper until the flames reached the bone-dry pine walls. One wall would catch, leading to the ceiling, then to the attic, where a hundred gallons or more of petroleum-based paints and outdated agricultural chemicals were stored. The Sioux Ranger District would be history in a matter of minutes.

George, the tavern owner and Camp Crook Volunteer Fire Department chief, radioed for help to Buffalo. "Complete conflagration" was the term he used. "That's it for the old school," he said. "Too late for the bucket brigade. Horton's inside."

A Powder River charter bus full of Type II firefighters from Pine Ridge Reservation idled in the street. It was one of the many crews ordered three days earlier to help put out the same Custer Complex that had gone out two years before.

Strain thought about his duties, then about Horton inside, where the old man burned like a Molotov cocktail. For the first time in his career, he balked at fire. There was a realism of consequences and an urgency to this fire he'd never experienced before. *What would Horton Wynn do in my boots?* He looked down at his boots, the steel showing through at the toes where the leather had been eaten by the lye made from ash and water. He thought of the Apache and Gila trout he'd caught during the past fire seasons that had melted together into one long sortie in his memory. He thought about bats. Kurt Strain learns to fly: Go Fish. He reached for the pis aller, his fly rod, which leaned against the fender of the volunteer engine. Then he met the strike-team leader in the yard. "Have your men put a line around it before it gets into the grass. Mop up when it cools. Don't forget to fill out your crew time reports. You're on your own for chow. De-mob when you feel you're finished here." He called the dog, who was running frantic circles at the edge of the intense heat, and headed back toward the Little Missouri.

"Sir," said the strike-team leader, "where are you going? I mean, is there anything else?"

The Indian stared at the burning house as Strain looked past him. The Lakota man knew he was witnessing the passing of more than one ghost. In Washington, D.C., this incident wouldn't amount to a cigarette burn on the circus-tent-sized corporate canvas. Strain stopped and turned, meeting the man's eyes. "I'm gonna fish through."

———

At night, on fires, Strain had often thought about what burning to death would be like. Not as immediate as an unsuccessful cavalry firefight, not as peaceful as the latter stages of drowning. "Down here," he mouthed to Mayday, who leveled the ship out at the cottonwood tops and hovered over the river. Strain cupped the hard hat containing the sample of Horton's ashes—mixed with ashes of newspaper, MREs, propaganda posters, lumber from the old school—and opened the door. "Care to offer an Indian prayer for the soul of this good man?" Strain asked the pilot.

Mayday just stared at the few working gauges on the instrument panel. "He sure burned hot," he said.

Strain hesitated. He should say something, but what? It was like having to pitch himself out the door. "Go with God," he said and flipped Horton into the rotor blast. The flakes of carbon blew back through the door, floating around the cockpit like confetti, then settling in the cabin's seams and cracks. "Goddammit," Strain said. The two had ash on their faces, in their laps.

Chances were a few of the ashes had made it to the river, where they would join the Missouri in North Dakota, then drift south to the Mississippi and the Gulf of Mexico. But a month later most of what remained of the old man would ride with the rich skiers into the untouched backcountry powder of western Montana and northern Wyoming. Then, when the snow turned to fire, Horton would fly fire for as many seasons as the Jet Ranger kept from wearing out or burning up.

Which happened, a year and a half later, on the Fourth of July.

The ship's bucket cable caught a utility pole. The cable snapped and backlashed into the rotors, shattering the blades and fire-branding Mayday two hundred feet upside down into the south face of a mountain northwest of Buffalo. The explosion lit the night sky like a Roman candle, the humidity dropped, and the wind picked up. That evening Kurt Strain, saw boss on a fire north of Cora, Wyoming, landed two limits of brook trout and the second- or third-largest rainbow of his life. The next Monday the Data General report listed in boldface Horton and Mayday's ten-thousand-acre, multimillion-dollar complex.

Calcutta

ubert de Sablettes hunted rabbits, on foot, with only a knife
and a basset hound in tow. He was a runner. He ran every
day—an addiction—even on the coldest winter mornings,
twenty, thirty below zero, leaving at dawn his home on
Klondike Street that was once the Methodist church, watch cap, a
water bottle belted to his waist next to the knife, and a buffalo-
horn *cor* to sound the *trompe de chasse*, calling Perch, the hound
that ran behind, who could barely keep up. Hubert, gaunt and
sinewy, ran up hills, over snowdrifts, into the sagebrush desert
until he flushed a snowshoe hare. Then he would chase the white
animal, sometimes for hours, until it became too exhausted to go
on and just lay there waiting for the knife, or died of an exploding
heart.

That was the hunt, the run, as described by the children who
claimed they had seen it themselves. Everyone wanted to have
seen it, but the hunts took place well away from town, on the vast

wastelands good only for gas wells and sheep grazing. Hubert
would sometimes run for five or six hours until his workout ended
with the kill. Then he would dogtrot back to town, Klondike Street,
carrying the limp hare by its hind legs, grimacing from the pain in
his own bramble-scarred legs. Some days he would stop in the
Hams Fork River and wade in the cold water until the swelling in
his legs subsided. This even in winter.

Rumor around Hams Fork, Wyoming, is treated with the cour-
tesy of truth, and rumor here had it that Hubert was a rich count
and that he was holing up in town, hiding in the high desert, a
refugee from France, where he had killed his wife by running her
through with a well-honed bayonet after hunting her in a frantic
chase in the forest. Around Hams Fork, Hubert was known as the
Count. It had become a childhood act of bravery to creep down
Klondike Street, into the churchyard at night, friends watching in
the bushes across the street, and peer into the lighted stained-glass
windows, pretending to be able to see more than vague shadows
inside. The metallic kitchen sounds were real: knives on sharpen-
ing steels and stones, the basset howling, and the tinny buzz of
late-night AM radio. And the smell was real, certainly, the smell of
garlic and hot goose fat and wild game frying.

———

Lizabeth Tanner lived next door. Sometimes at night she could see
the shadows of children chasing through the yard. The window-
peeking was childish, but she too smelled the food and heard the
hound and wondered what life in the church was like. Some days
she would see the Count walking and would notice the color of his
hair in the sunlight: grayish-white, like a summer coyote's. Perch
knew Lizabeth and liked her because she would sometimes lean
over her fence and treat him to a raw hot dog.

She was a carpenter. Thirty-four and single, she had made her living following the ski-town booms. Now she was a contractor, mostly doing remodeling work on the older homes in town, though the mine had recently laid off a hundred or so and work was slow. She had time to remodel her own home, do some fishing, read some of the books she had always promised herself she would, and build a dogsled. The sled she donated to the charity auction that followed the calcutta, the sled-dog-team auction where gamblers wagered on their choices for the upcoming race.

—

Like the gypsy circus in the days when Hams Fork had been merely an ashen coal camp, the dog race came to town each February. The day before the Hams Fork leg of the race, pickup trucks with mobile kennels containing the yelping spitz dogs paraded into town, sleds on top, straw and muzzles poking out of the whiffled boxes. The calcutta had become Hams Fork's winter version of the Kentucky Derby. Residents would eat from a prime-rib buffet, then bid on their favorite sled teams. Some of the lesser-known teams would go for a mere hundred apiece. Winners would receive a 30 percent cut of the money raised. The bulk of the money went to pay immunization costs for poor children. Chances of winning weren't great, but in a state with fewer than half a million residents and no lottery, the calcutta was still the social event of the winter. Following the auction was the dance.

—

Except to run, the Count rarely went out in public, but now he leaned nervously against the paneled wall of the Eagles Club and sipped his blush Chablis from a plastic cup as townspeople tried not to stare, and the auctioneer, an overweight man with a brushy mustache and 20x silverbelly Stetson, rattled off bids. *Hunerd dolla, hunerd dolla, I've a hunerd, do I hear two, two hunerd,*

hunerd dolla, I need two . . . Box wine and Budweiser, the calcutta was not fancy, but the building was warm and folks could catch up on gossip with friends from the other end of the county, people they saw maybe once or twice a year.

The Count, awkward yet privileged in carriage, wore his hair oiled down, navy blazer, white oxford shirt, Levi's, and handmade Luchese boots. The lobes of his ears and the very tip of his nose were purplish from multiple frostbite. His face was weathered, but he was extraordinarily fit. His leg muscles pressed like a horse's through his pantlegs. His supposed age around town sometimes varied by thirty years. The Count cupped his wine close to his chest and made his bids in regal gestures with his right forefinger, enduring the hearty bids of several Reno-wise ranchers and miners who had pooled their money in order to afford the big names in the sport.

The race director, a tan former musher out of Jackson Hole named Hunter, stood in the back wearing a long red driver's parka with coyote-fur trim and dogfood company logos emblazoned on the back. His job was to raise the anemic bids, show enthusiasm in hopes that the bidders would think he knew something they didn't. At times he would interrupt the auctioneer by walking down the aisle between the bingo tables in his arctic ringleader's coat and take the microphone. "Now, Dale's team has been training at altitude all winter long!" he might say with steely enthusiasm, or "Terry is especially hungry this race. He led through Dubois last year and he's not coming to town with the idea of losing again." Hunter's tactics worked for the most part, though he was forced to sit on several teams running a gangline of roadkill-fed curs. Hunter wanted to recoup his losses with the favorite, Guy de Calvaire, a French-Canadian musher training on the provincial tundra out of St. Louis, Saskatchewan. *Fifteen, fifteen, yow, sixteenhunerd, yow, seventeen, seventeen . . .*

The Count kept Hunter and the ranchers at bay and took the rights of the favorite. De Calvaire's team went for $3,500, the highest bid in the brief history of the calcutta. *Sold. To the man in the navy-blue blazer and the big checkbook. Hope you've got you a rabbit's foot.*

"Les chiens," the Count said softly. "Thank you. Marche."

When the crowd had topped off their drinks, the charity auction began.

"This sled is race-ready," said the race director, looking straight at Lizabeth, "and I admire the construction. Solid ash driving handle, crosspieces, brush bow, rear stanchions. Teflon runners. Everything welded together with rawhide joints. Some of our mushers are gonna wish they were driving this baby come a week from now."

The sled was beautiful, in the same linear way that antique gun stocks, oak letter desks, old saddles, bamboo fly rods, handmade cowboy boots, beavertail snowshoes, and wooden skis are beautiful. *We're gonna start the bidding on this fine piece of craftsmanship at three hundred dollars. Now who'll open the bidding at three hundred dollars?* Hunter's hand went up like the tail of the lead dog in the gangline as the crowd counts down the beginning of the race. *Three, now four, four hunerd, four hunerd, yow!* Hubert's hand went up at four. *Four, now five, five hunerd, need five, five!* A glass of cheap wine later, the Count owned an expensive handmade dogsled. Lizabeth watched Hubert run his hands along the lines of the sled.

The next item up for auction was a rust-colored Alaskan husky puppy, a cross between a Siberian, an American pointer, and a little something else built for speed, which had been bred by Hunter. Timber, the blue-eyed puppy, had stumbled over to the Count halfway through the calcutta to gnaw at the Count's cowhide boots. Every once in a while the Count reached down and scratched the dog's head. As the crowd watched him, Hubert slowly raised his finger and owned the puppy.

They stacked the metal folding chairs in the corner and the rest of the evening was the dance. Hunter, who had honed his dancing skills as part of a set of instinctive traits for Rocky Mountain survival, fared the best at the dance, dancing with every single woman and a few not single. A whistling cowboy dusted the floor with talcum powder, which covered the asbestos tiles like snow. The Noble Hussy Orchestra struck up a western swing. Hunter led Lizabeth through spaghetti turns and athletic dips.

By the third or fourth song the Count left his place against the paneled wall, pushing the sled across the talced floor toward the back door. Timber ran with the Count, hesitating when Hunter squatted to call him, but the puppy didn't stop until he reached the door.

In the heavy snow and halo of light from the parking lot, with the mid-tempo "Smokin' Cigarettes and Drinkin' Coffee Blues" at his back, the Count looked over his shoulder and saw Hunter dancing closely with Lizabeth. He kicked the sled through eight inches of newly fallen champagne, all the way home, the other side of town.

The sled had a special place on what used to be the altar stage of the church. The Count carried it through the double front doors and set it gently on its runners atop the carpeted stage. He spent the next hour or so admiring the sled from every angle, testing the flex of the wood, the runners, the joints. The old church was sparsely furnished, a couch along one wall, a table near the kitchen, and piles of worn-out running shoes everywhere, holes in the uppers, frayed laces, soles flattened slick and worn through. Timber chewed on a shoe and Perch jumped into the sled—the new centerpiece of the place—and watched his master.

That week KHAM broadcast special hourly dog-racing-trail-

condition weather reports and updates on how the racers were far-
ing on the legs prior to Hams Fork—Jackson to Moran, Moran to
Dubois, Dubois to Pinedale, Pinedale to Lander, Lander to Hams
Fork. From Hams Fork they would race to Afton, then on to the
neon finish in Jackson. The map of the course was drawn on a
Wyoming highway map in thick black marker and resembled, ten
feet and a glass of blush away, an outline of France. Guy de Calvaire and a pack of Europeans stayed tight on the leader, an American dog food tycoon. The course would become more hilly, the
dogs more tired. They would get a day of rest in Hams Fork.

—

The morning of the day before the Hams Fork leg of the race, a
howling dawn, Lizabeth awoke to a knock at her door. She tied on
her robe and answered it, holding tight to the storm door in the
wind. "Oh, Mr. de Sablettes, what a surprise. I'm flattered at what
you paid for the sled." She, like everyone, had heard the rumors
and didn't invite him inside, out of the sideways-blowing snow. The
Count had never knocked on her door, never been to Lizabeth's
home.

"It's beautiful," Hubert said. "I have it ready and thought you
might like to drive it."

"I didn't know you had a kennel," Lizabeth said, opening the
door wide to look at the sled in the street.

"No, just Perch and Timbre"—he pointed to the basset hound
sitting by the sled and the puppy in the cargo bag—"and myself."

"Well, I—" But Hubert had turned toward the sled and began
linking himself to the gangline with a caribiner. Perch ran to Lizabeth and sat, eyes pleading for a hot dog.

Hubert, in harness, looked back to the door, which Lizabeth had
pulled back tight against herself. He looked down to his feet. Then
back to Lizabeth. Hubert wore track shoes, distance flats, with

quarter-inch spikes screwed into the soles. No socks. "Won't you come for a ride? I have a beautiful new sled and now I need a driver." His voice blew away on the wind, but his English was careful and Lizabeth could read his lips in the early-morning porch light. Hubert stood facing forward, concentrating, waiting for Lizabeth but no longer acknowledging her. She reached down to Perch and rubbed behind his floppy ears.

Mumbling to herself that this was crazy, Lizabeth went inside to dress. She found her hat and mittens and stepped outside into the snow, where she could see each breath come nervous and fast. She led Perch back to the sled and wrapped him in the sled's red cargo bag with the puppy. Hubert stepped forward, pulling the slack out of the gangline. " 'Gee,' I turn right, 'haw,' I turn left. 'Whoa,' I stop, and you stand on the brake."

Lizabeth stood on the runners and lifted the ice hook. "Mush," she said softly, her breath rising upward.

"Sorry," Hubert said. "It's difficult to hear you in this wind."

"Mush!"

The brush bow lifted, then the sled tracked straight behind Hubert and leveled like a boat on-plane. "Hike!" They ran down Klondike Street in the low, muted light of the early-morning snowstorm, the crystals of snow the shape of tiny arrowheads. Hubert moved slowly, awkwardly, at first, but smoothed out and picked up the pace as his joints and muscles warmed and flexed. "Gee!" There were no cars on the streets, but the team set the racing dogs howling as they passed the parked mobile-kennel trucks awaiting the next day's competition. It was feeding time, and the dog handlers stopped chopping frozen salmon and beef roasts, set their axes down, and gawked as the little team slid by. A dream? "Trail!" yelled Hubert as they passed the dog trucks, "Trail!" The hundreds of dogs in town began howling at the event, drowning the steady pattern of Hubert's breathing.

Hubert had long ago become addicted to endorphins, the natural form of morphine his body produced through hard running. But as his running progressed, he needed more and more miles of it to produce the same effect, and the rush wore off faster. He ran harder and longer, running himself deeper into oxygen debt. Without a run he became dogged or edgy, enough that he had to avoid contact with anyone. So without running, he was convinced, he couldn't survive. Running had become his habitat, and if that habitat shrank, like a constricted heart, he would no longer be wild inside, and he would die. He could not explain this to anyone. Only the rabbits knew. The hares. The coyotes. Perch.

They ran the streets of town, a line of quick color in the storm, Lizabeth keeping one foot on the runners and pedaling the uphills. "Haw!" yelled Lizabeth, and they turned left and started up the steep hill of Canyon Road. The sled tracked true in the fresh snow that covered the sooty streets, though she found herself thinking about the design, about modifications she would build into the next calcutta's sled, mostly slimming it down, making it lighter. Most of all the sled felt heavy, the Count straining alone on the gangline. Next year she would pare away at the stanchions, crosspieces, and slats. The footpads would be made of something lighter than strips of old snow tires. Guilty, she tried to pedal when she could, but Hubert kept the pace fast enough that her kicks did little to propel them forward. Perch and Timber pointed their muzzles out of opposite sides of the cargo bag. Perch still looked back at Lizabeth with hot-dog eyes. Timber had fallen asleep to the rhythm of the run.

"Haw!" yelled Lizabeth. They shot down Elk Street, Lizabeth standing on the brake so as not to let the sled run over the runner on the long downhill. "Gee!" she yelled again, and they swung onto the Union Pacific service road that paralleled the railroad tracks. A yellow-and-black locomotive engine with a chevron snowplow over the cowcatcher blew its air horn as it slowly gathered momentum from a dead stop and finally passed the sled team at the other edge of town, on its way to the power plants of Utah with a load of coal. Lizabeth, warm in her down parka, lost track of time, but thought the Count must be exhausted. Crystalline rime formed on Hubert's fleece hat and wind-shell jacket. "You've got to rest!" she yelled. "Let's have coffee!" Hubert looked back, surprised. "Yes, all right," he said. "Gee!" she commanded, and Hubert made a right onto Antelope. "Gee!"—another right onto Third West—and "Gee!"—across Moose, back to Klondike.

Hubert was skittish in public. People avoided him and he avoided them when he could. He shopped for groceries at night, bundled in winter clothes, just before the IGA closed, though people still studied him and speculated what he must be eating based on the basketful of ingredients he bought. Green onions and bulk garlic by the pound. Fresh spinach and anaheim peppers. Potatoes, carrots, parsley, avocados no matter what the season and their price. Dried beans. Rye flour. Brown rice. Tabasco and balsamic vinegar. Port wine. Apples. "How do you marinate rabbit?" they asked each other, or "What on earth could he be doing with all that garlic?" Now Hubert held Timber on his lap, stroking his ears. Lizabeth set the cup and saucer before him on the kitchen table.

"Cream? Sugar?"

"Black, thank you."

The house now smelled musky, acerbic, of hard sweat and garlic. Sawdust and wood glue. It had belonged to a mine foreman in Hams Fork's early days. Lizabeth had taken out some of the interior walls and now it was light and spacious. Most of the furniture was hardwood she had designed and built herself. "You must be training for something. The Boston Marathon? The Beargrease? Iditarod?" Her question echoed against the hardwood floors of the house.

"No, I run for myself mostly," Hubert said softly. There was a long silence as they sipped coffee and crunched chocolate biscotti. The wind whistled in the power lines outside. Pellets of snow rapped at the windows. They could hear each other chewing and sipping. Under the table Perch grunted in his sleep.

"I must say," Hubert said suddenly, making Lizabeth jump, "I admire the sled, the work you put into it."

"Thank you. I'm glad I had a chance to drive it. Now I have ideas for a better sled next year."

"Yes. I respect those who always try to improve." Timber growled and jumped from Hubert's lap to pounce on the sleeping Perch. Lizabeth laughed and Hubert studied the animals wrestling on the floor.

"Animals are funny," Hubert said without laughing.

"I'm sorry," Lizabeth said, "but I have to ask this. What about the rabbits, the hunting? I've heard stories in town . . ."

"There are many rabbits. I marinate them, yes, in cheap red wine, then sauté them in much garlic, a little onion. It is good for me to eat. Protein."

"But why do you run and hunt them that way?"

"It's the only way I can hunt them. Without insulting them. I run because of this wilderness around us. I must run before there is nowhere left to run." There was a long silence, sipping sounds, a clock ticking. "Enough of me. Tell me, why did you become a carpenter?"

She paused, digesting what he said. "When I was little, my father said to me, There are only two respectable occupations. One's a bootmaker, the other, a carpenter. I never really saw myself as a bootmaker. I worked out of Telluride for a while. Jackson. Ketchum, Idaho. Just the summer months. I skied all winter, fished all fall. But it got so building saunas and adjoining bathrooms with fourteen-karat bidets in condominiums with names like the Bear Foot just put me off my feed. One morning I found myself two stories up, hammering a Swiss-style molding on a Kmart Alpenhaus in Red Lodge, Montana. I set my hammer down, took the nails out of my mouth, turned and looked behind me, at the landscape I was helping to exploit and ruin. I collected my pay and moved to the high desert. Hams Fork. My father always used to say that people were breeding like rabbits. It'll be a long time before many of them follow me here."

"I agree with your father. A carpenter is a very respectable profession."

"Yes. I've just decided to improve what's already here. I don't live life on a postcard anymore."

Hubert stood awkwardly, signaling his need to go. "I have something for you," he said, "because you know." He let himself out into the snowstorm and ran to the sled, with Perch and Timber chasing after him. The Count reached into the foot of the cargo bag and produced a cloth flour sack. He ran back to the door and handed it to Lizabeth. "You understand," he said, "you can do something good with these." Lizabeth opened the sack. Inside were a dozen or so hare pelts. She was puzzled, but she reached into the sack and felt the fur with her fingertips as if pinching salt, and rubbing the pinch into a roux. When she looked up again, Hubert, his dogs, and his dogsled were gone.

—

The morning of the sled-dog race, Lizabeth dressed warmly and went next door to see if the Count wanted to go and watch the start of the race with her. She wanted to look at the sleds and get some more ideas. She thought she heard a noise inside the church but there was no answer to her knocks.

—

Hubert de Sablettes ran. Under the power lines held high with silver standards and the cellular towers like church steeples on the ridgetops. Over the buried phone cables that allow the Californios to live in Teton County and commute daily to L.A. via their modems. The big bears were gone. The wolves. The mineral rights had been stolen from the Indians, who came from somewhere else and stole hunting rights from each other. It had all been wildness, before the polar ice caps began their melt. This place had become Europe, the only wilderness inside the hearts of a few.

The first mushers were French fur trappers who used the dogs to run their traplines. *Marche! Hike! Marche!* Now the top mushers in America are gaunt and hungry Europeans: Scandinavians, Austrians, Germans, and Frenchmen training out of Canada. They eschew heavy pac boots for running shoes that they duct-tape to their Gore-Tex pants to keep the snow out as they run, pushing their sleds up hills. The Americans have become thick and complacent and, though they can still afford the best of dogs, grow heavy on the sleds.

One musher that afternoon, an American from Grand Marais, Minnesota, told Hunter at the checkpoint midway between Hams Fork and Afton, that he had seen a man near the ridge, on foot, running by himself in the snow and rabbitbrush, twenty-five miles from town. The race director radioed in that they needed to call out Search and Rescue, that no one could survive up there, unaided in that wild country, the snow, wind, and cold, alone.

Honeyville

tah. Loaded down with honey. Our regular route. The December sun is coming up over Wyoming. While I keep a tired eye out for a state trooper's black-and-white, Wayne is driving and singing. *Got an old dog, ain't got much class* . . . The milk van strains as we tack up winding U.S. 89, a 6 percent grade, through Logan Canyon. We're wired on adrenaline, coffee, and money. *He's got three legs, and a hole in his ass* . . . The day is overcast, thick; it develops slowly, like a photograph.

On the broad side of the white panel van we restored—an old Ford Meadow Gold milk van with sliding doors and rounded panels—Wayne has painted a beautiful pale Indian maiden. Her hair is the color that you think is brown, but is actually red in the sunlight. She holds her honey dipper like a trident. Bees surround her. Below the maiden in crimson-and-gold letters: QUEEN BEE HONEY COMPANY. But her eyes! Her eyes are deep green, as if they go many fathoms inside her to inside the truck, and the honey behind those thin sheet-metal panels is laden with the power of love or magic or something else, something more. Studying the sunrise, Wayne says this: "Red sky at morning, sailors take warning."

The laws of Utah scare us. They are arcane and cryptic. They sneak up on you, like game wardens and ATF agents. Utah is a 3.2 state: weak beer. Everything good here is regulated by the state, which is run by the Mormons. The people of Utah are deprived, and where there is deprivation there is money to be made. But, as my father told me years ago, you can't legislate against what people want. I've memorized this road, the sagebrush and Mormon tea. In the vibrating rearview, underneath WELCOME TO UTAH, the sign will say "Still the Right Place." You can't legislate against what people need. The sign in front of us now reads:

WYOMING

LIKE NO PLACE ON EARTH

The sea was here once, a long time ago. "I don't get it," Wayne says, offering another of his jeremiads after the singing turns to humming for a few miles, which makes him winded. Wayne is an artist, a painter, and a student of history as well as the fermentative sciences. "Used to be the Mormons could have their whiskey, wine, coffee, beer, art. Then somewhere along the way someone with authority had a vision and put the kibosh on everything worth getting out of bed for."

Wayne and I offer them libation at a fair price. We have found a fortune to be made by importing U.S. Grade A Utah honey from the Beehive State, fermenting it on the lee side, and exporting Wayne Kerr Wyoming Mead back in. The Mormon men's illicit social drink of choice is mead—nectar of nectars!—and they're buying their own honey back, masterfully fermented, by the barrelful.

"Know the difference between a Catholic and a Mormon?" Wayne asks, fondling his beard. I shake my head east and west. "Catholic'll say hi to ya in the liquor store."

—

There are nights out here when the cavalry arrives in the form of a bright-orange snowplow. You can't mind the weather if you're going to live here in Hams Fork, Wyoming. Apocryphal stories about Wayne, about us, float around Hams Fork like flotsam and jetsam. He's building a wooden sailboat, the *Cuba Libre*, in his back yard. His dream is to sell all that he has, hoist the sails and the Jolly Roger, and become a citizen of the world. Live off third-world economies where a few greenbacks will make you a tycoon. Eat a lot of seafood and grapefruit. Make love. Drink good rum every morning. The air in Utah tastes of salt.

It is bad luck to sail into the horizon at sunset. A bee on deck is a sign of good luck. It is bad luck for a preacher or a woman to be on board, which makes Neptune angry. "Unless the woman is topless," Wayne says. "A topless woman is good luck."

—

Harriet is my girlfriend. She plays the tenor saxophone, and like aging mead, her hair is a slightly different color week by week. She's British and not a Mormon, though the Mormons are how she landed here. She doesn't like their rules; they did not tell her in England about their rules when she let them in her front door. Harriet calls them sodding Mormons, which in her British accent almost sounds like a compliment.

Now Harriet has submerged herself in Hams Fork. She waits tables at Habaneros, the Mexican restaurant next to Custer's Last Strand Beauty Salon on the Triangle downtown. She lives in an old shotgun apartment above the restaurant that she gets rent-free from the owners. The restaurant vents are near the window and her apartment smells like greasy Mexican cooking and old cigar smoke. The wallpaper is of yellowed Victorian flowers.

Harriet's hair now is the kind of blonde that is really brown until she steps into the sunlight. When things get slow she trades the ladies at the salon Mexican food for hair and nail jobs. She is beautiful, with sharp European features, and I don't know why she is my girlfriend or what she sees in me. She is wild and funny and makes me laugh. I sit and listen to her voice for hours and her stories, which are probably nothing more than small anecdotes, sound like high drama to me. Harriet likes to do things like hike up Sarpy Ridge, take her clothes off, and moon the town. She likes to say we were meant for each other, and this is something I truly believe myself, although I never repeat it back to her.

I know, when we're all together, Wayne studies Harriet the way an artist studies a still life.

—

I come from a family of artists. My grandfather was a bootlegger from Watonga, Oklahoma. He had a line of stills out in the red dirt and blackjacks. Once a week he'd load up his old Chrysler with lugs of moonshine and drive—fishing tackle hanging out the window—to Seventh and Broadway in Oklahoma City, where he'd deal them out of the sales manager's office of McDonald-Scott Chevrolet. Said he got the scar on the bridge of his nose from drinking out of fruit jars. His whiskey was the best that side of Wyoming—no Arkansas bathtub jakeleg. Grandpa distilled a special Christmas hootch for the local sheriff. He knew who to pay.

The Whiskey Road runs from Hams Fork—our town—to Honeyville, Utah. During Prohibition, Hams Fork was the prostitution-and-moonshine capital of the West, and Hams Fork Moon was famous. Now my grandpa is buried in Oklahoma, and Hams Fork is known only for its huge population of Mormons and its open-pit coal mine. The Whiskey Road is washed out and rutted, but we use it in the warmer months when the Utah State Patrol sets road-blocks on the Wyoming line. We've been stuck in the mud. We've broken down with a full load of mead. We've been shot at by ranch-ers. But we can always say we're just hauling honey. This is the can-o'-corn part of the job, right down U.S. 30 to our port of call, Hams Fork. If we get stopped, all Wayne has to do is say he likes honey on his pancakes. Wayne loves his pancakes. He catches his breath. *Wastin' away again in Honeyville . . . lookin' for my lost three-legged dog . . .* The Mormons know our mead is the best—the most medicinal, as they say—this side of the Continental Di-vide: our mead packs 16 percent alcohol. Stand next to the Hams Fork City Limit sign and you can throw a rock almost into Utah. This I have done.

———

Maybe sailing the Seven Seas is Robin's dream too, I don't know. Robin is the wife Wayne married. She's a bird-watcher and a math teacher. She's the kind of woman I'd like to marry but Wayne got to her first. The cat's name is Heck. Wayne says Heck's job will be to keep wharf mice out of the hold. Wayne says now he just sneaks around the yard and eats birds. Heck was Wayne's idea.

Like Heck, Wayne prefers the dark meat too. On Thanksgiving and Christmas, after quaffing much morning mead, Wayne jerks the legs off the hot turkey and hoists them in the air like Henry VIII or a Viking.

———

Late at night in summer we drive the honey truck up-country and poach shipwood on the National Forest. We choose the cleanest, straightest pines and Douglas firs, fell them and deck them, the hot buzz of the chain saw in our ears. Some of the trees we buck into ten-foot logs and stack inside the truck. Some we leave long and I winch them on top of the truck with a come-along.

Wayne's painting studio has become a workshop. An edger, a planer, a table saw, drill press, lathe. Sawdust covers the floor, the easels, the framed figures of buxom models. Sketches of boats are taped to everything. The log that will become the boat's prow is solid European maple, from a 150-year-old tree we felled at two A.M. in the bishop's front yard.

"A good boat is like a woman," Wayne says. "The malty smell of warm wood, the sanded lines of the bow, curves you can get lost in. You can fall in love with a boat." Wayne says that someday he's going to capture love in his art. He says "love" like it's the rarest of wild animals, never been snared before, and this boat is the most cunning of traps. I help Wayne with the heavy wooden pieces because Wayne has a bad back and cannot lift anything heavier than a camel-hair paintbrush.

A wooden fence surrounds the *Cuba Libre*'s skeleton in the back yard Wayne now calls the Tropic of Kerr. In winter, like now, the boat's backbone and ribs stick out of the snow like giant wishbones on a white beach, a whale beached in snow. I stand inside what will be the *Cuba Libre*'s doghouse and I'm like Jonah, Jonah of Hams Fork. You can tell the temperature by the sound your boots make—the colder it is, the louder the crunch.

Lot Young, next door, pretends to do yard work—raking snow, shoveling frost—so he can watch Wayne Kerr build his dream. Lot is caught in a role with many kids and one wife and can no longer have dreams. "Say, Noah!" calls Lot. "How long 'til it starts raining?"

"Not long now!" yells Wayne. "Just time enough for me to finish building and collect two of each kind!"

"How's that?"

"You know: two blondes, two brunettes, two redheads!"

—

When the Vikings died and went to Valhalla, the warrior maidens served them horns of mead: when the battles ended, the Valkyries became waitresses. Four o'clock is tea time. I'm on the tea standard now. Before I met Harriet, four meant a Coke and two cigarettes. Now, no matter, four means tea.

Our meadery is in Wayne and Robin's basement, where everything is safely hidden from taxes and regulations. Heck and I sleep in the basement. I keep a cot in what used to be Robin's sewing room. Every Saturday Robin changes my bedding. Harriet's futon is warm and her sheets are flannel, but I like the independence of being able to stay in the meadery sometimes, where I drift off to sleep to the smell of honey and yeast, and not enchiladas.

But in the afternoon—after checking thermometers, hydrometers, fermentation locks, sterilizing barrels—when the winter sun has started to drop behind Utah, I stroll over the Tropic of Kerr, through the gate, across the alley and the Coast to Coast parking lot, to Habaneros on the Triangle. Robin will be there, grading papers, forever grading papers, and we'll tear open little restaurant packets of artificial creamer and honey and drink tea with Harriet and eat sugared little greasy things Alex the cook fries up for us between real orders. It's in the four o'clock hour that it just doesn't matter that I have a chimichanga haircut, need some dental work, have no health insurance. I've lived here long enough to know this Wyoming wind could bring a tempest, could bring anything. The honeybees came on ships from Europe almost four hundred years ago. Now the bees are the figurehead of a state that doesn't even allow mead.

—

Sometimes I picture them on the *Cuba Libre*—Wayne in the pulpit, a mad Viking, gray hair and beard in the wind like an unfurled jib, spray over his bow. Robin is grading papers. Wayne could rape and pillage all of Great Britain while Robin stayed aboard to finish red-penning eleventh-hour geometry quizzes.

—

The only thing I remember about geometry class is that you are allowed one "given." This is my given: I know how to make mead.

The legend is that mead is an aphrodisiac, so in a way what I do is ferment love. The Mormon men drink mead for virility and fertility: It is believed that mead drinkers father more sons.

In the days of the Norsemen, when great men were made from the spit of gods, dwarfs brewed a magic mead from the blood of a poet. The dwarfs lured the poet into their caverns and ran him through with swords. They poured his blood into three jars and mixed it with honey. From this wort they brewed the magic mead. Anyone who drank the mead could have wisdom.

—

You already know about our Utah honey. We use high-quality European champagne yeast and yeast nutrient that we dissolve in hot water. I splash cold Hams Fork River water against the sides of the fifty-five-gallon honey drums to oxygenate the honeywort. The city has come around asking why we use so much water. "Could there be a leak?" they ask.

"I water my lawn and flush the toilet a lot," Wayne tells them, this in December, Wayne not having much of a yard in June anyway.

Then I pitch the dissolved yeast and yeast nutrient into the honeywort, add a blow-off tube to each drum lid, and wait. We don't boil our honey. The alcohol content is high enough to kill any contaminants. Kerr Mead is aged nine months, and when it is finished it tastes like sweet honey wine.

—

Everything, fermentation especially, and love too, I suppose, amounts to time. Sometimes the fermentation sticks. Just stops. The hydrometers indicate that the sugar isn't finished fermenting throughout the anaerobic cycle.

This is when we use yeast skeletons. Normally throwaways, these yeast hulls are the cell walls left behind during the yeast extraction process. The yeast skeletons absorb fermentation-inhibiting poisons produced by yeast when too much alcohol gets to them too soon. Unsticking fermentation is a little like magic.

Time in Utah is an odd concept. Utah is like another country, another culture altogether, less like Canada than Mexico with its odd rituals and ancient customs. They still have real live firing squads in Utah. I guess that it's the noble way to go if you're on Point of the Mountain's death row, say, for intent to deliver high-octane mead to Honeyville, or stabbing your girlfriend's lover in the throes of passion, and the final grain of sand just slipped through your hourglass. The last cigarette probably isn't allowed. They pin a paper target over your heart and buckle you into a chair. Take it like a man, good night, lights out. No last cigarette, no last belt of whiskey. So much in Utah is lost to time.

You have to be wary of the wild yeasts. They can live and propagate themselves in mead wort if your champagne yeast doesn't get the jump on them and kill them with the alcohol. There are thousands of types of wild yeasts in Wyoming. Let them get at your mead and what they make of it isn't fit for Utah or anywhere else.

—

Wild yeasts infected a dozen barrels of our mead once. It was like discovering your girlfriend or wife has been cheating on you—we felt violated. We're not sure how it happened—an infected syphon hose maybe. We loaded up the barrels one midnight over much cursing and drove to a river access above town. "Kinda like the goddamned Boston Tea Party," Wayne said as we pried the bungs off the barrels and dumped the mead into the Hams Fork River. The river under our flashlights turned blond as the bad mead caught the current and flowed through town.

—

Harriet was baptized in Utah, a baptism of sorts, anyway. She let the Mormon missionaries—white shirts, black ties and slacks— into her drafty East London flat one afternoon. They refused tea and told her stories about Zion: the brilliant deserts that smell of cactus bloom, the blue mountains that hold wild elk and summertime snow. Milk and honey. They described the contradictions for her without telling her in plain English that that's what they are, contradictions. They told Harriet about the brave British immigrants of almost two hundred years ago. They told her the miracle of Elizabeth Ann Walmsey Palmer.

E.A.W.P. had been one of the first Mormon converts in England. She immigrated to Nauvoo, Illinois, then whipped an ox team to Utah Territory and settled here in the 1860s. She was an invalid, and the legend—Mormon history—says she was carried into the lukewarm water of the Great Salt Lake and walked out unaided.

Harriet had been working in a department store in London. She packed a steamer trunk and worked her way here shoveling cow shit on an Argentine cattle ship. She came ashore in New York and rode the Greyhound to Zion.

She can't swim. Harriet waded into the briny water off Antelope Island last summer and had to be carried out by a photographer from Mona who was disappointed she didn't require mouth-to-mouth, but he had the powers of a bishop and proclaimed her officially baptized. She hitchhiked eastward and got as far as Hams Fork, where she met Robin in the IGA. Robin is the one who introduced us. Harriet's visa will run out in the spring. Legally, she cannot work at Habaneros, but the Mexican owner is cutting her a break. I could marry Harriet and make her legal, but it's something we talk over and around. Robin is the only one who is completely convinced that Harriet and I should get married.

—

Wayne bought a video: *Basic Sailing Made Simple*. Harriet is excited about going sailing with Wayne when he finishes the *Cuba Libre* and trailers it to the Great Salt Lake for test runs, as if the brine of that lake still holds another miracle, and sailing over it in a ketch with Admiral Kerr might produce some effect of love total immersion didn't. Who here wouldn't want to sail a desert ocean with Wayne Kerr when every day, everywhere you look is a sea of sagebrush. I know that, though beautiful, the lake is sterile and holds only the lowly brine shrimp.

—

We make love and drink hot cocoa. She's never said so, but the chocolate part is her favorite—the chocolate part is *not* my favorite. Even in winter Harriet plays her saxophone on the rusty second-story fire escape. She leans over the railing, hair wild over her face, and blows love into the unappreciative wind. "Isn't there an ordinance against that?" I've heard Mormons walking below say.

When it snows sideways down her alley she plays in the glow the streetlights make through the leaded glass of her apartment window. Now and then a big, slow winter fly, stunned by geography and cold, drones heavily around her apartment. Killing it seems too easy, so I slide the heavy window open and shoo the fly outside, where it has to face Wyoming on its own or die. I'm sure they crash-land in the snow and freeze to death almost immediately. Harriet has a sensual overbite, an elegant neck, sculpted British nose, sea-green eyes, pale skin, and she loves Billie Holliday. I've never had such a beautiful woman before. It makes me anxious, as if one day I will come back from Utah and it will all be gone. I don't know if she loves me or not. It is not a word we use between us.

———

Mead lasts. It gets better with age and can last for years; unlike so many things, my mead gets better as I get older.

Viking tradition had it that if mead was imbibed heavily for one moon—one month—after the wedding, then in nine months another celebration would ensue at the birth of a son. Having many sons was especially important in the days of constant war.

Wayne says mead was the drink of orgies. "Look at that honey moon."

———

Today we are on our way to Honeyville. The return trip. Full of mead. I'm not hungry, but I force down a piece of toast. It settles my stomach. Wayne is out of bed at high noon. He splashes water on his face, puts on his Rockies cap, ready for business. We check the oil, brake fluid, and antifreeze. We check headlights, taillights, running lights, turning signals, and brake lights. Tire pressure. Fuel. Horn. The trip to Honeyville, loaded down with contraband alcohol, is a bit more tense. Wayne drives, lapsing into song as we sail by the Wyoming Port of Entry at the edge of town. *Livin' on pancakes . . . watchin' my dog bake . . .* My back is sore from loading the drums myself.

Another thing about the trip to Honeyville is that we do *not* know who to pay off. Trust no one over there, Wayne says, and almost no one on the Wyoming side either, for that matter.

Wayne checks his mirrors and stops his humming to inform me of something. "You know, the sailors with the real huevos *soloed* around the world. Picture that, at the helm on a starry night. Next day it's rum and mahimahi at some maiden-infested island paradise. I'm thinking about soloing around the world in the *Cuba Libre*."

"What about Robin?" I say, but the old milk van leaks wind at its seams and rattles like a washing machine so Wayne doesn't hear me.

Just across the Utah border at Garden City we turn west and grind up the pass before dropping into Logan Canyon and down narrow U.S. 89 through the Cache National Forest and its timber, the thousands upon thousands of potential ship masts. After an hour of canyon we reach Logan. It's almost four, almost dark.

The most beautiful girls in the world live in Logan, Utah. Wayne says it's the gene pool. But considering the Viking tradition of mead, you'd think there'd only be sons. Little real love lives in this town, Wayne says. Everything in Logan is too pasteurized, too sterile, too filtered. The van lumbers away from each stoplight like a loaded ice wagon. Even with overload springs in the rear, the front end rides high, causing our low beams to glare off the windshields of oncoming cars. They flash their lights at us. Wayne flashes back. We drive on.

"So when are you going to marry Harriet and grant her citizenship?" Wayne is blunt.

I look at him in a way that says I'm thinking about business. His talk, I think, turns to Robin.

"They'll do anything for us. They cook. They do dishes. They scrub toilets. They have sex with us. They *raise* our *children*. And for what? All they ask is for one thing. Just one thing, and it's small—tiny—in comparison." A coffee dusk settles hard over the Cache Valley. The dashboard lights cast Wayne's shaggy face in a virulent green glow. "All they ask is for us to *love* them."

We brake not to hit a family of mule deer crossing the highway in our high beams. Wayne downshifts and honks without breaking his line of thought.

"Yesterday, old guy at the gas station. His wife was younger—or just less sick—anyway, she looks spry and supple next to this guy she's driving. She pulls up to the pumps, gets out, and pumps the gas. Ol' passenger-side Methuselah must have had his prostate suctioned out two days before. But he puts all his energy, all his strength, into opening the car door, setting his feet on the con-crete, and lifting himself upright so he can watch her pump his gas. This guy has had his life, but the wonderment was still there. I kinda smiled at him. That old man and me, warm sunshiny day, smell of high-octane unleaded, Antelope Street, Hams Fork. The meaning of existence passed between us right then and there."

Wayne pauses for a moment, a bearded, contemplative pirate. "A guy like you," he says, "women love you because they think you're the kind that will evolve with them. They really believe that's possi-ble. Me? I've always been me, always will be. Wayne Kerr." Wayne says his name like he's the Emperor of Wyoming. "I think Harriet's looking for someone to evolve with her. You're pliable, still a pup. Plus she wants citizenship. All in one package, what a deal."

"We're fine just the way we are," I say. He knows I don't like to talk about Harriet with him.

"Hey," he says, "what are the chances of Harriet modeling for me?"

"Don't go there, Wayne." I've been ready for this. "Not happen-ing. You can fire me and get someone else to make your mead, but I'd go back to chopping mackerel heads on a cannery barge off the coast of British Columbia before I'll let Harriet be painted by you." I know that Wayne's models are more than just models. Wayne says the closer he is to his models, the more texture and dimension his paintings have.

"I didn't say I wanted to paint her. I've been chewing on another idea," Wayne says. "We can talk about this on our way back up the canyon." Wayne lapses into song. *He's a taker, so he took her, 'cause he could take her . . .*

———

Though not nearly the highest, the Wellsville Mountains are some of the steepest in the world. They rise from the valley floor like steeples. Tucked up against the base of the Wellsvilles, across the range from Logan, and just east of Promontory, where a hundred and fifty years ago the golden railroad spike was driven that tied the East to the West and hurried this region on its way to hell, is the hamlet of Honeyville. Jersey and Holstein cows gather under streetlights along the roadside. Fields of dry corn and wheat stems butt against farmhouses along Main Street. The lighted marquee at the convenience store advertises three hot dogs for a dollar, ketchup available. Many apiaries. If not for the Wellsvilles and the neon absence of a bar or two, Honeyville could be in Illinois.

In the 1850s, Honeyville had been one of Brigham Young's forts, the most northerly outpost in Utah. Now cottonwood trees surround the block-square ward house, a brick-and-mortar fortress with a parking lot the size of a Wal-Mart. *What would ya do with a drunken sailor . . .* Wayne cranks the wheel to starboard and we ease past the ward house, toward the railroad tracks, until a weather-bleached false-front general store comes into our headlights. On the side of the store a sign:

Tolman & Sons

GENERAL MDSE

HARDWARE

&

COAL

"Time for business," Wayne says as he gears down and turns the headlights off. Now we're operating by moonlight. We pull our bandannas over our noses. The brakes squeak to a stop in front of the store. The figure of a man walks out of the shadows. He wears a western hat and a bandanna over his face. We're all highwaymen here. The silhouette walks to my side of the truck. I slide the window open. "Who be you?" the man says. His voice is deep and coarse.

"Anama," Wayne says. He had to explain it to me the first time I heard him use it. Wayne knows a lot more about Mormonism than some Mormons. "Anama" is a word used by special ops like the Sons of Dan, a Mormon militia whose mission is to stop threats to the faith. Wayne says Mormons make up huge percentages of men in the FBI and CIA.

"All wheat," the man says.

"All wheat," Wayne says. "All's wheat and honey."

With that the man reaches me a thick Arby's sack and the big door of the store slides open. Wayne takes the sack, looks inside, guns the engine, and the milk truck with us in it disappears inside the dark building. A swarm of men appear at the back of the truck and, excuse the metaphor, like bees, work at unloading the mead barrel by barrel. Bad-back Wayne and I step outside to wait.

Wayne counts the money from the Arby's sack. Satisfied, he takes a cigar from his shirt pocket, pulls his bandanna down, and bites the end off the cigar, spits, and goes about his lighting ritual of flame, puffs, and sucks.

"Here's your cut," he says. "There's enough there to buy your boss a Christmas present and still get Harriet a nice ring." Wind licks the bills he hands me. I have enough saved up where I could marry Harriet and put a down payment on a house. Wayne never asks what I do with my money.

Tall cottonwoods towering over the house next door block out most of the moonlight. The house is old, very old stone. The windows are small, as if designed to keep something out. "Those windows," Wayne says, pointing with his cigar. "I bet those window frames flare and on the inside they're normal size, maybe even larger than normal size. Meant to keep flaming arrows and mad Utes at bay."

"Why wouldn't they just be small inside, too?"

"So a Mormon with a rifle could set up shop inside one, a bastion. I bet those walls are four or five feet thick."

"No way," I say, pulling the bandanna off my nose. "It's only a house."

"Look," Wayne says, "the Mormons knew what the hell they were doing when it came to defense. I say those walls are four or five feet thick, and I'm willing to bet on it."

"Bet what?"

"I'm right, Harriet models for me."

"No bet, Wayne. I told you not to step into that territory."

"Okay, then, dinner. Dinner at the Habanero."

"Deal."

At that it is like we are powerless to resist taking a look. We have time. The noises from inside the building tell us they are still unloading mead and reloading the truck with honey. The dark house, like the gravitational pull of the moon, drags us toward it. Our running shoes slip in the heavy frost. We stand in a dormant flower bed—bad-back, beer-belly Wayne standing on my shoulders—when headlights sweep into the driveway and pan the house, less like a Hollywood opening than a searchlight at Point of the Mountain. A car pulls down the little lane. We just stand there, frozen. The lights stay on, the engine stops, the lights go out. The metered chime of a door-open bell. Dim glow of interior light. Hard heels click up the flagstone sidewalk to where I'm straining to keep Wayne Kerr on my shoulders. "My word," says an older female voice, European, British. "Pirates!"

Another car door opens, then after a time closes. Soft foot-steps—tennis shoes—run up the sidewalk. "Why look, Benjamin, pirates." The man or boy breathes audibly. "There are pirates in our flower bed. Heavens. Did your car break down? Now, you two men, come along inside this minute."

Wayne defies the confinements of his bad back and jumps off my shoulder with the agility of a gymnast and lands on a small bush. He rubs the cigar out against the sole of his running shoe, puts the stogie in his pocket, and looks around, nervously, as if watching grapeshot rain across his bow. The front door isn't locked. The woman opens it and turns on a hallway switch. "Come along, I'll fix us all some cider." The boy—he is more boy than man—studies us, his eyes full of pirates! He wears thick glasses with heavy frames. In the light of the entryway I can see his eyes are milky and heavy, like oysters in stew. "Well, Benjamin, intro-duce yourself," the woman says.

"Hello," Benjamin says. The syllables are long and carefully thought out: hell-low. He holds out his hand to Wayne and Wayne looks at me, then shakes it. Then I shake Benjamin's hand. The boy's fingers are short and thick, his grip soft.

We follow. I catch a glimpse of myself in a hallway mirror, flan-nel and running shoes. I look pale and worried. Then suddenly, I find myself with Wayne Kerr in the harsh light of this woman's kitchen. Smell of detergent and candles. The window above the sink is wide, but tapers toward the outside. The walls are every inch of four feet thick. Wayne is right.

"I'm Margaret," she says. "Margaret Cloud." Mid-fifties I'd guess, maybe sixty. She wears a dress, like a meeting dress. "I'm originally from the Old Country, from Goole. Zion is our home now." She takes a deep, appreciative breath. "Benjamin is my youngest son. It's just the two of us in Honeyville now. Peaceful it is. I have an older boy in Brigham City and a daughter in Salt

Lake." She pours cider from a plastic milk jug into an aluminum pan on the stove. "Do you need to use the phone?"

Wayne shakes his head no. "Well then, you must have business at the Tolman building. You must be honey merchants."

Wayne clears his throat. "Honey merchants, yes, ma'am. We buy honey."

"Oh, yes," Margaret says. "And what ward are you from?"

Wayne is taken aback. "Oh, ah, Montgomery Ward. It's in Wyoming." Margaret smiles warmly and nods.

Magazines and newspapers cover the table. On the walls are antique kitchen tools and curios—a hanging plate with a portrait of Charles and Di. A thimble collection. Ceramic egg cups. Tin flour and sugar canisters. Cereal boxes. A plastic bear half full of honey. A yellowed print of a sloop in a storm. Taped to the refrigerator, childish crayon drawings and a computer printout:

BENJAMIN'S HUG LIST

Mother

Aunt Evelyn

Uncle Earl

Brother Hyrum

Sister Rachel

"They're beautiful." It's Wayne. Margaret and I turn to see him studying a pair of old sailing-ship prints on the far wall.

"My father built sailing ships in Goole. Those are two he built," Margaret says. "Do you men like history? Sit down, please." She leaves the kitchen for the dining room. In a moment she returns, carrying a gin bottle, sideways. She hands the bottle delicately, like a baby, to Wayne. Inside the bottle is a minute and intricately detailed schooner. "I always thought of this as magic. My father built these at home, though he didn't allow me to watch. Bottled magic. It's done with thread, you know."

I sit next to Wayne, whose head hangs slightly, eyes wide, as he studies the ship in the bottle. I hadn't planned on being ambushed by a British Mormon. We had no Plan B for this.

"It's so real," Wayne says, and I know he's forgotten the mead, the money, and the men next door. "It's all there."

Margaret leaves again and returns with a large book she sets before us. Then she pours cider from the steaming pan into coffee mugs on the counter. "Well, this house was built in 1856." Wayne sets the bottle down, gently, like a baby, and opens the book to the first page. He points to an old photo of the house. "Honeyville was a fort then. Call's Fort, they called it. The Indians used to come out of the mountains and pillage. Upset the peaceful balance we have here today, you see." She sets the warm mugs in front of us. Mine has a unicorn on it. Wayne's has a big red heart embossed with *MOM*. I look at Wayne and we commence sipping. I put the mug to my lips when a bright flash of light fills the room.

"Benjamin! You should have asked these gentlemen if they wanted their picture taken."

Benjamin smiles wide, eyes big and round. He's captured us. He's captured our smugglers' clumsiness on his Polaroid. The white negative spits out the bottom of the camera and the instant chemicals go to work. Benjamin's smile turns to a confused frown. Wayne and I take shape on the negative like ghosts. "May I please take your picture?" Benjamin says. Wayne and I look at each other. Wayne shrugs and says, Sure, hell, why not. Benjamin snaps more photos and arranges them on the table like solitaire cards. Wayne sets his cider down and gathers the photos like a folded hand of cards.

The boy walks over to his mother and whispers something in her ear. Margaret nods her head. "Well, I guess you'll have to ask them, won't you."

Benjamin takes a deep breath and raises his chin. "May I please have my picture taken with you?" Wayne and I look at each other.

Margaret raises her eyebrows with pride. Wayne smiles and says, Hell, why not. He has ships in his eyes and nothing else matters. I can tell for the next few weeks, Wayne will be obsessed with working on his masterpiece.

We stand and Benjamin knocks into a chair positioning himself between us. I put my hands in my pocket because I don't know if I'm expected to put my arm around him. I feel a piece of paper between my fingers, a grocery list Harriet gave me in case we have time to stop off in Logan, but we're always so full of money, honey, and paranoia that we never stop on the way home.

Margaret aims the camera. "All right, say 'cheese.'" Out of habit, I almost say "whiskey."

"Cheese!"

This is the first word I'd said since coming into the Cloud home, and the word felt awkward in my teeth. The battery-powered motor rolls out the negative. Benjamin holds it, hands shaking, while we watch it develop, a face here, another, like children watching chickens hatch.

Yes, it looks like a mug shot—FBI photos in the post office.

"Hey, you're quite a photographer," Wayne says. "May we have them?"

"Yes," Benjamin says and snaps another Polaroid. "I'll keep this one."

"Oh, I'm afraid I'll need to have that one too," Wayne says. I always knew a time like this was coming. It's an inevitability in any below-board profession. This is where Wayne and I become Dick and Perry, violence where we hadn't planned any. "I'll buy all your photos of us," Wayne tells him.

"No, sir," Benjamin says.

"See, Benjamin, we're like Indians and you've captured our souls. You wouldn't want to keep our souls, would you?"

"No, sir, just your picture."

Wayne lunges for the photo but Benjamin dodges him and shoots out the back door into the Utah night. "Goodness," Margaret says, looking up from her history book. "He collects Polaroids. Shares them with his friends." Wayne looks at me and I raise my hands in surrender and thumb toward the door.

And when Benjamin passes the photos around the ward house on Sunday, the men in bandannas will receive visions of these particular pirates and our deliveries will no longer be wanted in Honeyville. I can't stop thinking about Wayne's love story—the old man watching his woman pump gas. Our latest career is over but I am thinking of Harriet, imagining I'm sitting at Habaneros watching her deliver steaming plates of greasy enchiladas with lots of Sonoran farmer cheese and onions. I somehow talk Wayne into stopping in Logan and we spend almost an hour wandering through the isles of Smith's, carefully checking off items from Harriet's list: organic vegetables, special cheese, marmalade made with limes.

The Wagnerian fat lady, the operatic Valkyrie, has sung over this state. It's over for us here. Like wild yeast, love lives here in the folds of Utah, and love shows itself to be more powerful than mead.

The rest is the scud up the canyon.

———

Back home Wayne stands at the bowsprit and works from memory, a photograph in his head. He clears the bark first, the Stihl chain saw wound like an eight-day clock, blue two-cycle smoke filling the air. Wood chips fly as he cuts toward the heart of a figurehead with a long, elegant neck, motherly breasts, eyes that are portals to the sea, a sensuous overbite. Hips develop, and strong, slender arms. The morning sun rises higher and brightens the snow on the Tropic of Kerr, though I can feel the barometric pressure drop inside me: a storm is coming. Wayne cuts the engine on the saw. His hot breath replaces the Teutonic smoke that drifts slowly eastward, toward Illinois. Heck slithers around the ribs, watching Wayne work, hunting for dark meat. With quiet, easy strokes of a rasp, Wayne smooths her full lips, high cheekbones, sharp nose, shoulders, breasts. I watch him work, and this seems to distract him.

"It's beautiful," I tell Wayne, rubbing the wooden smoothness of Harriet's cheek. He nods at me apologetically, blood rising to his head.

———

Like our Utah, the wild honeybees are no more. They have been replaced by domesticated apiary bees. But they too are being killed by the Chinese bee mite that lodges itself in the bee's breathing tube. The mites came over in ships full of shit stamped MADE IN CHINA.

Utah has driven me closer to Harriet, and Harriet loves bread. But Wyoming may be a memory for her soon because I have not yet asked her to marry me. What I wish I could brew is a stronger mead, a mead fermented from the blood of an artist. And if I drank this mead I would be the wise one.

Wayne says marriage is an island, and sooner or later even Greenland becomes small. It is Robin's spring break and she sits in a chair in the yard reading and watching Wayne.

Sometimes I have nightmares of Harriet playing a blues song on her sax while sailing back to England on a cattle ship. She's in the pulpit, where she can blow something Leadbelly and raw and tempt fate as if it were icebergs. Sometimes in my recent dreams I'm married to a Valkyrie.

Wayne's figurehead has the power to determine fate, both mine and Harriet's, I suppose. Wayne sails on, testing his own, a fearless Leif Eriksson, Jason, Noah, Captain Bly. While my fate seems stuck.

—

Snow knocks at the window. An April storm. We're not going anywhere tonight: the roads in and out of Hams Fork are closed. I knead the bread dough. The smell of warm yeast and rye blankets the apartment, fending off the foreign fumes from downstairs. While more dough rises, Harriet makes tea. She knows I take honey in my tea and she sometimes puts in too much. I watch her let the honey drip from the spoon into my cup and I can tell it's too much but I don't care. She is so beautiful standing there. I could watch her forever. Let it snow for forty days and forty nights.

Becky Weed

ust a boy of seventeen and Four Roses drunk, Romer Meeks had pancaked his father's Aeronca Chief onto Becky Weed's front yard, downtown Tea, South Dakota. He'd knocked out his two front teeth against his kneecap and spit a pulpy string of blood on the long grass next to the little airplane, which rested maimed over its buckled landing gear. He'd wanted to impress her. Now he'd have to tell his dad he'd broke his glasses.

Romer limped, casual as a scarecrow, to the porch where Becky and her family stood. Don't appear messy, he thought, the idea forming like foam in his consciousness. Don't appear hurt neither. Mostly, though, don't appear stupid, but it's maybe a little late for that. "What are you up to?" Romer said as he reached visiting distance, hiding the gap in his mouth with his tongue like an upside-down wolf whistle.

"My God, Romer, are you okay?" Becky asked, standing at the edge of the porch. Romer felt a throbbing in his chest.

"Just turn around and keep on walkin'," Becky's father said, staring at the toylike airplane for signs of smoke and fire. "Limp on home."

"But, Dad, what if he's hurt?"

"He ain't hurt that bad."

Romer did limp home, to be rejected by the Air Force and the Navy and the Coast Guard and Jackrabbit Air Freight, for reasons that ranged from arrhythmia to corrective lenses thick as the bottoms of canning jars. After another wrecked airplane he had to have custom-made shoes with the left sole cobbled two inches higher than the right, normal one, just so he could walk in a straight line. Fifteen years later, he wore black lizard-skin cowboy boots, little red airplane hand-stitched into the elkhide shafts, cloud of thread on leather weather, skywritten initials just below: *RM*.

Chasing bugs and nightshade up and down the long and short rows of eastern South Dakota, Romer laid malathion and Dibrom 14 fog over small town after small town for an outfit out of Sisseton called Sky Tractor; the poison settled into wells and backwaters, marrow, eddies, aquifers, and fat stores. Romer found himself gypsy-flying over Big Stone City, where, he remembered reading from the Weddings section of the *County Broad-Axe*, Becky Weed had moved (following a honeymoon in Hawaii) with her husband, the quarterback-turned-banker.

Jim Beam his drinking buddy the night before, poison and coffee sloshing in his stomach now, the checkerboard cropland surrounding the airport read like the cloudy irrigated topographical map of his memory. He'd come such a long way, scud-running the 250-horsepower '66 Piper Pawnee with a narrow Spartan cockpit like a fighter plane, a long way from the boyhood Chief that would fly backward at full throttle in a stiff headwind.

But now, in real time, he flew. A film of green engine oil and yellow motes of poison that dripped from leaky O-rings painted the windscreen of the Pawnee or his glasses—wasn't sure—causing the sunlight to prism his view, sweet vibrations and smell of malathion, alfalfa seed, and old tractor filling the cockpit as he taxi-bounded across the grass, synaptic bulbs firing, his liver feeling fine and clean as ever. Styrofoam Grande Café Java between his legs. Traffic control a smile and a wave.

Pawnee Whiskey Zulu. He took off heavy to the north, using every inch of runway in the thin summer air, pulled up and banked hard and buzzed town fast and low. That morning over breakfast— cigarettes, a jelly-filled—he'd sleuthed Becky Weed's (now Becky Catchpole's) address. Old fashioned pre-GPS telephone-book map in his lap lined with a carpenter's pencil, he nosed the airplane down and rolled left into a twisted horseshoe. Romer surveyed her half acre of yard and house in reconnaissance fashion, the end of the canopy rainbow resting at her patio, where the quarterback barbecued in a pink golf shirt. Becky Weed nowhere in sight.

Romer had held a fantasy, that of flying shotgun for the Animal Damage Control boys over to West River, shooting coyotes from a Husky with a Benelli 10-gauge, but the ADC was military in nature and he knew he wouldn't pass muster, many physical equivalents of flat feet. He'd have to stay satisfied with his summertime blitzkrieg on the delicate chemical balance in the nervous systems of arthropods. Catchpole the quarterback flashed a banker's wave at the pilot in the sky, Thanks for spraying, yes, the world needs fewer insects and more fliers like you, you'd qualify for low interest, damn sure would—Go Coyotes!—see me on Monday in my designer tie.

Romer waved back, tipped his wings as if to say, Remember me, Becky Weed? Romer Meeks, the only one who's crashed for you.

This one's on the county, city of Big Stone, Romer Meeks, Sky Tractor (by God!). He ruddered left, stall speed rising, circled and came in low, yawing above the ranch-style, out of trim, then leveled his booms over a 12-gallon veil of malathion, enough organophosphates to drop a murder of crows.

Becky Weed will not have to swat mosquitoes as long as Romer flies her evening air.

Atomic Bar

Two Bulls and I while away our days mining petrified herring for tourists. What we're really fishing for are the six-feet-long gar that the museums will pay good money for. But, like the Eocene horses, the gar are very rare.

There isn't much traffic in Alkali, but we manage to sell enough gasoline and cigarettes along with the three-inch Knightia fossils to eke out an existence in this ghost town, population three. Two Bulls' wife, Miriam, is a good cook and we eat like pharaohs, though her hand shakes more each year as she holds the cast-iron skillet out to us—she won't let us buy her a microwave oven. Some days Two Bulls can hardly stoop to tie his boots from the pain in his joints. He sees his arthritis as a good reason to lace his coffee with cheap whiskey. I see his arthritis as a good reason to join him and doctor up my cup as well.

In the past fifty of my seventy-some years, I have yet to find another perfect Eocene horse in the stone. But the one we have, the one I found when I was young, we keep in the back room of the store, where we can see it and touch it, and no government agency will come take it away and send it to a fancy museum in the East. In an odd way the horse keeps us company. A fish we could set loose, no problem.

There are still a few mustangs here in Wyoming. Sometimes, just before dark, I see one, a Roman-nosed Andalusian stallion I call Atom Boy. He comes to drink from a muddy spring in the foothills. The hair on his fetlocks is long and shaggy and his ribs show under his matted hide. He sucks the spring dry, then stands, watching, while it slowly fills up so he can suck it dry again. He does this until he gets his fill. Atom Boy stays out of the open—behind a herd of antelope, an oil pump jack, or a sandstone outcrop. He knows there are people who would shoot him for dog food.

Booms and rodeos come and go; the only thing consistent are the bottle flies. There is always talk of the mines starting up again, and Western Nuclear keeps a skeleton crew out there, pumping the shafts dry, letting them fill, then pumping them dry again; this, I suppose, can be written off in taxes. We could dig for fossils in the old mines, save for the water and radon. To the companies, Alkali is a dunghill. Whatever uraninite the country needs now comes cheap from the deserts of North Africa, where the Moorish Barb mustangs came here from. Western Nuclear doesn't understand that the smell of wet sage has a way of evening out your losses.

I still keep batteries in the old chrome Geiger counter. I get a boost from knowing our world is still radioactive, and no matter what the professors do with it, that energy comes from God's brown earth. The glazed dishes we eat from will set the Geiger counter to rattling. Thorium gas-lantern mantles are hot too. Sometimes our petrified fish kick up a few alpha particles when I hold the vacuum tube close. In this way I listen to the fish. The fish tell me what was. Every afternoon, over coffee, whiskey, or both, Two Bulls tells me what used to be, though I know because I was there too—Two Bulls just likes to put his Indian bent on things. The horse, Atom Boy, reminds us both of a story. It's an old testament.

———

Truman was President on that Sunday in early June when Mose drove up the tree-lined lane to the headmaster's office in his rusty 1939 Buick. I was shagging flies on the ball field when one of the boys brought word that Father Irons wanted to see me. As I entered his office, Father Irons forced a smile and introduced us. "David, I'd like you to meet Mr. Moses Dogbane. Mr. Dogbane, this is David Hadsell, one of our finest boys. Mr. Dogbane is in mineral futures."

A fossil of a man, wild-bearded, with stringy gray hair under a battered Stetson Open Road, he wore an old gray double-breasted suit, suspenders, and dusty cowboy boots. He nodded and shook my glove hand with his dirty right hand, while the stubby fingers of his left hand held a gold watch on a chain with a yellow elk tooth attached to the end. He wheezed when he breathed and made a nervous clicking sound, like a Geiger counter, with his tongue against the backs of his soft brown teeth. His breath smelled of whiskey and horseradish.

"I'm confident Mr. Dogbane will lead you to a bright future, son," Father Irons said as we stepped back into the sunlight.

"I'll put hair on your chest, young man," Mose said, tucking the watch back into his vest pocket, "you can count on that much. Hair on your chest, yessir."

St. Joseph's records said I was either sixteen or seventeen. This was correct enough, for I could hit a fastball farther than any fifteen-year-old, but I wasn't yet wise enough to think like an eighteen-year-old. Schoolwise anyway. Outside of school there wasn't much paperwork involved.

I packed my duffel and we made the long hot drive to Alkali, stopping only briefly in Casper for gas, oil, and a week-old *Tribune*. I noticed a matinee I hadn't seen, *Gun Smugglers,* advertised on the marquee at the Acme downtown. "What's *Gun Smugglers* all about?" asked Mose. "That a good one?"

"Haven't seen it," I said.

———

Mose was a prospector and a deal man. He started me out as a swamper for room and board and a pair of six-dollar field boots that gave me blisters on my heels the size of silver dollars. My room was a dim and dirty mop closet behind the bar. Board was beans and fried-egg sandwiches with mustard on bread you sometimes had to tear the green patches from, and once in a while a rangy chicken we killed ourselves.

Mose gave testament to my future. "Set your aspirations high," he told me. I thought maybe I'd like to play professional baseball, though as I grew a little older I realized that was only a kid's pipe dream. What I knew for sure was that I didn't want to be a priest. Mose wheezed when he told me what he thought I shouldn't become. "A cowboy couldn't pour piss from a boot if the instructions were printed on the heel. Thou shalt not be a dumbfucking cowboy, Davey, my boy. Best get uranium on your cranium. We're gonna leave the horseshit to the punchers and deal our way to the top."

———

Alkali sat like a sun blister along dirt-and-gravel spur highway 77—what the locals called Poison Spider Road—in the Paradox Basin.

A small wooden sign a hundred yards up the highway announced it: EAT AND DRINK AT ALKALI.

Somewhere in that big bowl of land was the geographic center, the nucleus, of the state of Wyoming. Standing in the middle of the pitted dirt parking lot of the Alkali Bar, the world was wind, sage, snakeweed, and sandstone. At the edge of the parking lot, where the Alkali Bar and a half dozen withered Russian olive trees met the desert, a pump jack sat frozen with rust, a dinosaur from the real oil-boom days of the forties. On the clearest mornings you could see Mount Sinai to the west. The tattered screen door of the bar would slap against the blue asbestos siding in the wind. Nailed above the door hung a rusty caulked horseshoe, for luck. KWRL out of Riverton played Hank Williams and Bing Crosby all day long; the tinny Philco radio buzzed with static from the army-surplus diesel generator that rumbled behind the bar, powering the town. At night Seldom, Mose's big wife, listened to AM sermons from Casper and Denver, hellfire and redemption at dusk. "Today, Mr. David," she would say, "today was so hot, I saw a coyote chasin' a jackrabbit and they was both walkin'." Alkali wasn't on most road maps.

———

Mose did magic tricks. He'd sit at the bar and drop a hen's egg into a milk bottle without it breaking. He could find the one-eyed jack on the first cut in his old dog-eared deck of cards. He could change a dime into a silver dollar, then back into a dime again. Sometimes he would change one of my dimes into a nickel.

A matted cur we called Pennzoil lived in a hole under the boards of the front porch. The dog had tapeworm and he stayed in the damp shade during the heat of the day, and in the evening came out and dragged his hind end across the parking lot. "Where's the wandering Jew today?" Mose said often. There would be days when not a single customer pulled in to so much as buy a Coke and walk around the oiled hardwood floor and study the framed black-and-white rodeo photographs of champion cowboys like Toots Mansfield, Harry Tompkins, Buster Ivory, Homer Pettigrew, Dee Burk, Ike Rude, Jess Goodspeed, Shoat Webster, and Casey Tibbs. On these lonely days, Mose would look at his boots and figure the price of diesel fuel to the price of customers' absence until the shadows crept across the floor and the preachers lit up the airwaves: "And the Lord shall make thee the head, and not the tail, and thou shalt be above only and not beneath." Like an evangelist, Mose recited familiar passages right along with them while Seldom rocked and nodded her head.

Mose had recently married into Alkali. One afternoon while I fought back the desert at the edge of the parking lot with a sickle, Mose strolled out to see how the battle was coming along. "Man don't know what he's doin', the desert'll get the best of him," he said. I asked Mose if Seldom was her real name. "Nope," he said. "Real name's Abigail." I asked him why he called her Seldom. "Because there's something seldom about that woman," he said. Wheezing from the heat, he shook his finger at the sky. "She ain't much to look at, but I have learned that it's better to dwell in the wilderness than with a contentious and angry woman." Seldom ate a raw clove of garlic each morning and tended to the town from a rocking chair on the porch while Mose made figures on the backs of old penny stock certificates that weren't worth a hill of beans. Seldom smiled often, though didn't much care for dusting. Dust covered everything in Alkali.

—

Mose was an antique, a product of the old days. He was part businessman, part saddle tramp, part hardrock mucker. In his day you had to be a jack-of-all-trades. Would-be mining brokers might raise a little capital and birth a mining company on the marble stock exchange floor, then go out into the hills and dirty their hands. Mose had humped a battered alligator-hide briefcase all over the West, not getting rich, more often not breaking even, for a good lot of his many years. He did it all, not having evolved into a specialist, and survived a heart attack, a near-hanging in New Mexico over an asbestos mine gone bad, and a bout with lung cancer to boot.

"Like straw for bricks, uranium is the nucleus of tomorrow," he said to me and every one of the few customers who came into the Alkali Bar. "Like straw for bricks." It was something he'd read in the Bible or the *Tribune*. He was going to get rich from ground-level atomic power. "There are folks down in Utah getting dirty rich," he wheezed between sips of the boiled coffee he called coffin varnish, "and these hills don't look no different than Utah hills." Mose had no intentions of breaking rock himself. He was going to booster his way to wealth. I had a feeling the rock-breaking was where I might come in.

Alkali Bar's daily special consisted of pinto beans in a jalapeño-and-chili-powder sauce Seldom made, every day, and it was the only thing customers could get from the kitchen—breakfast, lunch, or dinner. She never washed the giant cast-iron Dutch oven the beans simmered in, and a black char caked the inside of the big pot. Between bites, chewing and shooing bluebottle flies, customers would reply to Mose, "You don't say," or "That's what I hear." But most just paid for their gas and bottle of beer and hurried down the road on their way to God knows where.

Sometimes oil men, men who knew geology, would come in and Mose would talk uranium with them. Under the saltgrass and greasewood, there were ancient seas of oil in the Paradox Basin, but uranium was foreign to the oil men, just something they remembered hearing about in chemistry class in high school. Their checks were signed by the oil companies. They were lost in oil the way a person can get lost in time in Wyoming, and before you know it, an entire life passes by.

Mose and the geologists talked rocks. They talked vein deposits and mineralization. They talked radioactivity and economic feasibility. They talked about the nuclear-age equivalents of "fool's gold," radioactive elements that weren't worth that hill of beans to the Atomic Energy Commission but could excite a money-blind prospector. The men would finish their coffee and beans. Mose would lick a stubby carpenter's pencil, mumble, and scratch names and figures on the yellowed stock certificates. "For the Lord is my shepherd, but also my rock," Mose said.

———

A week after I arrived in Alkali and learned to pump gas from the pump that was set to give three quarts of watered-down Fire Chief for every gallon that rolled over on the register, Mose's Buick, towing a rusty open-top two-horse trailer, came rattling through the parking lot on its way back from Riverton. He sprang out of the driver's side, slammed the heavy door, and stomped over to the porch, where I was pretending to sweep. "Take a look-see at my new business card." He poked a small gray business card at me and Seldom, who was rocking in the shade of the porch and whistling through her teeth.

POISON SPIDER URANIUM CO., INC.

EXPLORATION AND DEVELOPMENT

J. MOSES DOGBANE, JR., PRESIDENT

RURAL ROUTE BOX I-A

ATOMIC BAR, WYO.

"Our uranium is the nucleus of tomorrow."

Alkali didn't have a phone.

"You're living in Atomic Bar, Wyoming, now. I've already notified the postman. I don't want to hear any word about Alkali except in the history books. And there's no sense thumbing through the history books unless backward's where you want to go."

He pointed toward the Buick. "Here, son, help me with this." He wheezed several notes, like an accordion, and started back for the car. I followed him, studying the mule and the wild-eyed horse in the trailer. A spirited mare, coat slick brown, not bay, but dark— almost greenish in the sunlight, like crude oil. She was blocky, with fox ears and a bowed Roman nose, big feet, and long, shaggy hair on her fetlocks. Her matted croup and thigh had been firebranded and cross-branded several times into an illegible maze of scars. She bucked hard in the trailer. "Here," said Mose. A wooden crate took up most of the back seat. Stenciled on the crate in black letters: NEON, FRAGILE, THIS SIDE UP.

We left the animals in the trailer while we hung Alkali Bar's new neon sign atop the corrugated-tin roof in the afternoon sun. "Beasts'll be fine," Mose said. "They can wait." Once in a while the mare would snort and kick against the tailgate. I worked without a break until just about dusk, when we finished jack-wiring the livewire into the hotbox in the mop closet, my room. Mose climbed down the rotting ladder, stuck his head through the east window, and said, "Okay, hit the switch."

Full dark sat on the desert and we had gone through a box of fuses by the time we got it wired right. Out of fuses, I replaced an element on the last fuse with a shiny new 1950 copper penny and flicked the switch again. The hotbox made a faint hum in the evening quiet. I ran outside toward the pump and looked up. In bright orange letters surrounded by a cartoonish outline of the bomb we dropped on Japan, it read: ATOMIC BAR. Mose stood erect in the glow, chin high, and struggled to contain his pride. His eyes reflected the neon like two new dimes at the carnival midway.

Early the next morning, with difficulty, we untrailered the mare and turned her into the corral. "You can just starve today if that's your attitude, you glue-bound fleabiskit!" Mose yelled. The mare ran tight circles along the rail, catching up again to the dust clouds behind her.

——

He turned the mule and me into the hills to stake our fortunes. I knew nothing about uranium or prospecting, though Mose told me that didn't matter—he would teach me all I needed to know. He gave us a pick, a shovel, a rock hammer, a couple of cold fried-egg sandwiches, a case of beans, an aluminum surplus mess kit, two tin canteens, three full canvas water sacks, a bedroll, an old United States Geological Survey topographical map, boundary stakes, a shiny chrome Precision Radiation Geiger counter Mose'd ordered from a catalogue, a surplus compass, a battered Mexican straw hat, and a weathered copy of the General Mining Law of 1872.

"Don't I get to ride the mare?" I asked.

"Oh no," laughed Mose. "That gal is bronc stock. There'd be something seldom about you after I turned you out in the desert on that devil. She's gonna subsidize our uranium riches until those checks clear."

"Well, what's her name?"

He watched her gait around the corral, kicking dirt, snorting, and butting her breast and throat latch against the top rail in anger. Mose studied her tantrum with pride, like he'd made her himself. "Atomic Bomb, starting today."

Mose stayed at the bar because, he said, he only had one lung left and the walking would do him in. Besides, I was man enough for the job, he told me, and he had a rodeo to run. "That hinny gives you any trouble," Mose said, "go ahead and beat him within a miner's inch of his life."

The mule was probably near the same age as me and was almost as rank as Atomic Bomb. A hinny is a cross between a stallion and a jenny. This one had white patches around his eyes, like a clown, and, like Atomic Bomb, had been cross-branded so many times that his ass-end read like history. The first time I pulled the latigo he jerked around, honked, and bit me on the arm. I fell to the ground, holding the wound with my glove hand, fingers inking red at the edges.

One-handed, with my bloody hand still holding my throwing arm, I hitched down my gear and threw a moldy canvas manty over the bulging panniers. Still not trusting him, the mule, I took the lead rope in my right hand and jerked him forward. He followed, slowly. We cleared the first rise and I might as well have been on the moon, alone with the wind and this goddamned beast. I figured since it was just him and me, I had the right to give him a name. I named him Asshole.

Mose had instructed us to do this: walk for three and a half days east, into the riverless Paradox Basin, the wilderness. He pointed to the morning sun and said, "There lies the Promised Land. The land of milk and honey. Do you see that?"

"See what?" I said. "I just see sand and skunkbrush."

"Look up there on the horizon."

I squinted between two distant mountains, like a rifle sight, at the sun coming up over Wyoming. That time of day you can actually watch the sun rise, like if you stare hard enough at the minute hand of your watch. All I could see was sagebrush, the tops torching in the brightness like they were on fire, burning. I blinked away the spots left in my eyelids and looked at my boss.

"There's money on the ground in those hills," he said. "Go find it." He slapped the mule in the ass and we lit out into the radiating heat.

I kept the Geiger counter switched on, strapped to Asshole's withers, the vacuum tube swinging along his shoulders with every slow step. Nothing but the irregular clicks of normal background radiation that is part of everything.

—

Asshole was a bloater. He'd swell up with air when I cinched the pack saddle down and adjusted the breeching each morning. Careful not to get bit, I'd try jamming my knee between his ribs. He would wheeze, but still manage to keep enough air in his belly. As we walked he would deflate and the latigo would slacken and the pack would slide. Again and again I'd have to wrestle with the heavy pack and cuss a son-of-a-bitch mule. It got so I could tell he liked the cursing. His ears would twitch and he would fill up with fresh air and let out a gleeful honk. Sometimes the pack would slide clear underneath him and I'd have to untie the manty and unpack and rehitch everything.

On the morning of the fourth day of walking, in the lonesome middle of Paradox Basin known on my U.S.G.S. map as the Gas Hills—known to Mose as Bumfuck, Egypt—I hobbled Asshole, turned him out to graze on Russian thistle, sandbur, and the sparse rough grasses, and started looking for anticlines, rock outcrops, and colored formations in order to begin staking dishonest mineral claims.

I walked-off a dozen 600-by-1,500-foot rectangles. At the corners of the claims I built foot-high rock-duck markers. I staked the perimeters. I filled out location notices on a pad of paper Mose had handed me before I left, described in detail the land the claims were on, tucked the papers in tin bean cans with Moses' business card, and left them on the claims. It didn't matter that the rocks were cold and worthless, just rocks; now Poison Spider Uranium Co., Inc., had property.

The last thing I did, before finding Asshole and packing him back up and beginning the long return walk to Alkali, was hike the claims with the Geiger counter. The needle didn't budge, other than the normal twitch from background radiation. Lack of uranium ore was not going to stop the company. Mose explained to me that fortunes were made inside your head and that presence of the mineral—geological whim—was just something to believe in if your world was small. We, he said, were going to raise a million dollars, split it like an atom, and sell the company. "Hell, we can move to California or Kathmandu if we want to!" said Mose. "I'm gonna buy a boat the size of a battleship and sail the oceans of the world. Like a pirate."

We were going to salt several of the bogus claims with euxenite, atomic fool's gold, bring investors out by the Greyhound load, hand them cold beers, and show them our future. They would see a claim or two for themselves, then our long, notarized list of claims filed. Then they would get out their checkbooks and Mose would reach them his ivory pen. Mose wanted the claims three-days remote on purpose. He wanted to discourage government men from taking too close a look. And he wanted to make the claims seem all that much more valuable, like El Dorado, for their remoteness.

———

The wild horses ranged from here south to the Red Desert, into northwestern Colorado, Utah, Arizona, and deep into Mexico, and north to the Pryor Mountains of Montana. They came out and into the open as the evenings cooled into night. I would sit on a rock and watch the horseplay. The mustangs were wary of me, wary of people. Sometimes two stallions would fight over a mare for their harems. Ranchers shot the stallions whenever they could get within rifle range, because a horse eats what a cow eats, and from a rancher's angle, there wasn't enough grass for both. And because the stallions would strut in and steal purebred ranch mares. Horse thieves.

—

My arm healed quickly. Asshole's dull teeth left a flat scar the shape of a goldfish. I took a short-sleeved pride in the scar because it marked me as a real cowboy, a mountain man, no matter that it was a damn hinny and not a grizzly bear that had bitten me. By flexing and relaxing my arm I could make the scarfish tail-dance.

Though I might just as well have been talking to rocks on the journey back to Alkali, I began talking to the mule. Asshole and I had involved conversations about the weather. About Wyoming. About girls and the Brooklyn Dodgers. I asked him, figuring that food was about as much as a mule had to look forward to in the future and his immediate diet consisted of greasewood leaves and snakeweed, if he could have anything at all to eat right then, what would it be?

I told him I was soon going to be rich. I told him that if he didn't pull another stunt like biting me, that maybe I could scare up an apple or two, maybe some sugar cubes or a carrot, when we got back to Alkali. And in the afternoons, when my brains were at the verge of simmering, my canteens warm as radiators, and I couldn't stomach the thought of eating another bean, I could swear that mule talked back to me.

—

Other than overpriced gasoline, pinto beans, and beer, Mose's spot in the road was known for one thing: the infamous jackpot rodeo. The Alkali Jackpot was an informal event that drew cowboys and Indians from miles in all directions. A few of the wilder cowboys scratching out their livings on the bigger summer circuits would even drop in on their way to the more prestigious and respectable events in Casper, Riverton, Lander, Sheridan, Cody, and Powell, because the Alkali pot could get near handsome, and because the event was held on a Monday, the second Monday every July. The men associated with the Alkali Jackpot didn't have real jobs to begin with, or they were cowboys who could work an extra Sunday to make up for their weekday absence. The Alkali Jackpot was a spectacle, like a car wreck, and the way most cowboys are wired, they couldn't stand not to look, even if a look was 150 miles out of their way.

The Indians from the reservation in Riverton didn't adhere to the Roman week. They would begin arriving late Sunday morning by the jalopy load. In their trunks were the cases of Old Stagg bourbon and wet gunnysacks full of bottled Old Style beer. The main event, drinking, began well before the second-most-popular event, bareback riding. Gambling followed the bronc riding for a close third.

The purse consisted of entry fees, the ante—no added money— but many wagers on the side. And sometimes there were fistfights due to differences of opinion. The rules were simple. No judges: Seldom clocked the ride with a pocket watch. If you rode your bronc the full eight seconds, you'd advance to the next go-round. The last man to stay mounted won the purse.

Small ranches would save their rankest horses for Alkali broncs. Many of the horses were the wild mustangs from the Paradox Basin that had been rounded up for rodeo stock. Left in the desert, their element, they were a miraculous and intelligent arrangement of chemistry. Roped, corralled, and often beaten, the horses became volatile, angry equine bombs. The cowboys possessed a lemonade-from-lemons pride in bad horses, and the prestige in rearing a rank horse and trailering it to Alkali was almost as high as sitting on the back of one for eight seconds. As many wagers were made on horses as on cowboys.

The Alkali Jackpot was the biggest bucking-horse sale south of Miles City. And though it was seedier, an underground Monday rodeo, the audience always included several large-hat stock contractors—the Barnums and Baileys of the Rocky Mountain rodeo circuits. Like Major League scouts, they were here to find and buy the rankest stock for the bigger events in brighter towns. An especially surly bronc could bring the owner several hundred, even a couple thousand, dollars.

—

"How's our fortune doing, Davey, my boy?" Mose said as Asshole and I walked out of the desert and through the parking lot. I limped from blisters but held my head up high.

"Okay," I said, noticing that Mose had been busy while I was gone. He'd built an announcer's stand for that July's festivities, hand-painted a sign advertising Poison Spider Uranium, and, beside the front door of the bar, nailed a poster with the familiar Wyoming license plate silhouette of a bronc rider underneath ATOMIC BAR JACKPOT RODEO! Slowly, things around Alkali were beginning to look a little straighter, a little brighter.

"Well, today we're gonna take a little trip. Hitch up the horse trailer and we'll be on our way. We'll have investors out here in a New York minute."

We stopped to file the claims at the Fremont County Clerk's Office in Lander. I liked Lander because it was civilization. If you were on the payroll you could order a hamburger or a malted and see a picture. You could watch pretty girls there for free. Summer dresses, white upper arms, freckles or no. I wanted to show a pretty girl the scar on my bicep. I wanted to tell her I was vice-president of a multimillion-dollar uranium company. Pretty girls did not stop in Alkali.

The courthouse smelled of floor wax, old books, and perfume. Our presence caused a buzz with the courthouse office girls and government men in newer suits, white shirts, and gold tie tacks. The uranium boom was still centered in the Four Corners area of the Southwest and hadn't hit Wyoming yet, though many geologists thought it was possible and only a matter of time. We had to smell something awful. Mose shuffled through a deck of business cards and reached one to everyone we saw like he was dealing them into our private game of Texas hold 'em, Omaha, or stud. He paid the filing fee at a dollar per claim with a brand-new hundred-dollar bill. "Yessir, even Ben Franklin is tight with Poison Spider Uranium." We walked out of the courthouse slowly, enjoying every step. Mose tipped his old hat to women and stopped to look at oil paintings of Indians and politicians.

We bought Cokes and gasoline at a service station where guys in white hats circled your car and checked everything, smiling. "Better get used to the good life, my boy," Mose said.

That day we drove south, all the way to Saratoga, where I noticed that *Mark of the Gorilla,* and *Stagecoach Kid,* starring Tim Holt, were playing at the Rialto. We turned left, east, then traveled for about fifteen miles until we came to the headframe of an old copper mine. Mose talked to a man at the gate and handed him a greasy envelope. The man nodded his head and waved us through. We pulled alongside a pile of old rock, copper tailings, and Mose shut the ignition off. The engine dieseled and the car bucked and died. He got out with the Geiger counter and flicked it on. The machine made a screech and the needle buried itself at the right of the dial.

"Uranium?" I asked.

"No, my boy," he said. "Euxenite. Pretty worthless. But not to us." I spent the next hour or so shoveling copper tailings into the horse trailer.

"This will make a man outta ya, Davey," Mose said between wheezy bars of a whistled tune. He was leaning against the trunk, eating a peach. "Your days with that idiot spoon are numbered. You'll soon trade your shovel for a suit and a new silverbelly fedora.

Mark my word." He studied the loaded trailer, then had me shovel the Buick's trunk full of the copper tailings too.

He started the engine, furrowed his brow, then turned the car off. "Fill the goddamn back seat up too," he said. "I'm gettin' me a new car soon anyway." The tires rubbed against the rear fenders as the old Buick belched green smoke and lurched toward the highway.

—

Atomic Bomb spent her time damaging the arena. I repaired gates and rails until Mose got tired of it and tethered her to a picket post out in the desert. "All right, you can just eat sagebrush and weeds if you're gonna make my life difficult!" Mose yelled at her. I knew that after this year's jackpot, he would unload her on the highest bidder and be done with her. Mose was determined to inflate that bid.

Mose tried to make her meaner, a better bucker, by throwing apples at her, a Wyoming version of Dizzy Dean. He saved soft and wormy pie apples and bounced them off her tough hide. She would start and whinny, the rope taut, then turn and stare Mose down, head lowered, rage in her eyes. After she thought no one watched her any longer, she took the rotten apples in her teeth and squashed them once before swallowing.

—

The next morning, Monday, after hen eggs, beans, and coffee, I saddled Asshole. This time Mose loaded him with two potato sacks of mine tailings in addition to our normal cache, throwing a double-diamond hitch to secure the heavy load. "A mule wearin' diamonds, if that don't beat all, eh, Davey?" The mule shook a little with each step, straining. Mose hollered after us, "Ain't gonna become a uranium tycoon polishin' your britches on a bar stool, son!"

Asshole and I cleared the first rise and a herd of three hundred or so antelope studied us carefully before exploding toward the west.

I hobbled Asshole and we camped that night along a chimney rock, the base blackened by hundreds of fires of Indians and hunters. I ran my hands over the thin fossils of little fish and ferny plants and tiny oysters that covered the layered sedimentary rock like ancient wallpaper. I sang songs the nuns taught us at St. Joseph's. I sang songs I heard on the Philco back in Alkali. I caught the miniature desert horned toads, talked to them, and let them go. "Go on, get outta here. See ya." I saw rattlesnakes and made gentlemen's agreements with them that they stay in the rocks and far enough away from camp not to bother Asshole or me. In return, I wouldn't shoot them. I did not tell them I didn't have a gun. I fell asleep to the soft jingle of Asshole's bell.

The salting was like sowing grain seeds. I stomped over the claims, dragging Asshole behind, throwing handfuls of the hot broken rocks, egging the earth on, daring the sandstone to turn into uranium. Alchemy. I could touch my future, feel it in my hands, and see it under my fingernails. A little Atomic Age Midas, where so many things I'd touched in my life before had turned to worthless dust. I could reach into those potato sacks and grab a handful of my tomorrow. The salting ore, this atomic pyrite, might well have been gold. I would have given such a bag of gold for a cold tin cup of water.

—

Before I left, Mose sat at the bar and reloaded a brick of 12-gauge shells. He opened a box of new high-brass Peters, unfolded the star-crimped paper ends, and let the lead buckshot spill into an old Hills Brothers can with a brown man in a yellow caftan drinking from a bowl. The Hills Brothers man, dressed for the desert, seemed at ease with himself; he had his coffee. Mose replaced the buckshot with euxenite pellets he'd ground with a machine hammer. Whatever we would shoot this hot buckshot into would set a Geiger counter crackling like a plague of locusts. "Enterprising folks have been shooting silver and gold into the walls of mines for over a century," he said. "We're pioneers, Davey, we're the first to shoot a salt charge into the Atomic Age." He explained that we were fixing to doctor up a special claim, a hidden one a little closer to home, to show investors who might not be up for a trip deep into the wilderness.

—

I began riding Asshole one evening, barefoot, wearing only my shorts, enjoying the last of the day's sunshine on my back and my dirty neck. He let me mount him, I think, only because of the great relief he felt not having to shoulder the sacks of salting ore. I was light as a skeleton. I kept the empty packsaddle on him; he was used to it. Having nothing but time, we'd work into riding bareback gradually. I whispered encouragement into his ear, things I thought at the time were true. "I'm not gonna hurt ya, boy. Just gonna ride around real slow like. Davey won't let nothin' happen to ya. Promise."

He stepped slowly. I didn't push him, for it would have violated our trust. We patrolled our claims, though there wasn't anything to defend them against, just the coyotes Mose called prairie lawyers.

The Geiger counter buzzed and rattled when we rode over the centers of the salty claims where the euxenite was scattered. The claims looked the same, but the earth was now more alive there. We made it so. Now the rocks could talk and I could listen to them on a D-cell-powered mail-order machine.

—

I dismounted Asshole because I didn't know where else to ride him and it felt good to walk around a little myself. I walked one of our claims, studying the contacts where the sandstones change colors from pinkish-purple to buff or gray. That's when I found the horse. A black fossilized scar in a dry wash now owned by Poison Spider Uranium, that up close looked to be the skeleton of a dog, a small collie maybe. But it was equine, horse-like, a model in a museum diorama. I touched the horse carefully, running my fingers along its dark lines—a map of life, then. The little beast bore millions of years worth of sedimentary pressure and had yet to evolve into the modern idea of horse.

Asshole walked up behind me, his bell tinkling softly. I started at a rattlesnake that turned out to be the Geiger counter still switched on. I jumped back. But we hadn't salted the claim this wash ran through. The black of the bones and the rich green-brown mineral inside the skull and between the ribs and vertebrae was pitch-blende, uraninite. I untied the Geiger counter from the packsaddle and waved the vacuum tube over the skeleton. The needle buried at the right of the dial as I traced the bones. The horse was embedded in a hot vein of pay uranium. Maybe the horse could make Poison Spider legitimate.

I rolled a small boulder in front of the entombed horse, then brushed our footprints clear with a sage branch. Whether or not it made Poison Spider an honest company, I had conviction that the little horse would get me a raise. The feeling that the horse meant something more than money gnawed at me, but I had started to think like Mose, a businessman. I thought of how I would demand a raise, how I would or wouldn't tell him about the radioactive horse. At this point in my career as a uranium man, I envied my friends still playing ball back at St. Joseph's.

Hungry, sore, tired, canteens empty, we walked out of the wilderness to the sound and dust of Mose, in the parking lot, cutting doughnuts in a newly painted atomic-orange surplus jeep. He waved his hat as he sped past me, kicking a cloud of soil in our faces. "We've gone mechanized, Davey!" he yelled between laughs and whoops. Asshole jerked back and I had to calm him as the gears of the jeep whined and the engine groaned. POISON SPIDER URANIUM in black stenciled letters on the side of the hood. I knew that this meant Mose was going into the desert with me. The trips that belonged to Asshole and me were going public, no longer our own. I didn't tell Mose about the horse.

—

After feeding and watering Asshole and Atomic Bomb that afternoon while Seldom rocked on the porch and Mose took a nap, I sat in the old jeep, just sitting and thinking and breathing-in the machine's old oil smell. The seats were torn and the sharp end of a spring poked at my back. Oil and water leaked from underneath, turning the parking lot a muddy prism of colors in the sunlight. A thin shroud of cirrus clouds drifted overhead, fair-weather reminders of the rains that track north into the Bighorns and Montana, missing the Paradox Basin, again and again. I clutched the steering wheel, slick with bearing grease from Mose's hands, and thought of how I'd tell my boss about the radioactive horse and the mineral deposits I was sure were pitchblende. We could forget the medicine show and become a real company. Maybe Mose would make me vice-president in charge of exploration. We could buy a Piper Colt to fly our prospects in and have an office in Riverton with a secretary and a shiny hardwood conference table the size of a mineral claim.

Just before dark, Seldom stirred beans and I swatted flies and sipped coffee at the bar. An evangelist from Denver told us that "He raiseth up the poor out of the dust, and lifteth the needy out of the dunghill. He will abundantly bless your provision. He will satisfy His poor with bread." A shotgun reported twice and Asshole honked in a pitch much higher than normal. Pennzoil brushed my leg and shot under the porch as I ran outside. Asshole lay on his side at the edge of the parking lot, near the corral, still kicking and trying to breathe with two hot red holes the size of TV trays in his side, as Mose bent over him stiffly, dousing the mule with gasoline from a galvanized-tin bucket.

"Shit fire and save matches! We're mechanized, Davey, my boy! Don't need no mule no more!" he yelled while striking the flint on his Zippo and holding the orange flame to the wet, flammable mulehide. Asshole combusted with a flash I could hear across the parking lot. Mose picked up the shotgun again, reloaded, and shot twice more into the flaming mule. "We're modern, my boy! Do ya hear me? We're modern—no more mule to feed!"

I wanted to yell something, but was not sure what. Instead, I just stared as the mule's flesh ashed and melted in the heat, and the wind fanned the flames that picked him clean to the skeleton. The uranium horse would be our secret, Asshole and me.

—

Mose, his Stetson pulled down tight against the wind, pointed and waved with his shotgun as if it were a staff. I drove the jeep, a new sensitive scintillometer mounted on the hood in case we passed over legitimate paydirt. For the first time all summer I became aware of my sunburns, my blisters torching holes through my soles. My knuckles were red from gripping the steering wheel. I kept picturing Asshole burning in the parking lot. I sped up and the jeep bucked through the sagebrush, a stiff and heartless beast. The gears ground and whined over the misfiring of the cylinders and the sloshing of gasoline in the tank under the seats.

"Don't let it get in your head to be a cowboy," Mose said, holding on where he could. "Because there ain't nothin' but disappointment in that." He spit a wet plug of tobacco into the wind. "Cowboy is an attitude'll plague you all your days. We're business-

men, young David. You don't get rich but by using your brain.
Cowboy is just a sure way to empty pockets and a broken back.
Embrace the future, son. We're purveyors of the bright-orange
sage.

"Let's get this job over and done so I can get out of this goddamn
desert, Davey," Mose yelled over the whine of the gears. "I'm
sweatin' like a two-dollar whore on miners' payday."

The temperature gauge ran warm for most of the trip, and when
we pulled up to the claim the radiator hissed and steamed. Mose
pointed to the drill steel and nine-pound hammer in the back and
began hobbling over to check his claim. "Here." He pointed to a
long and narrow sandstone table. "Jack here."

The hammer was heavy, very heavy, but awkwardly I hefted it
over my head and down on the head of the steel bar. The metallic
ring of steel on steel wasn't steady and rhythmic, but foreign and
irregular. Mose might have held the drill steel while I swung, but
instead he slowly walked the perimeter of his claim, reverently
studying it as if it were an altar of stone, while I struggled to rotate
the drill after each swing of the hammer.

When I had a shallow drill hole, maybe a foot and a half deep,
Mose stuck the barrel of the shotgun in and tripped the trigger. A
thin column of rock, sand, and smoke trailed up out of the hole.
"Get the counter." I ran to the jeep and brought back the chrome
counter. Mose yanked it out of my hands, flicked it on, and the
needle danced, and the counter rattled and Mose showed his
brown teeth. "See this hole," he said, breathing hard. "I want fifteen more here just like it. Only deeper. I'm leaving the gun and
the euxenite shells. I'll be back out tomorrow sometime."

I wanted to pump a radioactive shell into Mose's back, pump
him and the jeep full of euxenite holes. Instead I sat on a rock and
watched the cloud of desert follow the jeep into Alkali.

It was lonely without that Asshole but Mose's jobs kept me busy and after a while I didn't hate him as much. Soon it was time for the rodeo.

——

Sandy Two Bulls, a Northern Cheyenne Indian and a helluva cowboy, drove up in the Ford pickup he'd bought with a season's winnings several years before. There were pictures in the bar of Sandy. He always wore a white Montana-creased Stetson, pants tucked into knee-high boots, and short, sharp, drop-shank, star-roweled spurs strapped to them with leather thong ankle wraps that ran under his heels and up his ankles, like biblical sandals with cowboy boots underneath. His chaps were buffalo hide and, from a distance, the same color as the skin on his face.

I was standing on the porch, trying not to look too worked up about the arrival of the cowboys, but I couldn't hold my excitement. Sandy Two Bulls was here. He walked from his truck at the edge of the parking lot to Asshole's bones.

"Horse catch fire?"

It took me a second to realize he was talking to me. "Mule. Named him Asshole. Mose had him cremated."

"How's that?" Sandy asked.

"Mose says Asshole ate too much. We're modern now."

Sandy took off his hat to wipe his forehead and poked at the bones with the toe of his boot.

That evening, along with other Indian cowboys, Sandy practiced on the reservation stock trailered-in earlier that day. The Indians nosed their cars against the corral and turned their headlights on to light the arena. Under the yellow light of headlights and the neon Atomic Bar atom bomb, they would take turns riding and reriding the horses, bareback, until the stock were too tired to buck and the Indians were too drunk to pull themselves up and get back on, and rodeo whoops answered the faraway howls of coyotes until the batteries in the jalopies ran dead from lighting the arena.

The next morning, Jackpot Monday, more rusty pickups and stock trucks with cracked windshields and odd-colored doors, hoods, and fenders ground into the parking lot. The bar was packed full of cowboys, who ate Seldom's pinto beans and washed down the fire with boiled coffee. Bottles were passed around and the coffee got doctored up. The Atomic Bar Jackpot began just after noon.

Mose did his best to solicit more stock contractors that year, and representatives from Fuller and Howard out of Riverton, Roberts Rodeo Company from down in Kansas, Tommy Steiner out of Cheyenne, Bob Barnes Rodeo Company, Butler Brothers, and even Autry and Colburn attended the event, wearing cleaner shirts, expensive stockman's Panama straws, and custom Olathe and Paul Bond boots. They were here on strict business and tried to steer clear of the revelry. Mose thought he could interest them in uranium as well as his firebranded mascot, Atomic Bomb.

The men talked about her as "the devil horse." She ran nervous circles around her picket post before Mose had tied her to the jeep and pulled her into a small corral of her own to wait for her turn to buck. She kicked at him with her hind hooves, missed, and split a rail on the gate.

I drove. The orange jeep rimmed the arena like Atomic Bomb on her first day in Alkali. I stopped in front of the announcer's stand. In a white gentleman's Stetson, bright orange shirt, and green wool pants tucked into the stovepipe shafts of his boots, like a ringmaster, Mose strutted to the ladder, slowly climbed up, and took the microphone. "Ladies and gentlemen," he said, his voice big and full of echo and static, "welcome to Atomic Bar, Wyoming, and the world's greatest Monday jackpot rodeo!" A few hands clapped, a few men hollered, but mostly the sounds included antsy horses and stiff dry wind. "Folks, please rise and remove that hat for our great country's National Anthem." A needle scratched against the rim of an old record; then Bing Crosby sang "The Star-

Spangled Banner," the speed just a little slow, while everyone listened patiently with their Stetsons over their hearts. "Let 'er buck!"

No clowns, no barrel racing, no country-and-western singers. Not even bleachers. Just bronc riding and spirits. Cowboys and ranchers leaned against the fencerail as riders drew their broncs out of a hat and climbed into the chute to straddle angry horses with names like Inferno, Bearclaw, Cherry Bomb, Tabasco Tea, Bazooka, Hudson Hornet, Whisky, Tiger Boy, Gunsmoke, Jack Hammer, Old Mr. Boston, Tax Man, Custer's Mother, B-17. They were thrown by Party Girl, Soda Jerk, Lucky Strike, Enola Gay, Texas Ranger, Iron Moccasin, Free Beer, Aunt Ulcer, Howitzer, Spilled Milk, Don't Call Me Dude, Wrecking Ball, Truman's Mule. Cowboys were stepped on by Rocking R, Banshee, Dark Meat, Sergeant, Red Devil, Two A.M., and Fastball. Bones were broken by Daisy May, Hermosa Bar, Medicine Show.

A bucking strap was cinched tight around the horse's flanks. At most rodeos, the bucking straps were smooth leather. At Alkaki, the straps were thick lengths of rough hemp rope with a knot or two tied in the middle. When the cinch knot was pulled tight, the horse would bleat and honk and kick in the chutes. When the knot was pulled tight and spurs were raked across its ribs, the horse wanted to hurt a cowboy.

Atomic Bomb had been isolated at her picket post all day without feed. Mose wanted her mad and hungry for the finals, which looked like they would include Sandy Two Bulls and a kid from Powell no older than me with the name Buck Lewis.

Mose's wheeze filled the dead air between the semis and the finals. He looked at the sky, then let the word take him. "Now, ladies and gentlemen, allow me to be frank for a moment. You, ladies and gentlemen, and I, ladies and gentlemen, are atoms. Blessed atoms. We are particles, matter, patterns of molecules—protons, neutrons, electrons—arranged in the image of God. We, good people of the West, have long been plagued by the East, and I'm not talking the Reds of Russia. We here in Wyoming have been plagued by Wall Street locusts and Connecticut corporations alike, raping our resources and exporting the money *that* way by trainload after Union Pacific trainload. Why must we vow poverty? Good people, riches and honor are with me, yea, durable riches and righteousness. Like straw for bricks, let us see this great country into the nuclear age with the best raw materials from right here under the Big Wonderful." Sweat dripped from Mose's temples, tracked down the crags of his face, and disappeared into his brushy mustache.

"See the jet airplanes fly from California to New York and right over our heads. Why not fill our pockets with the idea that those planes will soon be powered with Wy-o-ming a-tomic fuel? The Lord has lain for us a wealth of treasures. We live in the greatest, most powerful country in the world. Why shouldn't you live in the greatest, most prosperous state in the union? Dear friends, this is no miracle of judgment—it is simply God's brown earth. And worth its weight in gold, though my uranium is better than gold, yea, fine gold. Allow me, fellow citizens, to mediate your covenant of wealth, for in the house of the righteous is much treasure. For your children, the children of Wyoming, I strongly urge you to invest in the fruit of thy ground. Invest in Poison Spider Uranium."

Mose, spittle in the corner of his mouth, his shirt soaked with sweat, wheezed into the microphone and bowed his head, less out of respect and relief than admiration for his new boots. He dropped the microphone onto the wooden deck of the announcer's stand and a shrill of feedback pierced everyone's ears and made the corralled horses buck and knock together.

Mose climbed down from the stand, went to the jeep, grabbed the Geiger counter, and walked through the middle of the arena to where Asshole's bones dried in the wind. He switched the machine on and waved the vacuum tube over the bones. "This hinny's been workin' Poison Spider claims and now he's giving off enough radiation to light a town."

The crowd around the mule parted to let a cowboy through. "I'll ride that mare against ya for it," said Sandy Two Bulls, pointing to the corral where Atomic Bomb paced in circles.

"What's that you say, Hebrew?" Mose said.

"For everything that went into that mule," Sandy Two Bulls said, his hand following his words across the desert. "All your gold mines. The bar. That jeep. This town. The boy." His finger stopped at me. The eyes of the crowd moved with Sandy's finger, finally shifting from me to Mose. Everyone was silent, anticipating a duel.

"Why, Two Bulls, you're drunk. You ain't even won this rodeo and you're talkin' my uranium. You're drunk. You're piss drunk."

"True enough. Everyone here will put up a stash. You can collect wagers on the side. The purse. My truck. The deed to my house in Montana. And I'll ride her first, wear her down for ya."

"You'd better make the finals here, first, Indian," Mose said. "Everything in time, everything in time."

———

The air was smoky from the forest fires burning west of Alkali— Yellowstone, the Bridgers, the Wind Rivers, and the Tetons—and the neon from Atomic Bar shone against the east like an artificial sun as Sandy Two Bulls straddled a stallion named Dog Rose. Two Bulls nodded and leaned back hard. He spurred Dog Rose out of the chute, then dug into the bronc's shoulders with his sharp spurs in a graceful and violent rhythm. The horse blew and bucked hard for eight seconds, ten seconds, twenty seconds, until he became exhausted and sore and Sandy Two Bulls rode him to a bleeding standstill.

Buck Lewis drew Atomic Bomb and three long seconds out of

the chute was thrown to the side, where his head got caught in the rigging. Atomic Bomb's horsepower ripped the young man's ear off the side of his head. A dozen cowboys walked the arena, searching for the ear. They tied his own dirty shirt around his head and drove him into Riverton in the back of a pickup, where he recovered enough to keep on living, getting to feel things, no longer a boy, though he never rode bareback broncs again.

——

Mose's speaking-in-tongues adrenaline still pumped through his veins and he wanted to put an exclamation point on his speech, but by now I could tell he was no longer sure of himself. Two Bulls had won the jackpot, but the cowboys still waited around for what had turned into the real event. The drunk crowd couldn't give a damn about uranium: they wanted to see animals break the bones of cowboys, and vice versa. This was their religion. I thought about what Mose'd said about being a cowboy, and I could see this as Sandy Two Bulls tried to position himself and pound the rigging on Atomic Bomb's back. But Mose didn't always practice what he preached. With his whiskey-thick breath, he was getting ready, strapping on his tarnished spurs.

Atomic Bomb bucked as much as the gates would let her, making Sandy Two Bulls have to hold on even in the chute. Then the mare let out a big breath and settled, saving her energy.

With a snort and several honks, she exploded out of the opened gate. She sucked her back, swapped ends, and drilled Sandy Two Bulls into the hard arena soil, then circled around to run over him, exact vengeance on him like a mad bull buffalo. Two Bulls made it up onto the fence and Atomic Bomb cut away and circled the arena twice before being waved back into the alleyway. Two Bulls limped over to me near the chute and blew to catch his wind with his hands on his knees. He spit in the dirt and smiled up at me. I ran and got him a dipper of water, and I knew I would tell him about my uranium horse.

—

Mose rested his boot on the first rail of the bronc chute. "Davey, my boy," he said, surveying his world by moving his eyes sideways, back and forth, like a lizard, "you gotta pay the fiddler if you wanna dance."

Mose mounted Atomic Bomb while keeping his left hand firm on the top rail of the chute. Gingerly, he forced his gloved right hand into the rigging, drew it tight as the mare snorted hard. He pounded the leather into his palm. Mose looked old, yes, but through his eyes shone a deep pool of youth. He wore the smile of a man about to enter through the ivory gates to glory. Mose's gates were solid uraninite.

"Ladies and gentlemen, I urge you to invest in Poison Spider Uranium! Let 'er go!" he yelled, nodding. The gate swung open and the spectators whooped and hollered, but the mare just stood there and a moment that seemed like an eternity went by as the horse took everything into consideration before commencing with what she did best. She was a high roller. She sucked her back again, accordioned, then swapped ends, her trademark. She runaway bucked and sunfished straight across the arena, and Mose looked like he would stay on her back out of some unearthly gravitational law that only applied to medicine men and evangelists.

Mose bucked away, then connected with horsehide, shot away again, daylight between, out and back, but clinging to the bronc, like an electron. The crowd was silent, watching with mouths open, listening to the thunder of hooves, the cracking of cowboy against bronc.

Atomic Bomb bucked him up, then off to her left side. A bloater like Asshole, she let out a powerful snort and whinny, deflating her lungs. Mose's gloved hand hung in the rigging as it slid around and underneath the mare. Like so much copper tailing, Mose's own weight pulled him into the maelstrom of powerful hooves, leaving his hat and handkerchief in the dirt, the elk-tooth watch behind to glint in the half-light like fool's gold, and his hand still in the rigging. Mose hung upside down in the hammer mill of hooves as Atomic Bomb rimmed the arena, her Roman nose held high.

Mose rode her barrel like a trick rider. Atomic Bomb passed so close to the fence we could feel her hot breath. Two Bulls and I stepped back from a cloud of Mose's whiskey and horseradish dust. Forever the salesman, Mose gave the crowd his best, most confident bloody-nose grin. In his eyes he was still a champion cowboy and a champion mineral baron, his fortune within reach of his thick fingers. His teeth had been knocked out and left in the dirt. But you can't sell stock in old teeth. Mose hung on.

When Atomic Bomb finished her parade, she jumped to clear the corral and something not horse made a hollow thud against wood, knocking the top rail and several spectators to the ground. The mare kicked up a cloud of desert and raced toward the east— a dark dot on the horizon the size of an atom—into the future.

Sugar City

onnie and I had just gotten married in the town hall in the tiny village of Jarbidge, Nevada, and were throwing back Angel Creek Ales at two dollars a pop in the Red Dog Saloon when Bonnie asked the barmaid how the most remote gold town in the lower forty-eight got its name. The barmaid let out a lungful of smoke and said, "Jarbidge's Shoshoni for 'a bad or evil place.' " This started Bonnie to crying big makeup-ruining tears. Names and their meanings meant a lot to Bonnie—she didn't take mine: Petefish.

—

"This is Mr. Petefish," I'd said. "I'm sick. I'm sick of a lot of things. In fact, I think I'll be sick until the end of the year." I'd already called in two weeks in a row and they had to pay me for my sick days, which had added up over the years. The principal phoned a couple of times in the late morning but I never picked up. Instead,

I'd suffer his nasally voice on the machine, thinking I wasn't missing much.

Burned out, we were selling in. Bonnie resigned from her secretarial job at Boise-Cascade with a traditional two-week notice on the first day I called in sick.

I considered myself a spirit teacher. My principal considered me lazy. I love teaching, but I needed to be able to sleep until ten, go in at noon twice a week, and tell stories until Happy Hour. Kids remember stories, not comma splices. I couldn't face the rat maze, the Pavlovian hell of bells and report cards. I taught through stories. While other teachers filled pails, I lit little fires. And fires are hard to capture without parables.

After I'd quit, I sold my Explorer—a vanity I'll admit I'd caved in to—for eight thousand dollars cash and disciplined myself to two cigarettes a day.

Bonnie quit smoking cold turkey along with her job. She drove a white four-hundred-dollar AMC Matador, like the one I drove in high school. I love that car. Bonnie's dream was to someday open a bed-and-breakfast in some quaint western town at the edge of reality. She'd told me this the first time we'd met, in a bar, her dressed in a leather mini, me wearing my teacher pants, at Happy Hour at five-thirty on a Monday night. After we quit, we decided I would take a seasonal job doing something romantic, like planting trees or putting out fires. We even had a little ceremony where we ate macaroni and cheese with jug wine, because we were saving money, and cut up our credit cards with scissors. It was fun, I thought. Bonnie paused as I whooped with joy when the scissors snapped a piece of my Visa across the room. She seemed a little quiet afterward, but I pretended not to notice. The plan was already in action.

Sell everything, flee Boise, get married, and find true happiness in living like coyotes. Hunter-gatherers.

We started out by driving to Reno, where I gave her the queen of

diamonds—the card, that is—and asked her to be my wife. I celebrated our engagement by losing ten thousand dollars at the
roulette wheel. The next morning we had breakfast and I never got
around to telling her. I figured it was something we could discuss
after the honeymoon when we needed the money.

From Reno, we headed to Elko for the thirty-five-dollar marriage license before making our way north to the most remote town
in the lower forty-eight. I thought it would be romantic and I
needed something grandiose for when we discussed our budget.

The drive was spectacular. After twenty miles of two-lane highway, we followed the signs onto a dirt road that wound for fifty
miles over cattle guards, through thick forests and green fields, up
and around mountains, heavenward, until we finally began a steep
descent that took us right into the village of Jarbidge.

"It's lovely" was all Bonnie could manage on the drive. The rest
of the time we were so busy looking at the scenery, we forgot about
each other.

———

The "bad and evil place" thing really shook Bonnie up. I had to buy
her another beer with her own money to try and calm her nerves. I
consoled my new wife by saying that Jarbidge was probably really
the last name of the first single-jack miner in camp, but the Forest
Service man nipped that idea in the bud by verifying the barmaid's
story from behind his own Angel Creek Ale.

"My wife swore the place is cursed. She lived here for almost a
year. Left without a word. I've been here for thirteen."

"It's an omen, Frank," sobbed Bonnie. "Our marriage is cursed."

"It's just a name," I said. I was ready to call for a paper bag if
Bonnie started to hyperventilate. "And even if the town is bad, it
doesn't mean our union is cursed."

"Yes it does!" she cried. "I had a dream last night that proves it
all!"

We all looked at Bonnie, waiting for her dream, me knowing this couldn't be a good thing.

"I dreamt that we were walking around town and I kept seeing all of these people in old-fashioned clothes. I would say, 'Look at that pretty dress, Frank,' or something like that, but Frank"—Bonnie looked me in the eye—"you couldn't see their faces. Now I know what it means. They were ghosts. I dreamt about evil ghosts the night before my wedding. That's a serious omen."

After that Bonnie cried into another beer. I loaded her into the old Matador and wrote *Just Married* with my finger in the dust on the trunk. "We can renew our vows somewhere else," I said. "Make a great anniversary."

"Where?" Bonnie yelled. "Las Vegas? The Elvis Chapel?"

The night before we had slept in the Matador and got up early to bathe upstream from town in the Jarbidge River. The cold August water shriveled my manhood, and I poured each of us a shot from a pint bottle of Ten High whiskey. Bonnie put on her new white halter dress, me in olive pants, white shirt, my grandfather's old tie. "I must really love you to do this," Bonnie had said, shivering while she poured herself another drink into one of the shot glasses I'd brought for this occasion. "Frank's Bar" was etched into the glass.

"It's a test," I said. "I'll not marry any girl who wouldn't bathe in a cold mountain stream on her wedding morning."

We drove to town with the windows down, the Matador's lifters knocking a little louder than I remembered.

Nevada covered our shoes, clothes, and hair like a layer of history by the time we got to the town hall, where Reverend Ron said he'd meet us and marry us for the small gratuity of a hundred dollars. If not for the whiskey, I knew Bonnie'd be worrying about the dust coating her new dress.

Reverend Ron greeted us from the porch of the saloon, clutching a Bible against his heart. The barmaid and the Forest Service man—witnesses—followed him down the street to the town hall. It was already in the mid-eighties. The Reverend Ron was some sort of outlier himself. The scene came straight from a hundred-fifty-year-old tintype: the reverend wore a deerskin jacket, faded jeans, a flared Civil War goatee, and leather sandals—Boise sandals! Boise seventh-grader sandals. They were all the rage.

I took a breath and grabbed Bonnie's hands. Bonnie shook. Reverend Ron's ceremony was full of cowboy-and-Indian hippie sophistry. Tears tracked down Bonnie's cheeks.

"All people of the world recognize marriage, and there are many common themes in all wedding ceremonies. With tremendous insight, however, and perhaps most significant to our western way of life, is a simply worded yet profound Indian ceremonial which describes the union of a man and a woman in this light: 'Now you will feel no rain, cold, or loneliness, for each of you will be shelter, warmth, and companion for the other.'"

Bonnie's crying became softly audible.

"At this moment you come before us as two persons, but there is only one life before you.

"Go therefore to your dwelling, to enter into the days of your life together.

"May those days be good, and long upon this earth."

Bonnie wept uncontrollably now, a cry of something I can't describe that was nowhere near deep joy. "We don't even have a dwelling!" she interjected.

"Aw, Sugar." I squeezed her hand and made her look at me until she smiled a weak smile.

Reverend Ron'd lost his place in the ceremony. "The ring?" he asked, clearing his throat.

Her ring: a simple, thin band that I prayed contained real gold. I had found it in a Nampa pawnshop.

"This band of gold that you now offer to Bonnie represents a circle. The symbol of the universe. The symbol of peace and perfection. Likewise, this ring is the symbol of unity, in which your lives are now joined in one unbroken circle of love and commitment that is never-ending.

"As Frank and Bonnie have before us pledged their love and commitment, each to the other, I declare, through the authority vested in me by the State of Nevada, they are husband and wife. You may seal this union with a kiss."

We did and walked out into the sunlight, holding hands, toward the saloon. No one remembered photographs.

——

Hot Springs, Nevada/Idaho was on our map. We both had a sad buzz on, made stronger by the winding forty dirt miles north of Jarbidge. We pictured a resort town at the mouth of the valley with a hot bath and a hotel room. I sped through town—a single wide trailer and shotgun shack with HOT SPRINGS painted on the side. The air smelled of sulfur.

Two shirtless and filthy Indian kids rode a swayback mare. "Indians," I said, thinking all the while that my students would love this story, ghosts and Indians. I could probably even make it into an Indian ghost story.

"Drive on," Bonnie said, pointing down the road. "I don't like it here."

"But Indians," I told her. "These are probably Shoshone or Blackfeet—would they be here if the place was evil?" We drove on and I settled for washing my face with a wet-nap.

——

Bonnie slumped against my shoulder and slept the fitful sleep of the depressed who don't have their medication quite dialed in. A rainbow air freshener that hadn't bothered me before hung from the rearview mirror. I ripped it down, looking over at sleeping Bonnie, and threw it out the window.

Night would soon settle on the southern Idaho desert, northbound, and I began to need the ceremony of eggs and a bottomless cup of coffee. It's the surest thing about the road, breakfast at any hour, and something to chew on when driving all night: loss and breakfast. Bonnie still didn't know about the ten-thousand-dollar donation I'd made in Reno.

Driving north and east in Idaho felt like driving in a circle.

We had wanted to get married in Nevada. I had, at least. It wasn't until after we'd arrived that I realized I'd sabotaged every childhood dream and wedding fantasy Bonnie'd ever held; this is something they never outgrow. There is nothing real in Nevada. Not the people. Not the neon. All faceless ghosting of hope. Where did those Indian kids go to school?

Women spend the rest of their lives chasing the fairy tales, only adjusting their expectations somewhat accordingly. The license was real. The marriage was real. Quitting our jobs was real. Nevada is the false-front moral equivalent of the façade we'd left in the city.

The Matador's lifters beat like a marching drum.

The gas gauge read E when I slipped into the Amoco in Sugar City. The neon of the Amoco was warmer than the casino glow of Reno. I smiled at the girl behind the counter as I pumped the Matador full of 85-octane. As the pump clicked off the gallons, I retraced *Just Married* in the dust of the trunk. Bonnie stayed asleep, not knowing we were in Sugar City. Not caring.

The streets were quiet and peaceful and represented a life that was still miles away for us. The pump clicked off and I waved at the girl behind the counter and got back in. The Matador probably needed a quart of oil, but I didn't want to push it. Surely she saw the *Just Married* in the dust of the trunk. Surely she wouldn't call in the drive-off on a newly wed couple with a whole life ahead of them.

Twilight turned to dark and the headlights began taking purchase on the signs and reflector posts of the asphalt ribbon that bisected a moonscape of spuds and sugar beets. The Blackfoot AM played consoling country songs from the halcyon days of Buck Owens and Merle Haggard. A yellow diamond with a black cow silhouette whiffled with bullet holes signaled more open range.

"Sweetheart," I said. I would say this and if she was awake, fine. "I need to tell you something about our savings. There really aren't any." No response from Bonnie.

I was chewing two chunks of Double Bubble and drumming to "Kansas City Song" on the vinyl steering wheel at seventy-five miles per hour when realization sent a double of adrenaline through my system.

"Son of a bitch."

I comprehended the very real yellow eyes of the black cow silhouetted against black U.S. 20. The late brakes took maybe thirty miles per hour off our velocity. I'd already resigned to hit the animal in the adrenalined fraction of a second before the sound of the car breaking.

Bonnie and I—no lap belts—hit the dashboard. Spiderwebbing glass and the crunch of metal as the wheels left asphalt and launched from a shallow ditch, and the two of us getting thumped around before the Matador came to rest in an irrigation canal fifty feet into a beet field. The radio still played . . . *Take good care of you . . .* The radiator hissed. I tasted blood, which I assumed was my own, but in the yellow light of the dashboard I could see it was dripping from the cow, broken like a watermelon, and suspended between the firewall and front seat.

Bonnie was silent, a line of blood running from her scalp, across the bridge of her nose, to her lips and chin. "Sweetheart, are you okay? Sugar, please say you're all right." But what scared me most was that I realized, through my pleading for Bonnie to be okay, that

I was really pleading for *me* to be okay—how much of this steady smear of blood that I prayed came from the heifer was mine?

I touched my face and looked at my hands.

"I'm okay, I guess," she said. And part of me was relieved, though part of me remembered that the unhappiness brought on by Jarbidge could have, in a cowy stroke of fate, been laid to rest in this field of sugar beets with the smell of raw hamburger, radiator coolant, and stagnant mosquito water.

Bonnie's door was jammed shut with earth. My door opened. I kicked it down on the hinges and it swung hard. I stepped into the shallow water and deep mud. Bonnie slid underneath the bloody cow to my side, her hair slick with wet, wedding dress tainted red. As she pulled herself out the door frame, the animal wheezed. "The cow's still alive," Bonnie cried. "It's suffering. You havta do something quick. Put it out of its misery. Kill it."

"How the hell am I gonna do that?"

"I don't know, do something. This is your fault. Use your knife."

I always carried a pocketknife my grandfather had given me when I was eleven. Blade extended, the thing wasn't over four inches long and I carried it for luck more than practicality. I walked to the cow and told her I was sorry, knowing this would be charged to my karma debt. "It was an accident," I said. I poked a little at the hide under her chin.

God, what a story. I forced the blade into the throat hide. It went in hard—like through a boot sole—and, even sawing, I could hardly move the blade. A new, thin stream of blood painted my shoes. I was thinking of adjectives to describe the scene. I kept sawing and the cow kept not dying.

The sounds that seemed to escape from the cut were horrible. *How could you do this?* she said in anguished bovine language. *I was only ranging.*

"Is it dying?" asked Bonnie. She'd pried open the trunk and found a sweatshirt to pull on over her dress.

"Hell, yes, she's dying, but it might take two fucking days. We're on open range. That means we just bought this cow." My fear for myself had surfaced and now went before Bonnie and drama, and she smelled it.

"What are we gonna do?" she asked.

"Wait for someone with a gun and a camera, I guess."

Things were quiet for a moment, except for the cow. I kept sawing and Bonnie began rummaging in the trunk again. She looked westward.

"Don't worry about the wedding—I don't think it was very official," she said.

I collapsed in the dirt and faced the sky. "Oh, this takes the cake. I'm giving up. I'm finished."

Bonnie's shoes clicked as she walked away down the highway, but I pretended not to notice. I was getting good at pretending not to notice.

How much time passed? A class period, maybe two.

"It's cold." My arms, neck, and knee had begun to stiffen. "It's cold, I said. Aren't you cold? Answer me, Bonnie."

Silence.

"So you're selling out that easy. I see how it is now." But my words were absorbed by the black soil of beet field and she couldn't have heard me. "Okay, I see how it is now." A car stopped—old Plymouth with round taillights like rat's eyes. No Bonnie. No flashlight.

I limped south, southwest through the volcanic soil, hoping before long to run into U.S. 26, where I could hitch a ride to Idaho Falls. By now Bonnie was in a warm car, talking to her Boise mother on the cell phone. Few things beat the warmth of a car heater, the inane buzz of the AM radio, but you have to be cold first to appreciate it.

I walked all night, fueled by fear and the cold. Millions upon millions of goddamn sugar beets. Enough sugar here to fill every sugar packet in every café from hell to breakfast.

Selling out had long ago become bullshit. Drinking coffee, stories, twelve-year-olds high on sugar and Yellow Number 5—that life didn't sound so bad now. Weekends driving into the mountains in my Explorer. Seeing friends at the bar.

I tried navigating by the stars. There were no stars over Boise. I felt as if I was walking in circles and gave up, trusting my instincts.

Sometime well after midnight it became apparent that a person could die atop all that sugar. Collapse from exhaustion and dehydration. Maybe just lie down and freeze to death on an especially cold August night.

The thin line of dawn began appearing. I adjusted my direction to walk due west. I could see the lights of a town that might have been two miles away, might have been twenty. Must be Rexburg, I figured. They'll have eggs in Rexburg. I limped to the beet elevator.

The letters on the elevator: SUGAR CITY, IDAHO.

I ran across the highway, not bothering to look even one way.

The Amoco was warm. There was a small convenience store with a bar and a few stools where customers could eat a cold sandwich and drink coffee from Styrofoam cups. I hadn't noticed the bar part before, when I was borrowing the gasoline. "I'll have a half dozen eggs over easy, sausage, bacon, hashbrowns, toast, white. Keep the coffee coming."

"Might be a ham salad sandwich left," the clerk, a kid not long out of high school, said without pausing her sweeping.

I found two sandwiches and unwrapped the cellophane and ate one in three bites without much chewing.

"Will that do it?"

"I'm full as a tick. Do you know that I can't pay for these?" I said, talking with my mouth full. "Guess I'm dining and dashing."

"It's on me. Actually, it's on the manager."

"I demand that you call the police."

"Sheriff."

"Then I demand that you call the sheriff."

"Nope."

"But I'm a fugitive! I'm a fugitive from Boise. I drove off with a tank of your gasoline. I've killed some guy's cow. I've stolen your sandwich."

"So if you drove off with our gasoline, where's your car?"

"I told you. I hit a cow on the highway."

The girl kept sweeping. "Sounds like bull. Look, I'm off shift in ten minutes and the sandwiches are free. The gas is free—I don't care. Now get out or not, but I'm going home in ten minutes, no hassles, okay."

Arrest would mean a hot meal and a blanket for a few days. I could sort out my thoughts, my future. Now I had to face all of Idaho with nothing but a windbreaker and a pocket comb.

She was finished with her shift—the best part of the day. The kind of accomplished tired that feels so good because you've put something hellish behind you. I imagine that the reason people run marathons is so they can feel the kind of tired that follows, where nothing in the world, not even Idaho, is bigger than a cold, hard-earned beer—no news.

My hunger delayed for an hour or two, I walked into the cold morning sun onto the shoulder of the highway. I felt light with nothing but hands in my pockets, no keys, no money, no responsibility. No wife. Nowhere to go but down the road. I could choose anonymity and poverty. I possessed the glorious luxury of choice that made me one of the richest men in the world. Only the beautiful, atavistic need to survive! Here I was at the crossroads of rock bottom and I could choose not to go up. I might choose to go to Mexico and live vicariously through a song. I could choose to go back to another classroom and tell stories while a real world spun around me.

I walked northbound, toward Blackfoot—the opposite direction from Boise. I concentrated on my feet, and the walking took my mind off things. A school bus passed without slowing. Maybe twenty minutes down the road, a huge early-seventies Lincoln slowed and wheeled to the shoulder fifty yards ahead of me. The Lincoln was green, patched with rust, enormous snow tires on the rear—reservation car.

As I neared I could read a bumper sticker: CUSTER WAS A PUNK.

Heads of long black hair shifted inside. The rear passenger door opened and a signal of smoke caught a breeze and blew toward me. They'd never been to Jarbidge, Nevada. What did I teach? Kids—I taught kids. A farmer in coveralls stood looking into his irrigation ditch as we passed, at his expensive heifer atop Bonnie's Matador. Friends and brothers, five Indians told stories of an Idaho Falls drunk, the Merit smoke sweet and white as saccharine.

Custer on Mondays

SUNDAY WAS A BATTLE

unday, June 25, was a battle. The last of the smoke cleared in the afternoon, the dust settled in the barley field, and the Sioux, Arapahoe, Cheyenne, Crow, and Seventh Cavalry called the horses, picked up the arrows, dusted themselves off, and headed downtown together for cold beers at the Mint. Most of the chiefs and officers had planes to catch in Billings, but the group got on without them. They'd pick up the Indian Wars again at next year's Reenactment of Custer's Last Stand.

On Monday morning, June 26, the day after the big battle, Owen Doggett came home from the Mint to find he was now trespassing on the dirt half acre he used to almost own. Everything the actor now owned formed a crude breastwork ten yards from the chipped cinder-block front step that led to the single-wide he also used to almost own. A buckskin shirt. A few T-shirts. Some socks. A faded union suit. A broken AM radio with a coat-hanger antenna. His Sage fly rod. An empty duffel bag. A brick of pistol rounds, and the title to the '76 Ford Maverick.

Charley Reynolds, the basset hound, was off chasing rabbits in the cheatgrass; he belonged solely to Owen Doggett now. Owen Doggett banged on the window of the locked trailer house with his gloved fists and yelled, "Sweetheart, I'll make you eggs!"

His wife had already begun her day's work, tying flies for an outfitter in Sheridan. Her fly patterns were intricate, exacting, and held the subtle variances of nature usually reserved for spiderwebs, mud-dauber nests, and snowflakes. Through the cloudy window of her workroom, Sue Doggett looked up from her vise and out at her husband in his riding boots and dirty wool tunic. She mouthed, "Read my lips: I am not acting."

THE SIOUX

Mr. and Mrs. Owen Doggett were married three years ago on a moonlit Monday midnight in Reno, Nevada, after meeting at a Halloween party and dating for exactly sixteen days. The engagement lasted an afternoon and a dinner. They took the red-eye out of Billings and stayed drunk for the entire two-day trip. They were married in the same clothes they met in—his custom Custer buckskin, her star-spangled Wonder Woman bustier. The wedding cost exactly twenty-seven dollars, bourbon and snapshots included.

Sue is a full-blooded Crow. Owen Doggett calls her The Sioux. And sue is what she is doing; she's suing the trooper for all he's worth. No negotiations. Sue gave him an old government Colt revolver as a wedding present. She wanted the valuable relic back. "Indian-giver!" he called her. He cannot afford a lawyer.

THE COLONEL

Owen Doggett is a local, an extra, a private. But Owen will tell you he's a trouter by heart, an actor by trade, and he has faith he will one day soon be the hero, the star, the colonel in the Hardin, Montana, Reenactment of Custer's Last Stand. "Call me Colonel," he'll tell you. He has to stay in character. "I'm an actor from Hollywood. Bred-in-the-bone." Right now he, his trouting buddy, and Charley Reynolds are on their way east so Owen Doggett the actor can audition to be the Black Hills Passion Play's substitute Pontius Pilate. The Colonel will not tell you he is only a private. He will tell you he may soon be cast as Pontius Pilate in a large-scale production of the second-greatest story ever told, the story of Jesus' last seven days in South Dakota. He will not tell you he is from Hollywood, Pennsylvania, and that he has to rent a nineteen-year-old grade horse when he wants to ride.

Hardin's current Custer is a Shakespearean-trained actor from Monroe, Michigan. He looks like Colonel George Armstrong Custer, owns a white stallion like Custer's, pulls a custom four-horse trailer, does beer commercials for a brewery out of Detroit, and calls his wife Libbie. It will not be easy. The Colonel is torn between what he wants to do, what his heart tells him—goddammit, you're an actor!—and what is to be done. "History is the now of yesterday," he says. In his own recent history, the Colonel has caught some nice fish, drunk a few beers, cheated on his wife, and watched some movies. He sees himself on the big screen—not in a factory, not in an office. He hasn't paid many bills, but "hell," he says, "we don't have a satellite dish and we don't get cable. That's a big savings right there."

Libbie Bacon Custer wanted her husband to be President of the United States of America. Sue Doggett wanted the Colonel to get a not-always-have-to-tenderize-a-cheap-cut-of-beef job. Not full-time necessarily, just something where the trooper worked more than one day every two weeks. But that would mean giving up a few Mondays—and Tuesdays, Wednesdays, and the like—of sore-lipping fish.

"Do I not bless you with much fish and bread?" the Colonel asks his wife.

"Whitefish and Wonder Bread every day isn't my idea of heaven," says Sue.

THE PRIVATE

The Colonel calls his trouting buddy, Ben Fish, Private. They might be knocking back a few Rainiers at the Mint. They might be boning up on the Black Hills Expedition of '74 over morning coffee at the B-I. They might be casting the Little Bighorn for browns and rainbows on a Monday. They might be, as they are now, rumbling down U.S. 212, on their way only a few hours after dawn, with Charley Reynolds in the middle and the Private riding shotgun. Just the three of them in the old oil-burning baby-blue Maverick, their forage caps cocked back on their heads, spitting the hulls of sunflower seeds out the windows. For the Private this trip is a chance to scout some new country, cast some new water.

The Private is a teacher. He has taken stitches in the back of the head where the heel of his pregnant ex-wife's cowboy boot caught him from point-blank range. He has lived in a U-Store-It shed for an entire January. The Private has slept in libraries and eaten ketchup soup and melba toast for breakfast. He has talked with lawyers he couldn't afford. He has lived in Wyoming.

The Private is learning not who he is but where he needs to be. It's a process of elimination. Sue gives him flies for simply appreciating them and showing her the little spiral-bound steno pad in which he logs which fly caught which fish under which conditions.

The Private is growing older, which means to him that it's harder to have fun.

"One week," he tells the Colonel. "One week and you'll have to find another couch to sleep on."

HARDIN, MONTANA

Every now and then responsibility picks up an ax handle and knocks the Colonel into government service. He delivers mail in Hardin on a substitute basis. "It's a job," he would tell Sue. It's a job.

Hardin is a rough town because it is one thing but also another. Most of it is not part of the reservation. But some of the town, across the Burlington Northern tracks, rests on the Indian land. You can see cattle over there grazing their way through the front and back yards of the trailer homes. The government prefabs are a little more in need of things—a window that isn't cardboard, siding that doesn't slap in the wind. The roads are mostly gravel and dust. There is the beef-packing plant, where many townspeople, mostly Crow, work. The Crow kids go to school where the Private, Mr. Fish, teaches history: Hardin Intermediate. The Bulldogs.

Every May the Bulldogs take a field trip to the Little Bighorn Battlefield. The Little Bighorn draws people from all over the country, from all over the world. Some of the students live less than ten miles from the national monument, and they've never been to it. Mr. Fish wears his wool Seventh Cavalry uniform, riding boots and all, and acts as if he were there on June 25, 1876, taking fire from all sides.

"Company dismount!" he calls, and the students file off the bus. "Form a skirmish line on the west flank of the bus and hold your ground. Any horseplay and you'll be back in second-period study hall so fast your head will spin."

Mr. Fish and the campaign-hatted guides lead the students around the grounds among the signs that read WATCH FOR RAT-TLESNAKES and METAL DETECTORS PROHIBITED. The spring wind whips their hair and makes it difficult to hear, though they understand. There are many questions. Sharp notes fill the afternoon like gun smoke as Mr. Fish bugles the students back on the bus. They talk motives and strategy, treaties and tactics, on the short bus ride back to Hardin.

The Colonel doesn't get called to work much. The Private has summers off and many sick days during the year. On Mondays they go fishing. Sometimes the Tongue River down in Wyoming. Sometimes the Powder River over to Broadus. Sometimes the Bighorn. But most often the Little Bighorn. They take sandwiches and keep a sharp eye out for rattlesnakes, Indians, and landowners. And it's often hot. Very hot. They fish other days, too, but always Mondays.

A SUNDAY DRIVE THROUGH CUSTER'S MONTANA

Driving east—going backwards—down U.S. 212, over the Wolf Mountains, through Busby and Lame Deer, the Colonel, Charley Reynolds, and the Private study through the yellow-bug-splattered windshield the country where Custer and his men camped on their way to the last campaign from Fort Abraham Lincoln, Dakota Territory. It's probably how the outfit would have retreated, if there had been a retreat.

"If you were captured by the Sioux, the idea was to shoot yourself before they had a chance to torture you." The actor steers with his knees, making finger pistols in the air over the steering wheel. "Troopers kept one round, their last round, for just that purpose. Shoot yourself in the head before they could cut your heart out while you watched."

The road is rough here and cuts through the charcoal remains of a forest fire that burned most of the salable Northern Cheyenne Reservation, but it gets better when they hit Ashland, back to everyone's Montana.

"Private," says the Colonel, not shouting over the rattle and thunk of the car so that his words are lost in the noise and it appears that he is just moving his lips, "know what the slowest thing in the world is?" The warm July wind rushes through the open windows and the gaps in the brittle rubber gasket surrounding the windshield. The Private is used to this Maverick lipreading.

"Besides us right now?" says the Private. The muffler and tailpipe have a few holes in them, like tin whistles, and the sunflower seeds taste like exhaust. "It's either us right now or a reservation funeral procession with only one set of jumper cables," says the Private. The speedometer needle is shaking at around fifty-one miles an hour.

The Private isn't laughing. Charley Reynolds isn't laughing. The Colonel's eyes glass over at the humble recognition that he's just told a joke everyone heard many campaigns ago. But as you get older—he is forty-one, nearly past his Custer prime—you forget. Everything turns to history with daguerreotype eyes and brittle, yellowed edges.

BUGS

Charley Reynolds stands on the Private's lap and sticks his nose into the fifty-one-mile-an-hour prairie wind. The Private lets his palm ride on the stream of air and dreams of becoming a scout. The Colonel talks numbers. Bag limits. Length, girth, weight. Hook size. Tippet strength. Rod action. He talks of the beefiest brown in Montana, the heftiest rainbow in Dakota Territory. "Pleistocene man used shards of bone for hooks," he says. "Indians used rock-hard spirals of rawhide until we traded steel hooks with them. Custer used steel."

What is different about Sue's flies, different from the flies tied by hundreds of nimble-fingered Western women for pennies apiece, is that they are tied for fish, not for fishermen and their aesthetics. Unless, that is, they are true fishermen and know the difference deep inside, like right and wrong.

Her flies have something of the ancient in them, borrowing from her ancestors on the frontier, as well as from evolution: her Darwinian ancestors, the fish. Sue tests her flies in an old aquarium in her workroom. The aquarium is stained, filled with the murky water of the Little Bighorn. With a pair of fencing pliers, she cuts the hook off at the bend and ties it onto a length of leader attached to a two-foot-long willow branch and flings it into the tank from across the small room. Weight. Aerodynamics. Flight. She is looking for balance. In the aquarium are several small rainbow and brown trout. Sue gets on her back, crawls underneath the aquarium stand, and studies the trouts' reactions to the new insects through the tank's glass bottom.

After only a week she throws a burlap water bag over her shoulder and walks to the river to turn the trout back into the Little Bighorn. "Thank you," she tells them, "thank you. Goodbye." She then unfolds the little pack rod from her day pack and ties on one of her new and experimental flies. She casts and catches new fish to help her with her work. Though it rarely happens, if she does not catch new helper-fish, she walks back to the trailer with the empty burlap bag, thinking about how she is going to adjust the new patterns. She enjoys being outsmarted now and then.

What matters is what an imitation looks like on the water, in the water, not warm and dry in a tackle shop that smells like chicken livers and epoxy. Sue's workroom smells like old wool, spruce, and duck feathers. Damp dog, river water, coffee. She rendezvouses with Ben Fish at the river and bails the aquarium out once a week, trout or no trout.

If it is late and he is drunk, the Colonel may tell you Sue ties the most beautiful, most perfect trout flies in the Louisiana Purchase. The Colonel calls them bugs.

THE TREATY

Mr. and Mrs. Owen Doggett celebrated their three-year anniversary by getting a six-pack of Heineken instead of Rainier and toasting the event at home while watching *She Wore a Yellow Ribbon* on video.

A week later, that belly-dancing night at the Mint, Sue said only this: "Three strikes, you're out." The faraway look in the Colonel's eyes was a sure sign he knew she meant it and he didn't shoot back, didn't ask about strike one, strike two.

Sue calls the legal papers the treaty. She'll get the waterbed and the microwave. The banana boxes of Harley Davidson parts. The eight-track player and turntable. The veneer bedroom set. The Toyota Corolla and the single-wide.

The third strike is named Salome.

SALOME ON SATURDAYS

Salome told the Colonel and the Private about the real live camels in the Passion Play on her breaks at the Mint. She is an actress. She works the Passion Play during the week and the Mint most Fridays and Saturdays. She also told the Colonel she could arrange a private audition for him because she happened to know for a fact that Pilate was moving to Florida and the director owed her a few favors that she'd probably never get a chance to cash in on anyway.

Belly dancing is hard work, she also said. So she took lots of breaks. She was not taking a break when Sue walked in after one of the battles to find her Colonel. Sue found him. The Colonel pleaded that it was all part of the act and belly dancing was an art form going back to biblical times and that it should be respected.

Horses, too, they have horses. Doves. Sheep. Donkeys.

THE BLACK HILLS EXPEDITION OF 1995

They stop in tiny Alzada for Cokes, oil, gas, beef jerky for Charley Reynolds, brake fluid, more sunflower seeds. The Colonel says to the Private, "You want to scrub them mustard bugs off the windshield?" It is Sunday afternoon when they cross the twenty or so miles of the townless northeast corner of Wyoming. Yes, the Colonel is trying out for Pontius Pilate, but they will fish, too.

"Nothing between this car and the North Pole but a barbed-wire fence," the Private tells the Colonel.

"Nothing between this car and the South Pole but Mount Rushmore and a fistful of gold mines," the Colonel tells the Private.

They cross the Belle Fourche River and see the Black Hills, the sacred land the Indians were afraid of.

"They heard thunder in there and thought it was the Everywhere Spirit," says the Colonel.

"Maybe they were right," replies the Private. "This wind does blow."

Spearfish, Dakota Territory. The sign at the edge of town has a trout with a spear sticking through it. "Trout are not indigenous to the Black Hills," the Colonel says to the Private and Charley Reynolds. "They were stocked, all of them. The Indians speared chubs and suckers. That's all there were."

The sun is shining and the summer school coeds are not wearing much. "Welcome to Calvary," says the Colonel.

The Colonel tells Charley Reynolds to stay in the car. The dog jumps onto the gravel parking lot of the Shady Spot Motel (phone, free coffee) and hightails it to a bush, which he immediately sniffs, then waters. The Private tackles him and lugs the hound back to the car.

The Shady Spot rests near the Passion Play amphitheater. Families here enjoy the steady increases in the value of their ranch-styles and don't mind the flash and rumble of the Crucifixion and Ascension three nights a week. There are coffeehouses and bookstores and no bad neighborhoods in Spearfish. No railroad tracks. No reservations. The Passion Play is here because the Mount Rushmore tourists were here first, and the Black Hills seem a fitting place for Christ to appear, should he visit America.

The elderly desk clerk looks them over in their forage caps, Bermuda shorts, T-shirts (the Colonel's Rolling Stones Voodoo Lounge Tour, the Private's Bagelbird), and sandals.

"You fellas with the Passion Play?" asks the desk clerk.

"We're Texas Rangers in town on a pornography bust," says the Colonel. "You rent by the hour, too?" The desk clerk does not think this is funny, is frowning. The Private nods. "Yes, we are here for the Passion Play. There a discount for that?" One dollar.

The Colonel then pays the two-dollar surcharge for Charley Reynolds after the desk clerk says, looking down at the dog no car can contain, "I see you brought a dog."

THE BOY COLONEL

Her flies are small miracles. Tiny damsels, Daisy Millers, opulent caddis flies in all colors and sizes. Shiny Telico nymphs. Little Adams. Noble royal coachmen. Muddler minnows and grasshoppers. Bead-heads. Streamers. Hare's ears. Stoneflies, salmon flies. Woolly buggers, black gnats, and renegades. She even invented a fly she calls the Libbie Bacon, tied with the soft hair from Charley Reynolds's belly.

"It's a shame that you'll now have to buy them, pay for them," the Private tells the Colonel. But their fly boxes are still worlds of insects: peacock hurl, elk hair, chicken hackle and deer tail, rabbit fur and mallard feather woven to life around a gold hook.

"And you won't?" asks the Colonel.

Sue gave the Private a full fly box as a Christmas gift the first year he moved to Hardin from Wyoming. Sometimes at night, when he's alone—most every night—and cannot sleep, he opens the box under his reading light and gently touches the flies and his heart speeds up a bit. When he would lose a fly—on a large willow, a snag in the river, maybe a fish—Sue would replace it with one of the same kind but yet different, one thing but also something else. None of her flies are exactly alike. The Private pointed this out to the Colonel, who still calls them bugs.

The Private started keeping the fly journal the first day he fished the flies Sue tied for him, the morning of the day after Christmas. It was bitter cold and the guides on the rod kept freezing, so that he would have to dip the graphite shaft into the water to de-ice the rod before each cast. Yet he caught more trout than ever before in his life.

While the Colonel ties fresh leader and tippet material onto his line, the Private looks through his fly box. Their plan is to take in tonight's Passion Play (free tickets) and do some fishing tomorrow after the ten-o'clock audition. From the motel room window, they can see Calvary, the sturdy cross as big as a pine tree, up the hill to the east of the amphitheater.

They were trying to have children—if not directly trying to pre-vent them is trying. Sue would often say, "I already have my hands full taking care of one boy. I don't need any more." This concerns the Colonel still. Even more so now. His mustache weighs at his lip when he thinks about it too hard.

SCOUTING

Spearfish Creek runs strong and clear through the Passion Play neighborhood. Today you can stand on any bridge in town and peer down at fish feeding against the current. Many healthy rainbow and browns. The Colonel's eyes widen as the men count the black silhouettes of trout feeding on the insects that wash their way. Heartbeats quicken. He calls this creek a river.

The detachment of three—a colonel, a private, and a basset hound scout—set out into the afternoon sun from the Shady Spot to scout the holes, the "honey buckets," they will fish tomorrow. There are many of these honey buckets running through the back yards of the people who don't mind living in the New Testament neighborhood.

As they patrol the river, the troopers wave to the grillers and the gardeners and the fertilizers and waterers, crossing now and then through the cool, calf-deep water in their sandals, though only some of the neighbors wave back—some sheepishly from behind their gazing balls and ceramic deer; some annoyed from behind their smoking Webers; some taken aback with beers in their hands as if, Honey, I think Colonel George Armstrong Custer in a Rolling Stones T-shirt and his basset hound just waded through our back yard.

THE COLOR OF SUNDAY

Salome did not tell them about this: the hatchery! How could she have left this out? The creek runs under a stonework bridge, and they wade out from the shadow of the bridge and peer through the chain-link and barbed-wire No Trespassing fence of what the sign heralds as the D.C. BOOTH FISH HATCHERY, EST. 1896. And for whole moments, minutes, they are old men outside the chain-link of the city swimming pool, Seaworld, Mainland, staring in.

Tall cottonwoods, oaks, and spruce trees, as well as the flowers that have been planted around each of the three stone-and-concrete rearing pools, reflect off the green-gray water. Two lovers and a family with a stroller and children walk along the boardwalk and gaze into the pools. You can, for a quarter, buy a handful of trout meal from the gumball machine bolted to the railing. Many signs: No Fishing.

A young woman in a khaki uniform sows trout meal from a tin bucket. The water boils with feeding fingerlings. Her auburn hair catches the late-afternoon light and is the color of Sunday. She is singing to the fry as she feeds them. Her hand dips into the bucket and she bows slightly and releases the meal. "I will make you fishers of men, fishers of men, fishers of men." Charley Reynolds chases a butterfly at the edge of the shallow water running over their feet, never catching it, as the men watch, mouths slightly closed, hearts racing. "I will make you fishers of men, if you follow me."

The lovers and the family stop to lean over the railing and look down into another pool, a larger pool. The father buys a handful of trout food and gives it to the young boy, who flings it all at once. The water explodes with trout, trout as big as—or bigger than—any the Colonel and the Private and Charley Reynolds have ever seen. "Good Lord, will you look at that! Did you see the size of those fins?" asks the Colonel. "Those tails!"

"Yes, she is beautiful," says the Private in a dry-mouthed whisper.

SUNDAY IN JERUSALEM

The Black Hills Passion Play draws people from all over the country, from all over the world. The Colonel and the Private have never been here. Young Christians in purple tunics direct cars, sell tickets, sell programs. An official program costs as much as it costs Charley Reynolds to stay at the Shady Spot. Outside the ticket office/gift shop there is a rather graceless statue, *Christ Stilling the*

Waters, by Gutzon Borglum, the artist who blasted four presidents into a mountain just south of here. The Christ of the sculpture looks less like he's stilling waters than waving to friends.

The evening is cool. The tickets Salome gave them are not excellent, not VIP tickets. The troopers are in the center, the fifty-yard line, but back fifty rows, back far enough to wonder how much real weight Salome pulls around here. But they can see downtown Jerusalem. They can see Calvary. They can see the tall cottonwoods that surround the trout hatchery a couple of blocks away. The troopers stand and remove their forage caps and place them over their hearts for "The Star-Spangled Banner." There is a sliver of moon, not yet a quarter. There is an evening star in the west. The fanfare ends. A blond angel appears in the Great Temple and recites the prologue, "O ye children of God . . ."

"It's going to be a long night—look at this program—twenty-two scenes," says the Colonel.

"That which you will experience today, O people, treasure well within your hearts. Let it be the light to lead you—until your last day." With that the angel disappears and the streets of Jerusalem fill with asses, sheep, armored centurions on white stallions, and laughing, running children.

When the play ends, the troopers are not besieged with passion, which is a little disappointing to both of them. An hour and a half of Sunday left. The actor has an audition in eleven and a half hours. Pontius Pilate is a muscular, tan, deep-voiced man. No long dirty-blond curls to his shoulders. No bushy handlebar mustache. It will not be easy.

FINS THE SIZE OF PRAIRIE SCHOONER SAILS

"Private, you awake?" asks the Colonel at a quarter to midnight.

"Yes," replies the Private. "Thinking about Sue?"

"No."

"The audition tomorrow?"

"No." Those fish. "Private, did you see those dorsal fins?"

CUSTER'S LAST STAND

They are out the door at midnight with an electric beep of the Colonel's Timex Ironman, waders on, vests heavy with tackle, wicker creels, rods in hand, Charley Reynolds in the lead, scouting his way up the creek. They wade through the same back yards, which are now dark except for a few dim yard lights and the electric blue of hanging bug lights and TVs through a couple windows. Walking, wading slowly, they have enough light to see by. They do not cast, do not hit the honey buckets they mapped in their heads earlier. "Just where are we going?" asks the Private. The troopers are advancing.

They stop under the bridge. Charley Reynolds is up ahead, rustling through some willows along the bank. They take the lines from the reels and thread them through the guides on their graphite rods. The Colonel reaches into a vest pocket and pulls out a tin fly box. He opens it and the insects come to life in the dim glow of a streetlight. Gold bead-heads, hooks, and peacock hurl shine in the low light. The Colonel selects a size ten delta-wing caddis fly, threads his tippet through the eye, cinches down a simple Orvis knot, and slicks the insect up with silvery floatant to keep it on top of the water.

"Fishing dry, huh," says the Private.

"I'm not yet sure what these Dakota fish like for breakfast."

The Private ties on a humble Libbie Bacon in a size fourteen that will sink maybe a foot below the surface in still water, but no more.

Upstream, Charley Reynolds finds a low spot where he ducks under the fence and into the D. C. Booth Fish Hatchery. The troopers watch the basset hound's silhouette as he sniffs around the ponds and lunges at the bugs ticking under the floodlights. "How the hell did he get in?" asks the Private. "Let's advance along the fenceline," says the Colonel.

They find the high spot in the rusty Cyclone fence. The Colonel goes to his knees and reaches his fragile rod and creel under the sharp steel mesh. "Just how low can you go?" he says and commences to crawl under on his soft neoprene belly, careful not to rip his vest or the three-millimeter-thick waders. He stands erect, brushing the dirt from his waders and vest. "Private, why don't you check that flank over there?" says the Colonel, motioning with his rod toward the tree-lined fencerow at the south end of the hatchery. The rearing ponds are lit from the bottom and they glow in the night.

"Colonel," says the Private, his rod leaning against the fence, both hands grasping the fence like a tree sloth, still outside the hatchery, still looking in. "Colonel, I can't go in there."

"Why in Heaven's name not?" asks the Colonel, nervously adjusting the drag on his reel between glances at the pools after the occasional light smack of a fish on an unfortunate insect.

"Because it's trespassing," says the Private.

The Colonel looks at him, his mustache arched in disbelief.

"Because . . . I'm sorry. I know we've trespassed before plenty of times, but this is different," says the Private. "And right now, I'm sorry, I haven't always, but right now I have just a little more left to lose than you."

"For one?" says the Colonel.

"A job, for starters."

The Colonel reaches into his wicker creel and pulls out the crow-black government Colt. He tucks it back under the fence, handle first, and says, "Here, there's one round in it. You know what to do if we're ambushed."

"You want me to shoot myself?" cries the Private.

"Chrissakes, no. Fire into the air, warn me." The Colonel leaps atop the stone wall and his rod is at once in shadowy motion, the graphite whip whistling in the still summer night. False cast, follow through, false cast, follow through—the fly stays suspended throughout the series of false casts, back and forth, not landing but rehearsing to land. Sploosh! The moment the delicate caddis kisses the surface of the pool, a giant rainbow trout engulfs it, bowing the rod at a severe angle while the Colonel arches his back and sets his arms to play the fish.

The rainbow breaks water and steps a few beats across the surface, tail dancing in the night, its fat belly reflecting white from the floodlights. The Colonel plays out line, careful not to overstress his leader and tippet. The reel drag screams as the furious trout takes more line, across the short pool, around its smooth sides, down, back to the surface, down again.

The Private watches this from underneath a willow tree, sentinel duty. Minutes go by and he watches with his mouth slightly open, jaw set, palms sweating against the cork handle of his fly rod. He can hear the Colonel's heavy adrenalined breathing and the high din of monofilament leader and tippet, taut as a mandolin string.

Two slaps at the water near the Colonel's feet and the trooper sticks a thumb into her mouth, grasps the lower jaw, and raptures the fish out of the water and into the night air. She is heavy with eggs, heavy with flesh and fins and bone. Upwards of twelve pounds and easily the largest fish the Colonel, or the Private, has ever played, ever captured. Her gills heave as he stuffs her headfirst into his wicker creel, struggling to latch the lid. The Colonel reties another caddis where the tippet is gnawed and stretched. He tosses the old fly on the sidewalk—bent hook, frayed elk hair and hackle.

"Colonel, let's get out of here, I think a car is coming," whispers the Private as loud as he can from a copse of ironwood that runs along the outside of the hatchery's southern length of fence. Fingers of one hand grasp his expensive fly rod, the other fingers curl around the smooth hardwood handle of the government Colt. But the Colonel is in the moment, back on the stone wall, casting in a frantic motion that causes the tippet and leader to jerk and the fly to land a moment after the heavy slap of the line on the water. Maybe the car will cruise on by. Maybe whoever is driving will not see the Colonel playing a big fish under the floodlights of the hatchery. Maybe whoever it is will not hear the gun crack and echo in the peaceful night. "Goddammit, Colonel, a car is coming!" yells the Private, the scout.

Another large trout takes the fly just as the million-candlepower spotlight pans the hatchery like a movie premiere and backs up quickly to light the Colonel on the wall, balancing against the fish, eyes filling with the realization that his stand on the wall is about to come to an abrupt end. He looks at the dark water, then up to the blinding light, back to the water, yells "Ambush!" looks at his expensive rod and reel, up at the spotlight, back at his rod and reel, before dropping them in the water with the trout still attached to the business end. He leaps from the wall and runs for Charley Reynolds's high spot in the fence.

Sploosh!

The government Colt lands in the rearing pond and sinks to the well-lit bottom, next to the expensive reel attached to the expensive fly rod attached to the expensive fish.

The deputy's boot pins the Colonel to the ground between his shoulder blades like a speared suckerfish, the trooper's tail end still in the hatchery, the other half of him a few feet away from the gently running creek he calls a river. His forage cap hides his face until the deputy whips it off and shines a heavy aluminum flashlight in his face. The deputy, a Sioux, looks at his partner, looks at the forage cap in his hand, and says, "Good Lord, we've captured the mighty Seventh Cavalry, red-faced and red-handed."

Charley Reynolds, now on the opposite side of Spearfish Creek, fords the river and licks the Colonel on the face. Insects flit around the yellow glow of the deputy's flashlight. "Have any more scouts in there, Colonel . . . Colonel Doggett?" asks the deputy as he reads the Colonel's Montana driver's license. "By the way, I'll need to see a South Dakota fishing license. The fine for not having one is pretty steep. The fines for illegal fish are pretty steep. The fines for trespassing are pretty steep. Randall, you bring the calculator? Now, about your scouts, Colonel."

The Private waddles out of the willows in his waders with his hands high, forage cap tilted down, rod in the air like a shepherd's staff. "I'm not armed," he says. "I surrender."

"Careful with the Colonel," says the Private as a deputy cinches the cuffs around his wrists. "He's got a gun."

"Why didn't you shoot in the air to warn me?" asks the Colonel.

"Shoot what?" he asks, looking the Colonel in the eyes. "You're the owner of the dripping gun."

The troopers sit, hands cuffed behind them, in the caged back seat of the Lawrence County Sheriff Department Jeep Cherokee.

"She must have gone fourteen pounds," says the Colonel. "A fourteen-pound rainbow on a number ten elkhair caddis. Put that in your fly book."

"That is something that belongs in your history book. It's your story," says the Private. "Not mine."

"This will probably mean we lose our South Dakota fishing privileges for quite some time," says the Colonel. "Private, it's a good thing we live in Montana."

The engine idles and the radio squawks periodically and the

deputies gather little bits of evidence from the scene of the trespassing, the slaughter. The troopers watch the deputies put the trout in a plastic garbage bag, twist it shut, and label it along with the creel. They watch the deputies fish the rod, reel, and pistol from the bottom of the pool, label each, and put them in plastic bags.

The prisoners wait in the Cherokee for what seems like hours. A car pulls alongside the sheriff's vehicle and a woman's silhouette gets out and walks over to the fence and speaks with the deputies. They show her the rainbow in plastic while she crouches, one leg in the dirt along the fence. After a moment the three of them walk toward the Cherokee. It is the Sunday-haired woman.

She looks at the prisoners. The corners of her eyes are sharp and pointed, like arrowheads, the centers glassy and reflective with tears. She is going to say something, and the wait for her to begin is agonizing. "They will take anything," she says finally. "They would bite on a pebble, on anything! Those fish will take a bare hook!" The prisoners see she wants to hit them, spit at them, shoot a flaming arrow through their hearts. Though she doesn't.

"Fourteen pounds, Private," whispers the Colonel, then whistles for emphasis after the woman turns for her car. "Fourteen pounds, I tell you. I was going to have that rainbow mounted."

"Owen," says Ben Fish the scout, Ben Fish the teacher, Ben Fish the trouter. "I'd as soon you call me Ben Fish here on out. I've gone civilian."

SPEARFISH ON MONDAY

After nine A.M., Lawrence County Jail, Deadwood, South Dakota. The men breathe easily, adrenaline gone, in the tired relaxation of fully realizing that fate has them and there is nothing they can do to undo all they've done. They had their photos taken with Lawrence County license plates around their necks. They have ink on their fingertips. They have called Salome for bail money, who said something to the effect of "Leave me the hell alone."

"Wild Bill Hickok was shot here in Deadwood," says Ben Fish flatly. "Shot in the back while playing cards."

The Sioux deputy walks into the holding room, what they call the tank, says, "Your basset hound is in the pound and your wife called. She's bailing you out. See you at the courthouse in two weeks," and sets a stack of carboned forms in front of the men to sign, and hands the former substitute mail carrier a hastily scrawled note:

Owen Doggett,
    Come home. Be quick. Bring Charley Reynolds and Ben Fish. I'm pregnant.

                                                              Sue
    P.S. You can't act as if nothing happened here. But I'm willing to work on it.

Owen Doggett reads the note once, twice, three times. His eyes show that he thinks it over deeply. He takes a long breath, exhales, and, without looking up from the note, says, "I suppose she needs me."

Salt, pepper, and Tabasco fly, and the men eat the scrambled county eggs in their cell instead of auditioning for Pontius Pilate at the amphitheater. "These eggs need mustard," says Owen Doggett. Ben Fish chews his eggs quietly.

"Owen, things are settled between you and me. I don't want to have to worry about the three of you."

FRIDAY IN OCTOBER

The prairie wind throws dirt and tumbleweeds against the classroom windows. Mr. Fish tells his eighth-graders that on the Black Hills Expedition of 1874 Custer lost a supply wagon full of whiskey and an expensive Gatling gun in a ravine along Boxelder Creek, now known as Custer Gap. He also tells them that Custer and four or five of his subordinates shot a bear. The bear was so full of lead and holes that it couldn't be eaten, couldn't be stuffed.

And he tells them this: "There was a troublemaker with the outfit, a private from Indiana. He stole food rations. He stole coffee, blankets, whiskey. He put locust thorns under saddles. He emptied canteens. One bright morning he cross-hobbled the wrong man's horse. The wrong man shot him in the chest. The chaplain said prayers for his soul and a detail buried him in the shadows of sacred Inyan Kara Mountain. Custer knew the dead man was a bad egg and judged the murder justified."

The class watches Mr. Fish and listens intently to these stories, the details once lost in the folds of history, brought to life again by the teacher, though some stories, for the sake of history, Mr. Fish just makes up.

MONDAY ON THE PLAINS

"I have an appointment on Monday," Mr. Fish tells the secretary. "I'll need a sub." He does not tell her the blackflies are hatching on the Little Bighorn. Or that he will be there all day, with his new trouting buddy, Charley Reynolds, fishing, reading, sucking on sunflower seeds, the two of them eating bologna-and-mustard sandwiches. He does not tell her his old trouting buddy, Owen Doggett, has to work on Monday because the packing plant never closes, never shuts down, and days off are best spent tending to legalities in Dakota Territory. The fine for fishing without a license—the teacher's only crime—can be paid by mail and doesn't show up on your permanent record. He does not tell the secretary that Sue Doggett just tied some tiny new blackflies that buzz and dance around a room on their own when a white man isn't looking. He does not tell her she gave him some.

Ash

er name was Ashley Elkind, but we called her Ash. She wasn't a smoke-eater like the rest of us, but she lived in the crew quarters, two bunks down from me, and she slept in nothing. In the mornings she'd get up in nothing, stretch, and walk to the shower room that way. It was something we appreciated at first, the surprise of it, the surprise of *her,* all woman, every curve, every fold and jiggle. Pretending to sleep, through the slits under our eyelids, like toads, we watched her walk across the cold pine floor—sunburned neck, arms and legs, nipples hard as pine nuts. But, alas, we got used to it after a week or so, because it was animal and because it was no longer new. And because she was big. Not sloppy. Not classically voluptuous. Big. She could hold her own.

Soon enough her buckwheat pancakes were what we mostly got excited about mornings.

We were what is called a Type II wildland outfit. Groundlings.

No parachuting into the torching bowels of the forest on fire. No helicopters or air tankers. No anything that would get us attention from our job title alone, like the Hot Shots from Logan or the tanker crews out of Greybull. We often worked at night and knew that if you stared too long at the fire, like a moon-blind horse, your vision could not adjust to the dark. But we stared anyway.

A Woodsy Owl calendar hung on the wall in the map room. We used a black map pen to cross the days off. We used a red map pen to mark the days we had fires. Red pins were used to chart fires nationwide; we got the situation reports every morning off the wire from Boise.

My girlfriend lived out east. She was going to graduate school in philosophy. She had been a cheerleader and still gave money to her sorority. Her name was Jennifer and she wrote a letter on blue stationery once a week that said, "It must be so lonely for you on those cold Wyoming nights." The way she said it was more like a question.

Ash came from northern Arizona and she would interpret dreams. The second thing she ever said to me was "Fire is a good thing, favorable to the dreamer." She carried a paperback of *The Wordsworth Dictionary of Dreams*. She had it with her everywhere she went, as if it were government issue.

She was a rangeland biologist. To the Forest Service, riparian land management means steak and wool; her job was cows and sheep. Deer, too. Antelope, some moose and elk, trout and cowfish. But mostly cows and sheep. She was pretty, but too bulky to be beautiful. "If, of course, the dreamer doesn't get burned" was the third thing she said. Red hair, less like a flame than a willow before the sap starts to rise in the spring.

—

We wanted fires. Smokey the Bear went straight against our grain. What we did was we fought fires, and it was as much a part of our inner selves as right and wrong. We might have pretended otherwise to appease Cappy, our boss, who had Tabasco in his veins but was up to his hard hat in politics, but we wanted fires. An evening dry-lightning storm was cause for celebration—"Tequila tonight, tomorrow we ride!" We liked the pay we got, but we loved fires more for everything infernal they were, everything volatile they could be. Our hearts worked like this: Flames or no flames, fire or no fire. Red or green. Hungry or satisfied. No sooty-gray in-between. Since fire was seasonal, the essence of temporary, that made it all the more precious.

—

They said about Hams Fork, Wyoming, our station, there's a pretty girl behind every tree. The nearest tree—small scrub pine—was thirty miles to the north of town. We would match up on the first days of every season, a romantic version of picking teams in high school gym class. I finally had a little seniority in the pecking order, but the other guys didn't want Ash for other reasons. There was a saying: "The summer's too short to dance with a fat girl." Maybe they didn't know or couldn't remember how long a slow, wet fire season could be. Ash was wide at the base like a spruce tree, sturdy and strong. I brought her Milky Ways and coffee with lots of cream and sugar. I couldn't say to the other guys she wasn't big, because she was. The beautiful girls in Hams Fork were mostly Mormons who lived in Utah and did not work for the Forest Service. Anyway, we didn't go into town very often, because there wasn't much to go there for.

On our dates Ash showed me where horned toads lived in the roots of sagebrush and the little mountain scorpions no bigger than Lincoln's head on a penny. "I never dream of fires," she said one afternoon while we were walking in the blue dusk. "I tend to dream of fish. Fish are a good thing. What do you dream of?"

The dreams that stood out in my memory were of railroad

tracks, spiders, sex, and tornadoes. "Sharks?" I said, not meaning it as a question.

The freckled skin around her mouth tightened and her eyes became cautious slits. She studied me. She knew it was a line, and not a very good one. I became convinced she could recognize a lie and know what kind it was the way I could smell smoke and identify the fuel. "To dream of catching fish is good," she said, finally, as if to take me seriously. "If you fail to catch any in your dreams, it will be bad for you."

"Does that include sharks?" I said. "What about sharks?"

She fumbled through her dream dictionary. "Sharks are not good," she said, frowning. She smelled like horsemint. It was almost Flag Day before she let me hold her hand.

—

I had my useless degree in English lit, which took me six and a half years to get. I majored in English because I liked reading. Or at least I didn't mind it. I wanted to fight forest fires during the season and do nothing in the wintertime. Maybe some skiing. Maybe read some books. It was that time of my life—my mid-twenties—when I hadn't yet realized that fortune wasn't going to fall from the sky, knock me down, and stick to me like slurry.

Many evenings Ash and I would hike up a deer trail to the top of Sarpy Ridge and watch Utah's lightning, which was better than our own. We'd take Cokes and a blanket, and it was like the Fourth of July. Some nights we would smoke the marijuana Ash had brought with her from Arizona. Most nights it would just be distant heat lightning. We would kiss or make animal sounds in the boredom—birds, coyotes, moose. Sometimes the lightning struck hard and green and beautiful, and it was like a celebration.

—

Ash was running a study up near the Montana border. She spent a couple days a week up there, counting warrior grasshoppers and Mormon crickets. When she returned, she spent most workdays behind a computer in the map room, long hair pulled back, gold-framed glasses on her big, wind-tanned cheeks, red and serious.

Her expertise was in riparian management, but she taught me that worms do not have eyes, but can sense light through their skin. She taught me that mosquitoes are attracted to the color blue. She told me about the Australian fire beetle. The females are colored exactly like the males, but are a good deal larger. "Size is everything in their mating habits," she said. "The males are attracted to the largest, strongest females." Road-train drivers would toss Emu beer bottles onto the roadside. Male fire beetles would come by the hundreds to mate with the bottles, which looked like big female fire beetles.

She taught me how to tell the temperature by counting snowy-tree-cricket chirps. "Count the chirps over thirteen seconds," she said as we stood in the desert and I held my Indiglo watch to my eyes, listening, counting. "Then add forty." We compared the Fahrenheit crickets to the thermometer she carried on her belt. The crickets were nearly right-on each time, give or take a degree either way.

I taught her that a smart arsonist can make a time-delayed incendiary device by mixing brake fluid and antifreeze in a Styrofoam coffee cup. Plant the little bomb in some tinder at night and stroll away. Once the temperature reached sixty the next morning, whoomph, fire.

It was a warm summer.

—

The camp's cat was named Cinder. He was black as a witch's cat, and during the day he insisted on sleeping on my bunk. He was a

mouser and his ears twitched when he dreamed. Ash bought him
half-and-half to put on his dry food. Some of the guys didn't like
cats and weren't above kicking him when he got in their way.

Raphael, the pilot, bunked out at the dirt-strip airport. He was
under Forest Service contract, and we used him for everything from
shuttling biologists around the desert to tracking livestock movements to searching for smokes after a lightning storm to dropping
boxes of fried chicken to us on the fireline. He was always reading
in the little hangar closet he bunked in, feet propped up on a parts
crate, sipping a Coke. He read pilot magazines and A. B. Guthrie
novels. Very often the Bible. I tried to not like him, but it was not
easy. He and Ash slept in a dome tent under the wing of his Cessna
when he flew her up to the border for the grasshopper count. She
told me when I asked about hotel accommodations on her trips.

His name was Raphael, but they called him Ralph. He kept to
himself and wasn't passionate about fires like the rest of us. The
whole of him didn't quite fit in.

He was a foreigner, from the East, olive-skinned and not tall,
with short dark hair. The little extra weight he carried made him
appear almost but not quite puffy. Not hard and lean like those of
us who swung chain saws and Pulaskis. Ralph was studying to be
a minister at one of those little Bible colleges in the Midwest and
he drove a 1972 Cadillac ambulance with a bike rack and a CD
player. "Don't you want to fly B-17s, Canadairs, Orions," I asked
him once, "instead of that little Cessna?"

"No," he said. "I am content with this." What I thought he
meant was that he was content with Ash.

Without thinking of the consequences, I asked him, "Does she
haul your ashes?"

"You don't need to know that," Raphael said. I expected he was
more than just sleeping in that tent with Ash. I expected he would
hit me and was a little disappointed when he didn't.

"Your survival in the wilderness might depend on it," she said, breaking the green-and-brown hopper's legs at the joints like expensive crab. She popped the insect into her mouth whole. The exoskeleton cracked in her teeth and her neck worked a little as she swallowed.

"Just let me die," I said.

"I can't help but to feel for him," Ash told me after her third or fourth plane ride to the border. "Raphael is an angel."

"What in hell does that mean?" I knew damn well what it meant to me, but I wanted her take on the matter.

Ash's eyes told me she would not answer, but not because it wasn't any of my business. In Wyoming, in the Forest Service, silence is an acceptable response, often encouraged.

That afternoon the mosquitoes were thick. I smeared my arms with government-surplus Desert Storm bug juice. The mint-green paint on my truck door had begun peeling where the sweat from my left arm smeared against it.

Though it looked like I was going to come up the loser in a toss of the I-Ching, I became determined not to let her go before October. She was something to hold on to for a summer in Hams Fork, something many, even most, people there did not have. That summer she was the only thing.

The Eternal Flame was the dump fire that would not go out. It had been burning for years, from deep in the ground where newspapers and plastic diapers and snow tires and condoms and motor oil and couches, beer bottles, and flashlight batteries smoldered and sometimes torched enough to shoot up a little flame, bigger than a pilot light, smaller than a campfire. Mostly it wasn't an eternal flame, it was just smoke. They covered it up, but it burned and coughed, burned and coughed. We would get called because from town it sometimes looked like Utah or the western heel of the Bridger-Teton National Forest was on fire. The Smokey propaganda poster over our kitchen stove showed a burned-over Oldsmobile in a black-and-white apocalypse. It said: HARRY'S TRASH FIRE GOT AWAY. DON'T LET YOURS. We knew it was just the dump, but we had to go.

Once there, we might walk out into the dump with eight-gallon piss-pumps on our backs and squirt some water on the little flame. Most often we just looked around at what was new in the dump and made comments about what could have been saved—a couch, a refrigerator, a TV, a mattress.

—

I lost a Third of July game of cards fair and square and had to be Smokey the goddamn Bear in the Hams Fork Independence Day Parade.

—

On a supermarket atlas, the southwest corner of Wyoming goes from Bureau of Land Management white to Forest Service green as you run your finger northward. The reason we needed range-land biologists was because of Lapland. The BLM sagebrush desert lapped into our Forest Service sagebrush desert, which slowly turned into thin scrub copse and eventually, as you got higher, thick crops of pine. Nothing is green in Lapland, save for the sage crowns and the few grasses in early spring.

The crew quarters was a good hour's drive away, over this moon-scape, from the nearest forest fire—the deep-pine fires that smelled like smoked Christmas—because Lapland sat between

Hams Fork to the south and the real woods of the north. Many cows. Many sheep.

The BLM men were government cowboys who thought like ranchers and had little patience for small and insignificant things like jackrabbits and coyotes. They wore cowboy boots and Stetsons and loved nothing better than running wild mustangs or control-burning thousands of acres of high desert. We couldn't blame them for that, though we did not always get along and often referred to them as the BM.

Our Forest Service people were government lumberjacks who had little patience for anything that did not grow tall and burn hard. We wore cork-sole logging boots and farmer caps, and we could put an edge to a chain saw in two and a half minutes with a pocket file, overhaul it in twenty with a Swiss Army knife. We worked like loggers. And most of us thought like pyromaniacs. "Let it burn to the road, burn her to the road!"

Ranchers leased BLM and Forest Service land for next to nothing and overgrazed their herds until a grasshopper would starve to death; mining and logging paid the bills. The cowboys called us the Forest Circus. The Hams Fork *Gazette* editorial page called the BLM and us "outmoded government tumors."

———

The reason we needed Smokey the Bear and his "Only You!" campaign was less apparent than why we needed Ash. For over fifty years Smokey had had an impact on kids and campers. He kept fire to a minimum. We, Smokey and us firefighters, did our jobs so well that the forest had evolved into an unhealthy monoculture of stunted ponderosa pine. In the draws too steep to log were the ironwood trees, pulpy cottonwoods, choked pine starts, and weeds. This treescape was what we called dense fuel, which burned like billyhell when it did catch fire.

Our fires were mostly caused by lightning. After a fire and the spring snowmelt, serviceberries, raspberries, fireweed, and bunchgrass would return. And wildlife—deer, moose, elk, bears, game birds, rabbits—would feed in the new meadows. Fires were a good thing, but millions of tax dollars went each year to try to prevent them and put them out.

Cappy said a forest fire was an educated devil who had made it to the top.

Raphael said fire was a symbol of God's presence; trying to prevent forest fires was like trying to prevent earthquakes.

Some of the townspeople said they suspected the Forest Service and the BLM were professional arsonists who set "job fires" intentionally so they could collect hazard pay for the long hours it took to put them out. I was invested enough in the firefighting game to know that this could be true. When I first started the job I would have been skeptical, but later I found myself thinking in ways that made arson justifiable.

—

Ash said, "For a woman to dream about grasshoppers portends she will bestow her affections upon ungenerous people."

—

Ash dreamed about grasshoppers. I awoke one night to hear her talking in her sleep.

"They're everywhere," she said. Her blanket was on the floor, and I could see her pale nakedness in the thin electric security-light filtering through the uncurtained windows. She scratched at her face and then, with a shudder, jolted upright, breathing hard.

"It's okay, Ash," I whispered. "Only a dream."

A couple of the other guys turned over, and Harley mumbled something about the Minnesota Twins. Out of nighttime weakness I whispered, "Do you want to come over here, bunk with me for a while?" The bunks were narrow, and I guessed Ash would take up more than half of mine. I wanted the temporal weight of her near me. We all did at that hour, though most would have denied it.

"No," she said.

The next morning over pancakes I told her I had had a dream about bears. "What does that mean?"

She stared at the poster of Harry's trash fire, chewing. Still staring, she swallowed and said, "Bear signifies overwhelming competition in pursuits of every kind. Killing a bear means extrication from entanglements."

"Custer killed bear in Wyoming," said Harley.

—

One evening in July I drove out to the airport to see Raphael about Ash. Ash was on a solo hike in the desert, something she often did after work. I wanted to get this thing settled. Maybe he would win out, but I wasn't prepared to spend the rest of the fire season sharing her. But I also knew this: No one won Ash. She wasn't anyone's prize, like the office girls in Rock Springs or Logan could be. Her attentions were a good thing during a lonely summer, but they were unpredictable and carnal and not something you wanted to have to suffer through a whole cycle of seasons. Her attentions were humbling when you found yourself counting on them.

The sun was dropping quickly behind Utah and the crickets were chirping. I walked by the old phone booth that waiting passengers used more for a windbreak than for communications—I'd tried to use it before and it never worked—and through the gate in the Cyclone fence, across the dirt runway to the rusty green hangar. The shiny white Cessna glowed in the open bay door. My bootsteps echoed off the steel ceiling. Raphael looked up from his reading.

I knew that he knew why I had come. "I don't think I'm here to break your nose," I said.

He bit his lip and looked down at the toe of his tennis shoe.

"Want a beer?" Turning to an old Norge, he pulled the chrome handle and a sheet of cool covered the little room. He took out two beers, and motioned for me to sit on the parts crate, the only furniture he had besides his own rotten-webbed lawn chair.

"We need to get something straight," I said, already feeling disarmed. There were little pieces of ice in the beer.

"Would it help if I broke *your* nose?" he asked.

"Might," I said. "It seems to be coming down to something like that."

"Got any pistols?" he asked. "We could have a duel."

"Nope."

"Swords?"

I looked at my hands and tried to make fists. "No swords. I guess it's looking like an old-fashioned fistfight." I took a hard swallow of beer, stood up and walked back into the bay. Raphael followed, and we stood in the big doorway looking at the dull orange horizon of Utah on fire.

"I get the feeling God's on your side and that bothers me," I told him. "Anyway, you can't hit me back—you're in minister school."

"I think you'd feel better about coming all the way out here if I clocked you a few times. Be glad to, actually. I could clean your whole plow, if that would make you all the happier."

"I thought so earlier, but I just don't have it in me anymore," I said. "I'll take that beating another day."

On the short walk back to my pickup the pay phone rang, once, twice, three times. I looked around, stepped inside, and picked up the receiver. "What would you do if you did have her all to yourself?" he asked.

My manhood and what was left of my pride were riding on the next several words to come out of my mouth. What I'd say would secure my place in the natural order of things for the rest of that summer. What I said was guttural and instinctive. I said what I felt, what was true. I said, "I don't know."

In that short arc between my ear and the receiver hook, it sounded as if Raphael said, "God bless you."

It sounded like he felt sorry for me.

—

Sage gets elderly and brittle when the natural fire cycle is interrupted, and the silver-and-black sage hadn't burned in years, so it was especially thick that summer. It was reclaiming the narrow two-track we followed to the ghost town some Sundays, so that it brushed at us as we rode by on our mountain bikes and left cat scratches on our arms and legs. But it smelled good, and Ash said it reminded her of some poem I'd never heard of. I said it reminded me of good restaurant chicken that you could get in Denver but nowhere near here. Ash could ride a bicycle like a banshee. It was hard for me to keep up with her.

Sublette, Wyoming, consisted of twenty-five or so limestone foundations with the skeletons of cookstoves, bedsprings, and flue pipes rusting away inside them. Tin cans, old leather shoes, and pieces of broken bottles stained blue and purple by a hundred years of sun. An old car chassis. Several steel mine vents. Tailings. A jail.

"If a town in your dreams looks dilapidated," she said one Sunday as we pedaled through, "it means that trouble will soon come to you."

"I'd say this town looks dilapidated," I said, "and you're about as much headache as I want to take on this summer. You might have to slap me just so I can be sure I'm not dreaming." Ash turned. She looked taken aback, as if the summer were so simple and natural and I had just unloaded something complicated on her that she wasn't wired to handle.

The jail was the only building relatively intact. Two cells not much bigger than closets. Ash and I sat in one, and I could tell she was wondering what it must have been like a century ago to have been trapped there. She let me kiss her on the mouth—garlic and marijuana taste. I awkwardly undressed her while licking the salt from her neck and little breasts, going lower to where the taste in the folds was animal.

I carved our names on a pine windowsill with my Swiss Army knife, knowing the wind and rain would sand the names and heart away in a matter of seasons.

In the brown willows along the little dry creekbed, she found a moose antler-paddle a bull had shed. I duct-taped it to my handlebars and we pedaled back to Hams Fork, coasting the gentle downhills.

On Monday mornings, when I would fill my truck with fuel, coolant, and brake fluid in the gravel parking lot, the Cessna hauling Ash would dip its wings as a goodbye, bank to the northeast, and grow smaller until it disappeared behind Sheep Mountain. I told myself that what I felt for Ash was not love, but I had no other name for it. I realized one Monday as the plane flew north that things weren't settled and that they probably couldn't be until October and the end of fire season, when settling things meant packing up and leaving them.

But the summer seemed to warm Ash in a less temporal way. She was a steward, a friend to the land, sure, but without me how could this have been enough? I thought she would have to want me, be grateful for me beyond all hopes. Wasn't I something out of her most enduring dream? As the summer progressed, it became apparent that she was helping me, showing me things bigger than fire and myself, holding my hand and pointing—see there! did you know that? It's possible that what she mostly felt for me was sorry.

———

Ash hated fire duty. It wasn't her job unless she was available. She called ponderosa pine "weeds." But though she groused about it,

Cappy made her keep her fire pack with her hard hat and fire-resistant Nomex shirt and pants in her truck. He made her keep her hand-held radio on her belt. If she was close enough to a smoke or if we were down on men, she would have to go. She was certified as a crew boss, certified to be in charge of twenty men, but putting out fire was beneath her. Or she was above it in that the suppression of fires has cause an ecological illness that will take decades of controlled burns to cure.

She would hide. And she would lie. I know this, because I watched her once. We were building water bars on a logging road about a half mile from where Ash was taking silt samples. At break time I grabbed two Cokes from my cooler and set out to take her one. When I got close enough to see her, I stopped and sat down on a stump and just watched her. She knelt as if she was praying in the silt along the little spring creek she was sampling. I watched her for maybe ten minutes. Finally, she looked up to the pine crowns and rinsed her hands and washed her face. It was a moment, a time where I didn't belong.

Without giving her the Coke—I drank hers, too—I returned to my crew. Half an hour later we got a call for an acre-large fire on Commissary Ridge. Cappy called Ash on the radio, asked for her location. She gave him an impossible legal: Township 28 north, Range 117 west. Alice Lake. "Taking tea samples above Alice Lake," she said. "I'm a good hour's hike away from my truck. Sorry, Cap, can't make this one," she said.

"Roger that," said Cappy. "Sorry you'll miss it."

From where she was praying, it would have taken her two, maybe three, hours to get into Alice Lake. You had to walk.

We returned from that fire sometime well after midnight. Ash was sitting in an old Naugahyde recliner in the crew quarters, wearing her cool-night T-shirt over nothing, drinking a beer, reading *Insects of Western North America.* "I suppose you guys want pancakes," she said.

—

The Thursday after Raphael and I finally locked horns, Cappy left the *Gazette* on the kitchen table. He had circled the article in the Police Blotter with a red map pen: FS MAN IN DRUNKEN RUCKUS. The reporter used my full name, which seemed foreign to me, the neon details of the fight belonging to someone else. I had already settled with the bar owner, and neither Raphael nor I was about to press charges.

—

I began watching her wake up again—my left eye half-closed with swelling. And I soaked her pancakes with syrup to soften them up, make them easier to chew.

I worked. I slept. I drank. At night heat lightning ringed the sky around Hams Fork. Several mornings it rained. No fires.

I wrote a couple of long letters, telling Jennifer I missed her and dreamed of seeing her in October. I carved a six-foot-tall pine-log grizzly bear with a chain saw one long weekend and had Harley help me drag it into the crew quarters, where I set it up between my bunk and his. I was glad when Ash said it gave her the willies, like it was staring at her all night.

The better part of August came and went. We had no fires to extinguish so they put us to work stacking slash piles and painting trees for timber sales. We prayed for fire.

—

One afternoon I ran over Cinder while backing my engine into the shop. I don't know why he didn't get out of the way, but he didn't. The dual tires rolled over him, squashing him flat. We had to use a snow shovel like a spatula to scrape him off the concrete. Cappy said we didn't need a goddamn cat around anyway. Ash didn't say anything.

In late August, Raphael abandoned her; he had to get back to Bible school in Nebraska. The way she limped around when he left—in his ambulance, like a portent, kicking up gravel dust in the crew-quarters parking lot—we knew it was over for good. He'd strung her along like any of us would have done, or did.

—

Ash stopped making pancakes. "Eat some oatmeal for Chrissakes," she told us the morning after he drove away. She stopped going for long walks in the desert alone. She stopped going to church—Hams Fork New Psalmody Free—on Sunday mornings.

I took to walking in the desert northeast of town by myself. I carried a rucksack and spent a good deal of time thinking thoughts I was later ashamed of.

After work the day before Labor Day, I mixed brake fluid and antifreeze in a Styrofoam cup and set it in the desert near the dump, so we could blame the fire on garbage.

—

We were hunched around the kitchen table trying to coffee away our hangovers, when Cappy walked in and told us we didn't look like firefighters, we looked pitiful. "Goddammit," he said, "every Mormon kid in the county is gonna be downtown and our public-relations point man smells like a distillery." He meant, in particular, that I looked and smelled pitiful, especially considering I was slated to be Smokey again, for the second time that summer, my third straight Labor Day parade.

But we'd gotten a call half an hour before—the Eternal Flame—and Harley and Chuck had gone out to see about it.

I was experiencing acute déjà vu: after coffee, Ash would be off to her grasshopper study in the north, sharing her tent with a new pilot.

Harley sounded concerned on the high-band.

"Bit of a problem here, Cappy. Better give the boys at the BM a ring. Their desert is burning and ours is catching. Over."

"You wanna give me a size-up? Over."

"Roger that. Break."

We waited, staring at the radio.

"Yeah, Cappy, looks like twenty-five or so acres are lit up, and there's a stiff wind out of the west, northwest. I'm a little concerned—this pitchy sagebrush is some serious fuel. You might consider sending every gandy dancer we got. And a BM dozer."

Ash's face fell and she got up to grab her rucksack and head for the airport. Cappy looked up from the radio and glanced at the wall map. "Get your Nomex, Ash, you're swatting flames today. There's nothing between that fire and town but five thousand acres of dry sage."

"No bear duty," I said. "There is a God."

Ash threw her fire pack on my engine and jumped in the cab. "This is beautiful," she said. "I've got nothing better to do today than put out a trash fire." We passed a BLM lowboy shuttling a D-9 dozer up the dump road. The fire was sending up a thick column of smoke the color of young thunderheads, and thin tendrils of flame were visible from five miles away.

The wind picked up even more and the dry sage torched and ran in the direction of Hams Fork. Another BLM Cat started cutting line along the edge of town, soon aided by two more colossal dozers from the open-pit coal mine that supported the community. The plan was to flank the fire at the city limits with a Cat line and back-burn and push the head to the northeast, away from improvements and toward the river.

Ash and I ran the burn-out operations along the Cat line on the southern flank. Bandannas over our faces like road agents, we worked as a team. The idea was to burn the fuel from the Cat line back toward the actual fire's momentum. I would drop a line of burning diesel fuel with the drip torch well inside the Cat line and Ash would walk behind me, filling in, cursing this carcinogenic duty. I couldn't see her through the smoke, and it was easy to get disoriented. With burning-out in heavy smoke, it was possible to walk toward the fire coming at you. Or you could burn yourself into a corner. "Are ya with me?" I'd call, sometimes coughing out the words.

"I'm with ya. Are you with me?" she'd answer, her voice hoarse from use and smoke. The intensity of the fire had driven us to relying on each other, needing each other. She looked to me for direction here in my element. I'd show her the way through, hold her hand until the smoke cleared.

"Roger that," I'd say.

Several hours had gone by when a Llama helicopter beat the wind overhead, filling drop-buckets in the Hams Fork River, then dumping its load at the head of the fire.

Ash and I found ourselves in a bad place. We'd burned ourselves into a warm corner and gotten turned around in the smoke. "Want me to call in the helicopter?" she asked, coughing.

"Not just yet," I said, breathing hard. Calling in the helicopter meant a beating for your pride. It meant you'd made bad decisions and weren't as good at your job as you could be, or as good as someone else was.

The main fire bore down on us from the northwest, and our escape route in the burn-out torched twelve-foot flames. It occurred to me then that if the main fire ran over us it would keep going, jump the Cat line, and burn right through downtown Hams Fork; my nearsighted pride would be responsible for the devastation of the entire town.

"We're about to get roasted, you bastard! Suck it up and call in."

"Okay, yes, goddammit, now!" I yelled. Ash was already on her hand-held. I realized that this time my stubbornness could kill another, not just me. For the first time all season I was concerned with something, someone, others, rather than just myself. I could see my world from the outside and it was small and rotten.

"Echo Charley Hotel, Elkind on net. We need water in a bad way."

She gave Charley Hotel our approximate location—where we were supposed to have been—and we could hear the rotors beating their way toward us.

"Roger-wilco, I've got you, Elkind," said the pilot. "Hit the dirt." Sage branches snapped and chunks of wet sand flew as three hundred gallons of river water cut us a new safety route.

"Thanks, Charley Hotel," Ash said when she caught her breath. "You're a godsend."

The fire coursed a definite track to the river, sparing Hams Fork. The sky tasted of ash. We took some lukewarm water and a melted candy bar, the sunset behind Utah a salmon-colored haze, and climbed onto a parked truck for a better view. The desert was cindered, lifeless. In the distance we could see the orange glow of the dump. The fire had taken the little shack and the wooden fenceposts around it, leaving snarled barbed wire surrounding four acres of hot embers that sparked in the wind. All of the surface trash was gone—the sofas, the televisions, the mattresses. What survived, and would last for centuries, was the refuse buried deep in the ground, like coal or fossils.

The main fire was setting spot fires that stretched along the desert horizon. We were strapping our headlamps onto our hard hats for night duty, when Ash pointed back toward the main fire.

Well in front of the fire's head, a herd of two hundred pronghorn antelope fled toward the river, pushing eastward. Behind them, just in front of the real heat, a wall of grasshoppers—an entire plague of them—pushed eastward, the roar of their wings louder than the roar of sage combusting.

"Warrior grasshoppers," Ash said.

The river was wide and murky and could have been oil for all the smoke. Hundreds of the hoppers didn't make the jump and landed in the water; the surface boiling with feeding whitefish, rainbow, and brook trout.

As we watched the fish fattening on the insects, the fire spotted across the river, igniting the far bank. The grasshopper wall ran out in front. My fire could burn to the Atlantic Ocean for all we cared. We both knew October was coming. The natural cycle of things would take back the desert.

Winter Fat

oe Jackman is privy to a mysterious world of Freemason-like codes and handshakes and genealogical records. My history with his world began 175 years ago in Illinois when one of my cousins was present at the shooting of Joseph Smith, founder of Joe's church. My cousin was part of the mob that stormed the jail holding the prophet. I'm not sure if the cousin did any actual shooting or not, but my family's relationship with the church has been tainted ever since.

Field mice the size of barn cats gnaw into the burlap sacks of wheat Joe stores in the pantry for the Apocalypse. But Joe sees the rodents' place in the order of things. He sets a livetrap for them and transplants the fat devils out in the snow, though they always manage to get back in, bringing friends. He considers himself fair, Christian. He hunts big game the old way, the noble way, in the higher country, on skis, with a black powder rifle. He lives off the lean of the land, trout and venison. He tithes religiously.

Joe has just one wife, Beth, and many kids. They barter for vegetables and cereal and fabric to make clothes. They dig wild garlic and gather raspberries from clearings in the Bridger National Forest north of Hams Fork. They do not subscribe to a newspaper. No TV. Joe works sixty-hour weeks as a pipe fitter. For birthdays and Christmas he makes his family durable things—barbecues, ice-fishing stoves, meat smokers.

The kids hunt the roadsides for valuable aluminum beer cans and stash their coins in piggy banks Joe creates from lengths of pipe with the ends capped, carriage bolt legs, scrap-steel ears, a curly nine-gauge wire tail, and a nickel slit cut in the top with a torch.

On hair-cutting day it's Who's Who in the Bible as Beth calls names and clips heads to a uniform slightly round shortness, moving down the line of towheads.

When Joe gets mad, which isn't often, he says "fetchin', friggin', fudgin', flootin'," etc., etc. No coffee—hot Tang for breakfast.

Joe works at the gasification plant, a castellated snarl of pipes, stacks, and boilers making an elaborate skyline on the desertscape, which turns bituminous Carmel County coal into gasoline. On his lunch breaks, after he's downed his venison summer sausage sandwich, he'll make his kids scrap-steel animals, like a clown makes balloon wiener dogs. The steel creatures are sprung from the nature Joe spends so much time observing, and the beaver, antelope, elk, fish, moose, and bears are more alive and real than any rag doll or sock monkey. More alive than any bronze effigy in a city park.

—

I did time at the State Pen in Purgatory. I was soon given trustee status and work detail for good behavior, working the State Pen's cattle ranch, cutting on horseback, branding, riding fences, night herding. I was in the cattle business in Purgatory long enough to realize that there isn't any real money in rustling cows anymore, that the West is driven by other aspects of the dollar, most visibly, metals. I got out of prison a little early for good behavior, gave up horses for a knobby-tired bicycle and a fourth-hand Subaru wagon with a ski rack on the roof. Bumper sticker: EARTH FIRST! *We'll mine the other planets later.* When I moved back to Hams Fork, rumor had it I took to cross-branding statues. When the one-and-a-half-scale bronze bull elk disappeared from its cement perch in the town triangle the winter after I got out of prison, folks began to point fingers, but Joe defended me. I didn't much care for the word "thief."

Hams Fork had been infamous for the Southern Hotel, a Tudor brothel down by the railroad tracks along the river. Now empty, the hotel once drew clientele from four states, many government offices, and myriad religious denominations, until the early 1980s, when an insufferable task force of angry housewives saw the doors and windows boarded by a posse of long-faced sheriff's deputies. Now the Southern Hotel stands full only of rats and memories, leaking and broken.

Without the cathouse, Hams Fork figured they needed that bronze elk. A twenty-five-cent postcard showed the beast under *Greetings from Hams Fork, Wyoming.* The Chamber of Commerce, Jaycees, Lion's Club, and Rodeo Boosters held a meeting with Sheriff Bagwell. They wanted restitution.

—

There is an old Indian saying that if you stand by the river long enough, sooner or later all your enemies will float by. Joe stays out of the loop of town politics. In the beginning, he had not been aware that an ex-con was back in town. He had not even been aware of who the ex-con was. We met when I rode one of my newer mountain bikes through what I didn't know was the Jackmans' vegetable garden.

"See here!" yelled Beth, throwing her sinewy arm in the air. "You're riding through our fetchin' vegetable garden!"

I stopped. "Thought it was a weed patch."

Joe stared at the bicycle and me on it, dressed like a rodeo clown. "Yeah, well we've been busy with other things. Nice day for a bike ride, anyway. How many speeds that thing got?"

"Twenty-four."

"Holy Moses. Where you live?"

"In an army tent down to Oakley. I'm camped on the BLM."

"Well whatdoyaknow," said Joe, still studying the derailleurs.

Beth was weeding in the vegetable garden the next day when I floated by on the Hams Fork in a dented aluminum canoe. "Good day for a garden," I called. She looked up from her work, her thin face frowning as I passed by.

I traded Joe that canoe for a half of venison.

A few days later, while Beth stayed busy inside, I moved into the aluminum snailback trailer that sat on blocks behind Joe's lopsided double-wide. From the bathroom, Beth's view of the river was blocked by the trailer. This put her more on edge. "You two are becoming quite a pair to draw from," I overheard her tell her husband that evening after a meal of venison liver and rice.

Beth was satisfied, though, when I convinced Joe he needed a new house and we could build him one easy as pie. First we tore the old one down, piece by piece, while the family lived in tents by the river. Then I helped Joe frame a new cabin, a modest three-room bungalow tucked back against a wash across the railroad tracks on the scantily industrial, more feckless side of town.

The new home was built from almost-brand-new Highway Department pine snowfence I got a sizable deal on. Joe and I went at the cattle-truck-load of lumber with a skill saw and a claw hammer and had it framed in less than a week. Running water and electricity in less than two. The plumbing is done in copper, the old way, with brazed joints, no plastic PVC pipes.

The roof is aluminum, Lincoln Log green, and coated with a Teflon-type finish so snow won't accumulate. A Roman archway crowns the kitchen and small dining area. The fireplace we masoned from stones gathered along the Hams Fork River that runs through the back yard just after the river oxbows at the Hams Fork Sewage Treatment Facility. A cedar sauna. A mudroom.

In a corner of the living room stands a half-scale bronze Benjamin Franklin, a housewarming gift from me. Franklin has long hair down the back of his neck, round spectacles, an inquisitive expression on his face, and a belly hanging over his trouser buttons. Franklin wears a soiled Stetson Open Road and cradles fly rods in his oxidized-green left arm. Beth thinks the statue hideous and often keeps an old cotton sleeping bag draped over it.

—

The elders admired Joe's dedication in showing an outlaw the road to reform, to salvation. The whole gesture was so *Christian*. The truth is that Joe didn't know me from Adam. He only knew that he liked something about me.

One evening a group of church elders paid a visit to Joe—vigilantes in slacks. Beth shooed the kids outside and served the men lime Kool-Aid and brownies while I lay on my down sleeping bag in his trailer and read sporting magazines. In nervous mixed metaphors and confusing analogies, Joe told the deacons that he was making progress with me, that it's tough to teach a wayward sheep new tricks, that a slick-brand cow can't be registered overnight.

"Your effort with Mr. Beers is very noble," said a gaunt man in a bolo tie and a golf shirt, "but perhaps there are times when one simply can't make chicken salad from chicken droppings."

"Look," Joe said, "every time I drive down to the Ben Franklin for a quart of oil, I miss seeing that elk. But the beauty about this land is that you aren't prosecuted until proven guilty." He was almost pleading.

"Who shall be prosecuted in the court of the Lord?" said the bishop.

"He's right," Beth said in a guttural voice when the mob left. "What are you trying to do, get us excommunicated?"

———

I traded like Jedediah Smith, Jim Bridger, Jeremiah Johnson. I swapped skis for meat. I swapped skis for fruits and vegetables. I swapped bronze park art for chain saws and skis. I swapped skis for mountain bikes and a kayak. I swapped a canoe for fishing rods and rifles. I swapped rifles for televisions. I swapped an old pedal sewing machine for an antique button accordion I couldn't play very well. It had been about three years since I'd moved to Hams Fork. Business was good. I swapped televisions, rifles, and skis for cash at one of the few pawnshops in Salt Lake City I could trust.

———

Joe often gets laid off from his pipe-fitting job for weeks at a time. He fishes. He skis. He hunts. He creates sculptures in the stout log workshop he built from old telephone poles. Joe winces a little whenever I call his creations art.

I tell Joe the two of us are the last of the frontiersmen. "We're tougher than two-dollar steaks," I say. Joe makes his own snowshoes. I was convinced if I didn't give him new skis every year, Joe would whittle them himself out of a green ash log. He is that much the craftsman.

———

It's tradition. On the eve of the first of November of every fall, Joe invites me over for birthday cake. "I'm putting on my winter fat," he says, something wild in his cheek. "Like an old bear."

"I'm getting a little thick under the chin myself," I reply. "But I sure as hell could use a slice of birthday cake."

"Well, it won't be from scratch. It's a mix from a friggin' box."

Joe sings old songs with titles like "Joe's Got a Head Like a Ping-Pong Ball." He will not eat pork and certain seafood because it says not to in the Old Testament. He won't eat bear because a bear without its hide looks human, the way the muscles and fat are stretched and layered. Just about everything else, Joe eats.

After chocolate cake, I excuse myself and go out to the trailer for Joe's birthday present. Back inside the house I hand the gift to my friend. Tears well up behind Joe's eyes and he says, "Aw, fetch, new skis." A year ago, as well as skis, I had given Joe a pair of hand-tooled cognac calfskin Paul Bond cowboy boots with cricket-killer toes and a Rocky Mountain elk stitched into the stovepipe shaft. Not once has Joe ever asked me where I got anything.

To Beth, I give expensive appliances she would not otherwise have—a commercial mixer, a nearly new microwave. In the spirit of the season, it is not her place to ask if the gifts were stolen. She has to accept them, which she does. To the kids I give shiny newish pocketknives, compasses, many watches.

The kids clear the table of paper birthday plates and someone pops in an eight-track tape of Freddy Fender or Roger Miller or Abba, and the entire family and myself hop and flail our arms about until after midnight in the little living room that smells like deerhide, used socks, rough-cut pine, and old maps. It is Hams Fork's only celebration of winter, only snow dance.

———

Joe is six three, over two twenty, and quite a little more in the wintertime. I am shorter, and thick like a fighter. I'm not as graceful on skis, but I ski hard and fast.

Working all night most nights, I sleep until midafternoon. I wake, fix coffee, and make the blue trout tattoo on my bicep jump and dance for the smaller kids, who circle me. In the evenings after work, Joe, myself, and the kids ski Sarpy Ridge and Green Hill, above the Hams Fork valley. They like to climb to the top, take a quick look at the town between their skis, and try to glide their way down, slaloming between the sagebrush, crashing often in the rocks. They hit patches of granite and gravel. "I hit a big flootin' rock and took a chunk out of my bottoms!" Joe yells to the wind. "Get out the p-tex candle."

"I bet you have another birthday coming up," I tell him. Between the two of us, we own a virtual quiver of skis.

Joe and I and the kids will sometimes hike all day, to the tops of the small mountains north of town, and ski the best snow, the powder between the thick groves of pine trees. We wear wool army pants and baggy sweaters, wool Andean mountain caps, and clouded green glacier glasses. We crash through branches and the sound is like bull elk charging through the timber.

We sometimes ski by moonlight the twenty cross-country miles to Cokeville on nights so clear and cold that water bottles freeze solid and it is too painful to stop long enough to eat the peanut-butter-and-serviceberry-jelly sandwiches or the hunk of venison salami we carry on our backs.

But Sunday is His day, God's day. The family goes to service in the morning, visiting members of the congregation in the afternoon, and are back in evening service before sundown. Joe cannot ski on Sundays. I try to tempt him, but Beth only glares at us both like heaven will thaw before her husband plays on the Sabbath.

On Sunday nights, after the churchgoers begin bedding down, I often stop by to tell him how things were. "The powder was a foot deep if it was an inch," I tell my friend. Each Sunday it gets better and better.

Joe looks at the ceiling, then down at his new Paul Bond boots. "Aw, fetch!"

Some Sunday nights I bring Joe a newer thermos or a shiny pair of poles without bends and scratches in them.

—

Beth began ordering subscriptions to the Hams Fork *Gazette* and the Diamondville *Camera*. The Casper *Star-Tribune* and the Logan *Herald Journal*. She clipped stories about the regular statue heists and photos of vacant concrete pedestals; where bronze beasts and heroes used to stand, there were only sheared bolts and cables. Police sketches of a suspect that looked not unlike me. She kept the clippings tucked inside the Hams Fork phone book, and whenever Joe went to make a call, stories floated to the floor like December aspen leaves. When I came in to borrow the phone, I made sure I put Beth's clipped articles back between the pages.

—

We hunt the old way. In the dark of early morning we load the dogs and family into whichever of the three old Scouts is running and drive as far north as Sawmill Road is plowed. Everyone straps on cross-country skis and we ski for half a day into the deepest country. We talk and laugh and sing hymns and folk songs. Beth hands out jerky, bushel-bargain oranges, and off-brand candy bars. Joe's big baritone leads the singing:

> *Oh, we'll shoot the Buffalo,*
> *Yes, we'll shoot the Buffalo,*
> *And we'll rally round the cane-brake*
> *And shoot the Buffalo.*

The day we shot the big cow was a fine one, bright and sharply cold due to the high-pressure system that splits the clouds here most winter days, leaving us in a barrel of fresh sunshine. We tow pulks made of bright plastic children's sleds with thermoses of hot chocolate and army-surplus wool blankets—the smallest kids wrapped in them—and meat saws and licorice and egg-salad sandwiches on week-old bread. The older kids pull their own sleds. Everyone sings.

> *Oh, the hawky shot the buzzard,*
> *And the buzzard shot the crow,*
> *And we'll rally round the cane-brake*
> *And shoot the Buffalo.*

The dogs howl from joy and the cool air fills with dogs and laughter. We ski hard, fueled by the fat our bodies have stored for winter. The morning is distinct, definite, like the day's first cup of coffee or that very first sip of cold beer in the evening after a long day of thrashing around in the Wyoming outback.

Last fall had been wet and warm and the grasses still poked well above the snow and the big elk were slow to come down into the lower mid-range country. We planned to meet the elk halfway, near Electric Peak. That country was difficult to get to in the wintertime, even with a snow machine, due to a tricky system of stream crossings and closed Forest Service roads.

The kids sang softly as they gathered sticks for a noontime fire.

> *Oh, the Buffalo will die,*
> *For we shot him in the eye,*
> *And we'll rally round the cane-brake*
> *And shoot the Buffalo.*

"Dad, what's a cane-brake?"

"The reeds around a stock pond, son." Joe unsheathed the black powder rifle I'd given him two Christmases ago. It's an in-line .54-caliber Buckhunter with a cutaway bridge, black fiberglass stock, and an eight-power scope. From three hundred yards it could put a hole in an elephant big enough to throw a cat through.

I shoot an old Sharps .50-caliber buffalo gun I'd swapped for a pair of skis. The gun isn't worth eight eggs for accuracy. But the shoulder kick and the smell of the barrel bluing and the walnut stock and the hot brass shells take me back to the plainsman I was in a former life and I am happy for the sport it puts into the hunt.

When I get ready to fire the Sharps, Joe does his best to count and account for all his kids and his wife and dogs, rounding them up and behind me and my frontier cannon. When we're looking to fill the freezer, we stick with the fiberglass Buckhunter and the eight-power scope.

We saw jackrabbits. We saw many hawks. Sparrows. A bull moose (neither of us had drawn moose tags that year). Coyote tracks. Fox tracks. But not elk. We tracked around the Electric Peak country, up Turkey Creek and Prospect Canyon. We'd leaned against our ski poles and were chewing and spitting little pieces of licorice in the snow when one of the towheads said, "Look! Up on that knob."

We glanced up. Joe said, "Well, Holy Abel." Two hundred yards in front of the hunting party was God's symbol of plenty: a milky-white shorthorn beef heifer that weighed no less than twelve hundred pounds.

Joe glassed the bovine through his binoculars. "She's a ways from home," he said. "She's wearin' the Broken Antler brand. The Broken Antler. That up around LaBarge?"

"I do believe," I said. It was getting on toward late afternoon and still no elk. "You in the mood for beef?"

Beth called out, "Joseph Levi Jackman!" It was all she said, eyes wide as Susan B. Anthony dollars.

"It's good meat," Joe reasoned, not looking at his wife. He chewed at his lip and thought. The pipe fitter's shaggy mustache was iced with respiration. Hot breath blew from his nostrils like cigarette smoke. He looked at me. I reached out and Joe unslung the Buckmaster and gave it to me. "You gonna shoot that white elk?" whispered one of the smaller kids.

"This is a McDonald's elk," I said, greasing a patch, tucking it under the lead ball and ramming it home. I pulled the bolt and thumbed a percussion cap into the breech, then, still mounted on my skis, sighted for the beef heart.

Bloooom! The recoil slid me back a few inches, but the heifer just stood there, still chewing her cud.

I must have missed, I reasoned. I stood staring, not blinking, and the afternoon sunshine on the animal made it appear warm, golden. "Joe Jackman, my friend," I said, "I just ask that you don't tell anyone I missed a standing cow."

I started reloading. Beth glared, re-sized-up the net worth of the man she had married and the outlaw he had befriended.

"Wait," said Joe. He squinted his eyes and his temples wrinkled and twitched as he birthed thoughts that seemed to come as hard and complex as gasoline wrung from coal. For a moment, as we all watched our father, husband, and friend, the wind quit blowing, the birds quit singing, and no jet planes passed overhead. "He maketh peace in thy borders, and filleth thee with the finest of the wheat."

Then, "Get the saws, kids! No sense in wasting a dead cow." The heifer's legs buckled and the meat of her dropped to the snow.

—

The moon was high overhead and the night cold had landed hard under Electric Peak by the time we got the game skinned and butchered and the cuts papered and packed accordingly in everyone's sleds. Joe took Beth aside and whispered to her until her face slackened. Holding Beth's hand, Joe led a prayer, thanking the Lord for the day's quarry, the fatted cow, and the opportunity to be where we were.

The moonlight was enough that we did not need headlamps. We sang the way home, the way we did after every successful hunt:

Oh, the Buffalo is dead,
For we shot him in the head,
And we'll rally round the cane-brake
And shoot the Buffalo.

At the Jackman house the sleepy kids worked from rote to put their equipment away and store the packaged kill in the old International Harvester freezers. We heard Beth say "Oh oh" and Joe walked to the pantry, stepped inside, and let fly with a "Fuck!" that echoed off the trailer walls like the report of a Sharps in a box canyon.

Eyes stayed wide as his wife hollered his full Christian name for the second time in twenty-four hours, and for a moment you could hear the collective quiet of the whole Wyoming early morning. "Forgive me," he said. "Fetch! They ate my boots!"

Joe posted an offspring with an air rifle at the pantry door, ready to fire upon the little outlaws who ate the Paul Bond elk-embroidered boots. "I'll get 'em, Dad."

The night herders traded two-hour shifts until time for church, which I promised to attend in order to give thanks for the prosperous hunt. I was out of my trailer in time for breakfast—pancakes and eggs. Beth was silent. A Jackman held out two field mice the size of balloon animals by their tails, BB-shot through the hearts.

"Remember, Dad," said a daughter, "that time a mouse chewed his way through the plastic lid on your can of peanuts and he ate so much he was too fat to fit back out the hole, and when you went to open the can he was still sitting in there eating peanuts like tomorrow wouldn't come?"

Beth cooked the beef for dinner, pushing it around in the cast-iron skillets and smelling it, curiously. At the dinner table, Joe blessed the meal. "Heavenly father, for it says in Joel that ye shall eat plenty and be satisfied, and praise you, the Lord our God, who hath dealt wondrously with us: His people shall never be ashamed. Amen." The steak was tender and the tame taste of beef was such a delicacy to everyone that they ate everything, gristle and all, even Beth, who studied each piece before she put a bite in her mouth. I told a story about the worst steak I had ever eaten—a desert steer out of Vernal, Utah—and the cut was tough as the sole of an old ski boot.

Beth grew more talkative with each mouthful. We laughed about the time I had brought over a basket of Maine lobsters I'd done some swapping for in Rock Springs. Joe had leaned against me and whispered, "What's it say in Lamentations about eating these buggers?" I shook my head and told him I didn't know. The passel of kids stood gawking at the lobsters as they screamed and knocked against the sides of the big stockpot of boiling salt water.

"This beef beats everything," Joe said. "I've never felt so satisfied."

When every cooked scrap of beef was gone and the children lay sprawled out on the floor, bellies full, eyes drooping, we talked about Frederic Remington's fine bronze *Coming Through the Rye*. Joe pulled a book from the shelf with a picture of the bronze and Beth watched us lean our heads over the picture to study it. "They aren't young," I said. "The riders are gristly and rough, but not young, getting older, putting on just a hint more fat each season. But alive as all hell." I leaned back in my chair so I could look at Joe as we talked. I liked to watch him process what I said. It was almost as if I could see the mechanics of his brain working in his eyes.

"What's apparent in the wild glints in their sculpted eyes is that it isn't over. It's a race for discovery. They're riding out of their present, pistols blaring, and toward something as wild and new and beautiful as their past."

"You wouldn't steal that museum statue now, would ya?" Joe joked. Beth cleared her throat from behind a pile of dishes at the kitchen sink.

I told Joe Jackman he should branch out, expand his work. "Think about what you could do with wax and molds." There was a rare moment of complete silence. "I'm fixin' for high ridin'. I'm off to see the elephant."

"The what? Where's that?"

"Black Hills. I hear that Costner fella has an artistic herd of American bison up there at his new casino, and I'd like to have me a look at them. I'm feeling the need to do some traveling."

"Back soon?"

"Not before things cool down again. Summer I expect. And if the Apocalypse comes, and the skies fill with smoke and the horizon glows with fire, just think of all the beer we can brew with that cache of wheat. I'll send you a postcard." Beth winced just a little as she sat back at the table with us, but her face smoothed and her frown was replaced with a slight smile. Me, working a piece of gristle in my cheek, I winked and said I knew where Joe could come by a river of bronze.

"Joe . . ." Beth started, but Joe wasn't listening to her. His face beamed and he slapped me on the back. Beth stood to put the children to bed.

———

The warm Chinook winds come out of the southwest to the mountains above Hams Fork. Snowmelt causes the Hams Fork River to run high and fast, carrying with it flotsam—beaver dams, pine trees, fence posts—through town, over the Jackmans' vegetable garden, and nearly to their front door. The kids run trotlines from their bedroom windows and catch fish between pages of homework.

The river pushes to the porch of the old Southern Hotel. Three sheriff's Blazers are parked in the mud surrounding the historic brothel. Radios squawk and bootsteps rap up and down the rotting wooden porch. The half-inch plywood has been pried off the front doorframe. Inside, the deputies are dusting for fingerprints, but the fingerprints they find on the twenty or so statues are of the hundreds of small children who'd worn bronze elbows and noses to a shine in city parks throughout the West. The deputies walk through the hotel slowly, pointing and taking pictures, as if touring a museum. From a dank corner of what had been the parlor, arms crossed and jaw set, like a statue, Beth studies the diorama. Joe is at work making art with steel pipe, oblivious to the accusations flying out of his wife's mouth. He is making a crude buffalo sculpture as a Christmas present for his friend. A surprise.

Tall and expensive, with giant hands, Abraham Lincoln watches steely-eyed over a deer, an antelope, a wild-eyed mule. A clean-cut cavalry trooper that may or may not have been Colonel George Armstrong Custer fearlessly strokes a little grizzly bear. A mangy gray wolf herds a quarter horse. Several stoic hard-rock miners push an ore car containing a stony mermaid. Jesus Christ, hand held high, waves at a familiar Indian. A shiny green pig noses a miniature tyrannosaurus no bigger than a pony. A puffy Jim Bridger hoists a stringer of trout toward Lewis and Clark, who look lost and worried. Having tumbled into a dogpile are a camel, a black bear, Brigham Young, and Thomas Jefferson waxing confused, and the famous Hams Fork bull elk.

—

The Louvin Brothers on the AM singing "The Christian Life," my little Subaru whines through the uranium-rich hills of central Wyoming, halfway to western South Dakota, the easternmost edge of the West. Yessir, there are buffalo there, fat with bronze, and they stampede through the parking lot of the biggest resort/casino this side of Las Vegas. Deadwood will be a walk in the park.

I'll send Joe a postcard from Gillette and tell him I've been thinking we should someday soon go to Mexico, drive and not stop until the beers cost a nickel and the *carne asada* is free, fish for marlin on the fly. Hope Beth doesn't get the mail.

When We Were Wolves

A n Oregon boot was a heavy iron cuff with an iron brace that ran down your ankle and under your arch. The idea of course was to discourage migration. It was invented by some crackpot warden at Salem with too much free time on his hands. We had Oregon boots in Wyoming in 1949 and walking in them was like walking across the exercise yard in ice skates. We did that, too.

We learned to act and think as a gang, a team ("There is no 'I' in 'team'!"), apostles. And this is what we saw quickly: Christianity in prison carried privileges. We got what is called "good time," time off our sentences, for attending services. We got free subscriptions to *National Geographic*. We got Sunday oysters in our gravy. We got all the bad coffee we could drink. Instead of making gravel, bucking grain, peeling potatoes, or pressing license plates, we dusted pews and crafted Nativity scenes out of plywood and wind chimes out of tin fruit-cocktail cans and baling twine.

As Wolves—we were the Wolves—we were well on our way to *really* good time. We wanted to play hockey, and if we had to attend Pastor Liverance's Wednesday-night Bible Study to do it, what the hell, so be it. Like the apostle Paul, we were former Commandment breakers on the road to Damascus. And Cheyenne.

The Hole is where you went for fighting. It didn't matter who started it. We naturally didn't much care for one another, but we learned to suppress our darker instincts for the greater good of the whole. It was teamwork, sportsmanship, brotherly love out of necessity.

"Behold, happy is the man whom God correcteth: therefore despise not thou the chastening of the Almighty: For he maketh sore, and bindeth up: he woundeth, and his hands make whole," our chaplain told a small congregation of us early one sunny Sunday morning. "Gentlemen, faith and the execution of goodness is your fast ticket out of here."

The Oil Cup was what the best hockey team in the Rocky Mountain Oil League got to keep. The *Purgatory Camera* ran a photo of our governor, Brandall Owens, hoisting the gold Oil Cup at a backroom press conference in Cheyenne. Pastor Liverance, an ex-Canadian and ex-hockey player, wanted that cup on his altar in Purgatory like it was the Holy Grail itself. The chaplain sat in on parole hearings and his opinion mattered.

"Gentlemen, I want that cup," he said every afternoon before practice. The pastor said it like a man possessed, a pirate, or Captain Ahab, staring past us at the sagebrush sea of opportunity that cup would bring for his advancement. We saw it as our opportunity, too. His advancement was our freedom. The Wolves wanted out.

It reads somewhere in Genesis that "While the earth remains, seedtime and harvest, cold and heat, summer and winter, day and night shall not cease," and the Wolves didn't either in our efforts to master hockey. Most of the time the yard was dry and dusty, and the dirt and sand caked our faces and stuck to our hair oil. When it rained we laced up our skates and practiced in the mud, running up and down the greasy yard in these powerful high-kneeing battle stomps, chasing the makeshift puck we carved out of an old snow tire, then slapping it in the general direction of the chicken-wire goals. In late October it got cold enough for the wall guards' spit to freeze when it hit the ground, so Warden Gordon had them hose down a quarter-acre section of hardpan that stayed slick and frozen until April (not counting a brief January or February thaw), wherein we skated in the brown slush.

We lifted barbells and dumbbells. We performed sit-ups and jumping jacks. We ran laps in our Oregon boots. We got to where we could skate in a straight-enough line without falling down. Our ankles grew strong and knotted. Some days the chaplain would watch the team from the watchtower and yell encouraging words from above. "That's it boys, that's it!" Warden Gordon chose the team color, atomic orange, and our colleagues made our canvas game uniforms in the garment shop.

We got new blue dungarees and striped hickory shirts to wear on the bus. The guys in License Plate honed our blades to razor sharpness. Pastor Liverance passed out brand-new Gideons. We didn't necessarily like each other, weren't buddy-buddy. But we kept our eyes on the pastor and stomped and skated together for a greater good—the good time we would get if Liverance got his Oil Cup.

At night in our dim cells we read stories about Cain and David and Max McNab and Gordie Howe and John the Baptist.

———

In those days geologists here from Texas and Oklahoma had just discovered oil four miles under the earth in the Cambrian Layer, and though it was harder to get at than the shallow seas of crude in the South, oil began spouting up all over our high desert. Rookie crude barons with new mad money thought it might be fun to own restaurants and roadhouses and big new Chryslers and Lincolns and hockey teams, and thought it might be even more fun to sell a lot of tickets and pit their hockey teams against a band of hooligans from the Wyoming State Pen.

Governor Owens was a pale, gaunt fellow who saw Wyoming as a colossal gold mine. Brandall Owens thought a prison team sounded like a good idea; therefore Warden Gordon thought it sounded like a great idea. The Wolves took right away to thinking of the whole shitaree as divine.

———

Pastor Liverance must have thought he was scoring in some big spiritual face-off because he had volunteered out here, was here because he *wanted* to be—the Pope of Wyoming himself. A short man, he teetered around the pulpit on stiff new dogger-heel cowboy boots as he spoke, keeping his arms out for balance as he clunked around the wooden platform, like the tall man on stilts at the rodeo circus or a dude from out east. Or like he was wearing hockey skates in church. He never did get used to those boots and the extra two inches of height with which they endowed him.

"What's your take out here, Pastor?" the Wolves asked at that first Christian rendezvous. No one *wants* to be here. Permanence isn't Western in nature. You take what you can get, or get what you have to take, and move on, get the hell out. *Vamoose.* Looking down and shifting his narrow eyes, he told us: "It says in Luke to sell all that ye have, and give alms. Provide yourselves with purses that do not grow old, with a treasure in the heavens that does not fail, where no thief approaches and no moth destroys. For where your treasure is, there will your heart be also."

"Say, is there a Pope of Wyoming?" I asked one evening during a Bible Study smoke break. " 'Cause if there ain't this guy's trying awful goddamn hard for nothing."

"Yes, there is," said Belecki. "Like there's a King of Canada." Rich Belecki was our forward, our ringer, our finisher, though the Wolves rarely started much in the way of offense that he might finish. Belecki was a white-collar, silver-spoon pretty boy previously from British Columbia, who wound up in prison by embezzling money from some oil company slush fund. He'd grown up with the game, and his family sent him valuable things like a radium-dial watch and spanking-new hockey skates. He was forever rubbing down the rich black leather with mink oil. The rest of us had never skated in our lives, and some of the figure skates the Salvation Army gave us were *white*. We supposed Liverance would have to settle for martyrdom or governor. Or they could make him warden. He told us we must protect Belecki on the ice at all costs.

—

On the chaplain's desk in his dank little office behind the chapel was a photograph of Maurice "the Rocket" Richard in his Canadiens uniform, his hair oiled down slick and his arm around Liverance in his white chaplain collar and black wool getup, the pastor's hair slick and greasy too. Pastor Liverance smiled away like Christmas in the photo—teeth a yellowed gray from the Chesterfields and big fifteen-cent Webster Golden Weddings he was forever smoking—like he was thinking, "This shot will soon look great on my desk." I didn't know who the Rocket was until Pastor Liverance showed me his Canadiens scrapbook. Richard was the Canadiens' goal-scoring prima donna and was subjected to many opponents' illegalities on the ice: bad checks.

—

On the side of the bus we stenciled WYOMING STATE PENITENTIARY CHRISTIAN WOLVES. I told the team I read in *National Geographic* that packs of wolves brought down camels on this very desert just a few million years ago, and it was those camel bones making the oil men rich today.

Rob LeBlanc, who sounded French Canadian but who was really a semi-commercial catfisherman and car thief from Cameron Parish, Louisiana, said, "We have oil in the swamps. We have wolves there too and they eat chickens, ducks, and rats, and sometimes big things like children."

Big Jimmy McGhan, an ex-marine, ex–horse thief, and the Wolves' physical leader, said, "Remember, gentlemen, a lion from the forest shall slay them and a wolf from the desert shall destroy them."

"Yeah," said Fowler, a third-degree batterer and a second-line wing. "And beware of false prophets, who come to you in sheep's clothing but inwardly are ravenous wolves!" The rest of us just looked at each other with foreheads wrinkled.

The license plates on the bus were yellow and said *Wyoming* JESUS in black next to a black cowboy on a black bucking bronco. All our games were away games. All games we lost by digits the scoreboards couldn't handle.

We lost to the Sheridan Savages and the Casper Cutthroat. The Ogden Americans and the Greeley Giants. We got routed by the Vernal Vikings, Rapid City Chiefs, the Fort Collins Grizzlies. Pocatello Roughnecks. Rock Springs Miners, Billings Badgers. And hammered by the Cheyenne Buffalo.

The other teams were manned mostly by Canadian exports: some guys who were maybe on their way up to the NHL, but most who were on their way down from leagues in regions very cold and dark. Men gaining on thirty, even forty, who hadn't learned enough about anything other than hockey to make a living. Men who weren't yet willing to give up their game to support themselves as professional cattle thieves or liquor-store robbers. So they found themselves in the Rocky Mountain Oil League, playing in dim and ratty rinks and dodging the beer, the snowballs, and the rotten potatoes that were regularly chucked onto the ice by the Oil League fans—who got into more fistfights than the players. But there were worse places to be, which we reminded them when we rolled into town from Purgatory in the Jesus bus.

Our strong suits did not include puck control or shooting. Or skating. We weren't native to it, so we didn't turn or stop much. But we could run. And we could skate fast, as fast and as hard as any team in the Oil League. We had conviction and spirit. And Lord, could we check!

We were the second-hardest checking team in the Rockies, maybe in America, maybe North America. Thirty-five-mile-an-hour, head-on checks. Train wrecks against the boards with a Canadian in between. And the other thing about our checks: we checked as a pack.

Big Jimmy McGhan checked the hardest of all of us and he could call the pack with the look on his face—the way his eyes glassed and sparkled under the black bristle of his eyebrows and the gray shine of his furrowed forehead, the way his neck flexed. He would snarl and light in on a target and hightail it down the ice like a mad monk, and we other Wolves raced and followed Big Jimmy to the kill—"awhooooooooooooooo!" The first Wolf, Big Jimmy, would be all their guy saw: Whump! Bless you, brother! Then Whump!-Whump!-Whump! And if Lovelock, our goalie, decided to get into this: Whump! That is to say, if the big check was right at the beginning of a period and no Wolves yet paced the penalty box.

Meanwhile the crowd would be screaming and yelling in language not Christian in nature and one of the Canadians—looking over his shoulder, tail between his legs—would have nosed the puck into our goal; and the police sirens wailed and the light behind the net flashed red and the organist played a jazzy Bulgar tune that wasn't at all like a hymn but that all the fans knew the words to, as greasy vendor items rained down on us and the refs escorted the check victim under the boards away on a Big War surplus stretcher. And it would be shoulder slaps and howls on our bench as we changed lines and another five got a shot at them.

But no fighting.

Not with the other teams. Not with each other. Not even a tickle. Not even if it wasn't initiated by a Wolf. Not even if they well deserved a good ear-boxing or a cuff across the gums. No matter that fighting is part of the game, and every other team in the league would be justified in starting what in prison shoptalk is called a riot. The governor and Warden Gordon wanted no bad headlines in *Time* magazine, no bad what they call in politics public relations. They made it clear that a fight would result in the immediate extinction of the Wolves, to hell with any survival instincts we might possess in our genetic makeups.

The other Oil Leaguers didn't know we weren't allowed fisticuffs, and we still intimidated the hell out of them. They just figured the first one in the Oil League to mix it up with us would be the first one in the Oil League to cross the Canadian border in a plywood box. They didn't know we weren't that bad. Half of us had never killed anybody. Or that we skated with Jesus, whose game plan didn't include fistfights. But what they didn't know didn't hurt us. So we continued to check like feral dogs, to intimidate the hell out of other teams, to avoid fighting—and to lose games. This in a time when general managers handed players twenty-five bucks under the table for initiating a ruckus. It's what the legions of Oil League cabin-fever fans paid to see. It's what the fans wanted to do to each other, would have done if it were legal. Sometimes they did it anyway.

Photos of the games appeared in the *Cheyenne Eagle*, the *Rock Springs Rocket-Miner*, the *Billings Gazette*, under captions like PURGATORY PRISONERS PELTED AGAIN and WOLF ERADICATION UNDERWAY. Dirty kids knew us by name. Women with animals and flowers tattooed on their skin wrote us letters telling us where their animals and flowers were. We lost on the radio. Live, following Milton Berle's *Texaco Star Theater*, on the big Cheyenne tower that broadcast us all over the Rockies and deserts surrounding them: 0–21–0.

—

Then things started to change. Some of the Wolves were slowly picking up the more tame rudiments of the game. It was as though thirty-five-mile-an-hour checks were beginning to bore them. Belecki's adolescent puck control really started to come back to him. LeBlanc learned to turn in big arcs to the left and would sometimes even abort checks in favor of following the puck. Lovelock, the goalie, got the hang of staying in the goal crease. Nearly everyone could skate all the way across the ice to the penalty box without falling down. Pastor Liverance became even more inspired and started writing a *book* about Christian prison hockey as if he were writing a sequel to Exodus, a sort of how-to guide, as he was a real pioneer in the sport. I memorized new Revelations dealing with ice and the end of the world. They set one of our Wolves free.

One morning we were just boarding the bus for God-knows-where in the crisp winter sunshine and Big Jimmy McGhan said, "Wait a minute." The Wolves all looked around and sniffed the air like we knew something wasn't quite right, who knew what? and Big Jimmy put his finger on it and said, "Where in heaven's name has Lucky Shepard been? How long we been playing without a backup goalie?" This is when Pastor Liverance told us Lucky had been paroled, had gone home to his mother in Meeteetse two weeks ago. "Think about the game, will ya?" he advised us.

It was like being born again.

We put extra oil in our hair. We did jumping jacks and push-ups twice a day. We had the boys in License Plate hone our blades after every practice and every game. We learned new verses about hope and heaven and committed them to memory. "The Lord looseth the prisoners, let's hit the road!"

——

"Okay, who we playing tonight?" we asked Pastor Liverance, trying to enter the world of the profound. The subject of who we played was beginning to matter to us. For the first time we saw that Christian battle had a direct bearing on our sentences as professional Wolves.

Especially if we were battling the Cheyenne Buffalo.

Cheyenne was different. The Buffalo were owned by a guy named Stumpy Wells, a greasy-rich petroleum tycoon who seemed to be forever trying to make up with his billfold for the fact that he was four feet tall. Stumpy always wore a gray eleven-gallon hat (he was bald too) and when he sat on his billfold he was bigger, much bigger, than any man in Wyoming. He recruited the best of the worst, guys actually *banned* from Canada, exiled to Wyoming like it was some Egyptian penal colony. Besides being able to really play hockey, these guys were tougher than harness leather. Maybe they'd beaten a ref to a bloody carcass north of the border. Maybe they'd killed somebody. Maybe they'd spent time in a Yukon hoosegow, busting rocks on the tundra. We could only guess, which we did. What we did know was that these guys were now Stumpy's toadies, his northern-import goons. They took cheap shots at us—spearing, hooking, boarding, holding, tripping, high-sticking, elbowing, slashing, spitting, punching. And Stumpy's refs got paid by Stumpy to let it go.

Though the Buffalo played in the seedy Bull Barn downtown, Stumpy Wells bought a genuine used blue-smoke-belching Zamboni with working headlights so that their ice was the smoothest and blackest and also the slickest in the Oil League.

And this: The Buffalo had cheerleaders. Stumpy owned a couple of steak houses named Jugs where the waitresses were all very busty and wore lots of bright makeup and tight, pink-fringed cowgirl outfits. The Jugs girls became the Buffalo Gals on their nights off. They tapped out onto the ice in pink cowboy boots between Zamboni swaths and bounced up and down to some Bob Wills 45 that Stumpy picked out himself and played over the fuzzy public address system. There wasn't a Wolf alive who didn't think about what it would be like to begat with one of the Buffalo Gals just once.

They also had a tame buffalo cow, a mangy hoof-and-mouth victim named Petey some guy in Wild Bill getup led slithering around the ice between periods. She drank beer and ate corndogs and dropped steaming cow pies on the ice. It was all pretty much a two-bit circus, including the games. The Buffalo checked harder than we did.

—

The bus ground out of the prison gates and rumbled through downtown Purgatory before turning east onto the highway for Cheyenne. "We're on our way to Boomtown, gentlemen," said Pastor Liverance through the sports page of the *Cheyenne Eagle*, and the bus got really quiet except for the buzz of tires on asphalt and the whir of the heater fan blowing out cold air. "Aaaaaahaaaaa," whined Pastor Liverance, imitating Bob Wills in a mousey falsetto, which he did when he was excited—a more frequent phenomenon now that his hockey team had players who could turn. Pastor Liverance's *V* was beginning to stand less and less for *volunteer* and more and more for *victory*. "Gentlemen," he said, waving his pencil like a staff, "I want that Oil Cup on my desk. I want it *next* year. I want to be the spoiler *this* year, tonight. I want the lousy end to the Buffalo's season to be because of Wolves."

We still didn't like him. We still didn't much like each other. We still didn't quite trust him the same way we didn't quite trust each other. But we saw that the pastor could help us, and we hated the Buffalo at a primitive level, someplace down deep where we couldn't help what we felt. And as Wolves, we tried our damnedest to love each other the way it says to in John, Peter, Colossians, Thessalonians, and Romans. We liked seeing the parole-board-sitting chaplain in high and gracious spirits.

Our pre-game Bible-and-prayer meeting in the locker room was attended by various walleyed members of the sports-page press. Our locker room still smelled like cigarettes—and hot urine since our last limp through town when Big Jimmy McGhan pissed on the radiator. The reporters snapped bright photos of us Wolves drinking reconstituted orange drink and chewing 'Nilla Wafers while LeBlanc cited the First Samuel he committed to memory on the bus trip to Cheyenne: "And the behemoth said to David, 'Am I a dog that you come to me with sticks? Come to me and I will give your flesh to the birds of the air and the beasts of the field.' "

"Amen, brother," the pack howled in rough unison to the snap-snap-snap of bright flashbulbs.

The multitudes had come from the jerkwater towns and down from the hills and we could hear the crowd amassing in the smoky arena. They were already booing. "This evening the Lord will deliver you into my hand, and I will strike you down, and cut off your head; and I will give the dead bodies of the host of the Philistines this day to the beasts of the earth; that all the earth may know that there is a God in Wyoming."

The reporters scribbled on their notepads like crazy men. One of them in an expensive Stetson porkpie said, "It mentions Wyoming in First Samuel?" and Lovelock told him, "Well, hell, yes."

"Gentlemen, let us pray," Pastor Liverance said. We looked at the reporters from the corners of our eyes until they took the signal and bowed their heads and held their hands together in front of them. "Dear Heavenly Father, for it was you who brought them out of darkness and the shadow of death, and break their bands in sunder. You who heareth the poor and despiseth not your prisoners. And though the rebellious dwell in a dry land, you bringeth out those who are bound with chains."

Real somber, as if our old backup goalie had died and gone to heaven, Lovelock broke the post-prayer silence and said, "Remember Lucky."

"All right, everyone on the ice," Pastor Liverance said.

—

We skated a couple of laps and, sure enough, were pelted with the Lord's deep-fried bounty as well as cigarettes and other smoking curses from above.

Stumpy stood low in a high VIP box with Governor Owens, in his silverbelly stingy-brim Stetson, and Warden Gordon, who drove over in his long gray 1950 Lincoln Continental with license plates that read *Wyoming* WARDEN. The three of them smoked twenty-five-cent cigars and laughed and elbowed each other, and the Buffalo Gals brought them drinks and lit more cigars with lighters shaped like oil derricks.

The three refs warmed up to an up-tempo organ version of "Three Blind Mice." Cheap bottle rockets and Roman candles popped and fizzled dimly above the dark coliseum ice. We skipped last laps and went straight for the bench to avoid getting peppered in the smoky dimness with an airborne something big and hard. "Ladies and gentlemen," said the announcer, "please note that these athletes skate at speeds of up to fifty miles per hour, and at these speeds a penny from the stands can put an eye out." It began hailing nickels. "Now, please welcome your own Cheyenne Buffalo!" The Buffalo skated by in a yellow-and-brown streak and rapped the boards in front of our bench with their sticks. The crowd made a pretty impressive stampede sound by stomping on the wooden seats with the leather heels of their boots.

"God bless you, brothers!" we howled as the Buffalo sped past. The organist played a bouncy barroom tune, and the Cheyenne crowd howitzered more food aimed at our bench. The Buffalo Gals bounced in rare form. Petey dropped another steaming buffalo pie onto the ice. We were wet and sticky with Cokes and beer and mustard. All this before a covey of Cub Scouts ran around the ice with the American flag and the Wyoming buffalo flag and the dumb bunny behind the organ pumped out "The Star-Spangled Banner" at polka speed.

"Let's play the spoiler tonight, gentlemen," said Pastor Liverance, dodging a corn dog. Meaning of anybody in the Oil League he would like to see not make it into the playoffs because of the Wolves, it was these goons.

And for almost an entire period we *were* spoilers. The spoiler part happened when the puck landed in front of Belecki after the face-off and he shot from mid-ice. It hit their goalie's chest pad and dropped to the ice, and as the goalie, Guy Somebody, was about to be checked hard by LeBlanc, he panicked and fumbled it with his glove and it fell to the ice again, where he kicked it into his own goal with the heel of his own skate. There was a vast silence in the crowd that turned to awkward boos and hisses. The Wolves had scored their first goal ever in their last game against the Cheyenne Buffalo, a feat that would make the sports pages across the West and that everyone in Cheyenne would damn well know about. The Wolves were *winning*.

We circled the goal, raised our sticks in the air, and howled at the top of our lungs. This is when the Buffalo began to act like the earwigs in the mess hall when we dropped Tabasco on them.

The Buffalo coach, a former Kamloops goon named Carl Carlsbad, whose nose pressed flat across his face to the left, nearly touching his ear, like it was Scotch-taped, sent in a hand-picked line of superenforcers, guys designed to inflict pain and bodily harm. They wanted to hurt us, and they did. We weren't checking—we were *being* checked. We'd gotten a taste of scoring. We liked it. We tried to do it again. We linked passes together. We set up an actual and sincere power-play offense that Pastor Liverance picked from a book. We *turned* and *stopped* and the ice sprayed from under our skates like pine whittle chips. We got the wind knocked out of us against the board lettering—EAT AT JUGS, in fat red letters. We took advantage of four of their goons sitting in the penalty box, and we scored again.

And all this without so much as a single rabbit punch—2 to 0, Wolves—and yes, it was something while it lasted. And yes, we could almost believe the Lord was skating with us on the frozen field of battle.

It didn't last, though. After two periods of play, the scoreboard high above read like this through the smoke of free cigarettes and blue Zamboni exhaust:

BUFFALO 27

WOLFS 02

EAT AT JUGS

But we'd scored two goals. Warden Gordon visited the locker room between periods to call us *his boys* and say, "This will indeed look good on your records." We taped our cuts and faced off and began the last period of our season, hell-bent on scoring again.

We did score again, and that is when they brought out the Czech, and our lives as semiprofessional hockey players came to a headlong end.

The Buffalo came out at the beginning of the third period performing crowd-pleasing, boredom-induced stunts like honest-to-God double axles. They also came out checking particularly hard, and, while four Buffalo sat in the penalty box, LeBlanc snuck the puck into their net, bringing on the howling for the third time in our lives.

We'd caught a rumor the week before of a Cheyenne giant everyone thought was a janitor who spoke rough English in grunts and growls, and who caught mice in the rink with his bare hands and skinned them. And of course a reporter asked him what the hell he was doing and he said, "Making a hat." The rumor, apparently, was true. I swear the giant was nine feet tall on skates and five hundred pounds. He stomped out of the Zamboni gate wearing goalie gear—like a dinosaur or a gladiator—but he didn't go to the goal crease.

The Cheyenne crowd went crazy; this would be better than Big Time Wrestling or *Texaco Star Theater* any day of the week. The organist pounded out a very bad "King Porter Stomp" as the giant in skates skated in awkward, taunting circles, flicking his stick like a blackjack while the Wolves on the bench watched with gums showing. A very fit five hundred pounds. He left half-inch-deep troughs in the ice where his skates had been. Our Big Jimmy McGhan didn't seem so big anymore.

And he scored goals. This was mainly because we kept well out of his way. We skated around him, watching our backsides, knowing that one mighty swing of that stick would amputate a limb or land us with the Lord or maybe even somewhere else, depending on other systems of judgment outside of Wyoming State Penal. Lovelock stayed with the net until the very last minute before bailing, but it was shameful what we were letting the Czech do to our pride. Within five minutes of his appearance they scored another ten goals, making the score 37 to 3. This was the score when time ran out on Belecki, and he became a martyr.

The Buffalo paraded in circles behind the Czech when the puck squirted out of the herd and Belecki danced it down the ice and into their net for goal number four. The Czech, in awkward pursuit, let out a grunt that raised the hair on the backs of our necks and checked our Canadian Wolf into the boards with a sickening thud that echoed over the crowd. Belecki just lay there, an unconscious pile of pads and blood, helpless in his white-collar naïveté, and something inside all eleven of us—something natural, but from a place deep and dark and forbidden—snapped.

The Wolves' gate swung open and Liverance stepped onto the ice and calmly walked across the frozen water in his black suit and cowboy boots. Instinctively, we knew where he was headed. The look on his face was peaceful, knowing, as he loosened his tie and unbuttoned his collar. And not even waiting for Jimmy McGhan to call the attack, we all fell upon the Czech, a thread of black and a pack of atomic orange, in what we called in grammar school a dogpile. My hands and fists felt disconnected, working on their own without conscience, directed from that heart of wildness and boiled instinct all of us possessed.

The other Buffalo circled and watched, not daring to get involved, as we pummeled the giant's body and the soon-to-be-exchaplain dribbled his skull against the rink, making a slush like cherry snowcone where it dented the ice and where we spoiled our hopes of this lifetime and very probably the next.

—

A few months later Wyoming went from a black and greasy state to an orange and atomic promised land. They discovered immense uranium deposits in the Bear Lodge area—Devils Tower—and the Uranium Boom was on. Former hockey fans lost interest in oil and took to the hills with picnic lunches and Geiger counters, searching for buried treasure.

Brandall Owens lost the next election to a uranium-fat Republican from Casper, but before leaving the governor's mansion he saw to it as promised that the Wolves left hockey for good, and that all twelve of us were buried so far under the penal system that Armageddon was a damn sight more probable in our lifetimes than parole.

The Cheyenne Atomics played bush-league hockey in the South for a year or so before fizzling.

—

As I near my allotted three-score and ten, I think about the Czech every new day of this life. They say his eight-and-a-half-foot skeleton was displayed in a sideshow that traveled eastern Europe in mule-drawn circus wagons. Though I really don't believe much else, I believe assuredly that when the Wolves fell upon him, he didn't feel a thing. His eyes just glazed over and his soul just flew out and went where all ghosts of animals go.

I read in an old yellowed *National Geographic* that there are no more wolves in Palestine. I read in the *Cheyenne Eagle* that there are no more wolves in Yellowstone.

The book, Pastor Liverance's manuscript, is called *Wolves on Ice: Prison Hockey from the Inside Out*. It's long yellowed, like old teeth, and sits in the corner under a stack of ancient magazines. And every year the parole board refers to the book as "a sad history." This morning at breakfast, between stories I've heard a thousand times about Maurice "the Rocket" Richard, Liverance asked me, Say, did I suppose they still had Oregon boots in Oregon? "I doubt it," I told him. In the spirit of progress they have found something else. Our purses have grown old. We are men.

Albatross

olf for Wayne Kerr was as unnatural as the missionary position. Now, three swings into his pre-season practice session,
bad-back Wayne found himself turtled on the ground, night
coming on, only a mile from home, mercury dropping fast.

At first he didn't feel anything but surprise—his thick down
jacket and store of winter fat had padded his fall. Islands and
berms of dirty spring snow decorated the course: Wayne had fallen
on a half-exposed sand trap. *My God,* he thought, partly joking
with himself, *this isn't what I meant by wanting to die on the beach.*
Pain like a broadhead in the back shot along his spine and down
his left leg when he tried to move. He could lift his head, which
gave him a good view of the north side of his belly and a short
stretch of the willows that lined the Hams Fork River.

He reached for his golf bag, slowly, testing for pain. He'd barely
touched it with the blunt of his mitten when he remembered he
had left the fucking cell phone on the truck seat.

Early confidence turned to cold fear when he realized he couldn't get up. The thermometer at the bank had read thirty-nine degrees on his way by—it might easily drop to below zero after dark. So this is how Custer felt, he thought. Wayne Kerr's Last Stroke. Panicked breaths made dense steam in the air over the artist. His fingers and toes grew numb, a sign that his body had already begun reserving calories to warm his vital organs. First thought: *I can't move.* Then: *Robin knows I'm here because I told her where I was headed. She'll be here shortly. Lord, please before the onset of hypothermia.*

A solo merganser—little bastard of a duck—descended over Wayne on its way to lighting on the newly open river.

April is still winter in Hams Fork; Easter can't arrive without a snowstorm. Below-zero temperatures are normal at night. Spring might happen in May, when townsfolk begin to think about gearing up for the new golf season. Now, capsized on the snow, Wayne's jump on the competition may have cost him his life.

Don't worry about the problem, he thought. *Concentrate on the solution.* He stared at a cloudless sky—sure sign of a cold night. He remembered reading that Tibetan Buddhist monks could, through intense meditation, raise their skin temperature by fifteen degrees. But his mind wandered. He thought of how luxurious, how glorious the cab of a pickup truck with a broken heater would be right now. The turquoise truck, a Chevy Apache, sat three football fields away from Wayne, who, on the edge of paralysis, was afraid to move. He realized how cold his fingertips and toes felt, wiggling them until the blood moved back in, a good sign. He shuddered. "Shivering is good," he mumbled. "Shivering will warm me."

———

Picture a two-horse double-axle trailer full of oil paintings on Masonite. Wayne's newfound popularity had stemmed from his series of murals featuring buxom, topless nymphs doing Western things:

wade-fishing for rainbow trout, riding bareback, mushing a team of huskies into the frozen Wyoming tundra, fly-fishing while mounted on a quarterhorse standing midstream in a braided river, panning for gold, dealing cards, shooting pool, drinking whiskey. Snowboarding. The paintings were a big hit with the professionals—doctors, lawyers, investors, who could relate so strongly with the paintings' siren songs—and saloon owners, who found that the murals, when hung behind the bar and billiards tables, kept the rounds coming almost as fast as Wayne could whip the paintings out.

As is the case with painting, proficiency in golf requires practice. Wayne was not, by breeding or finishing, a golfer; he had other motives that he intended would propel him beyond the imminent ego-demolition derby of the art world. Wayne had always thought the whole idea of donning zany trousers, pink shirts, and studded bowling shoes to graze around an overfertilized lawnscape was silly—pedestrian billiards for day drinkers—but he believed he could push his art on the monied set while researching golf culture from the inside. So just because he didn't know the difference between a baffie and a niblick, why should the only real artist in Hams Fork be woodshedded? After a few preliminary practice sessions he would be ready to participate in the Hams Fork Pro-Am, as well as begin work on the opus that would seal his retirement: a series of life-size, highly authentic topless golfwomen. Only then could he set sail for the world on the boat he was building himself. He would never again return to this ten-cent town and thirty-below winters.

Wayne had left the new Foot Joys at home and laced up his weathered Sorel pac boots. *By playing in mittens now*, he reasoned, *think how deft I'll be in golf gloves come June.*

Wayne had long suffered from a chronic bad back. He had thrown it out lifting heavy compressed-air tanks for his portable airbrush. Wayne approached painting with the savvy of the best insurance adjustors—gotta be in the field when the hurricane hits.

He hadn't counted on being in the field all night long, nightfall, and bitter arrows of cold.

"Just a few swings," he had told his wife, Robin, a bird-watcher and dog-lover and math teacher by nature. "An hour of uncoordinated slogging to knock off the rust."

When Wayne hadn't returned home well after dinnertime, Robin took this to mean he would be closing down the Dry Cow or the 189 or the Location, and as she had to get up at dawn to prepare to teach middle-schoolers how to be people, she fell asleep and wouldn't miss the ruptured artist until morning, then not until after her second cup of coffee.

Wayne kept his eyes snaked downward, watching the frost build in tiny crystalline sculptures on his beard.

"Hello! Hello! Over here!" he shouted. Then, weakly, "Help." He knew his voice didn't reach as far as the highway, or even to the Hams Fork River that ran along the west edge of the course.

Wayne tried propelling himself with his heels, like a boat, but moved only a quarter inch with each kick, and each kick caused his pants to pull back in cruel proportion. The pain ripped down his back and into his left leg, which ceased to kick. The artist's capillaries, now dilated with exercise, transported the heat to his skin. Wayne's sweat-soaked cotton underwear, flannel shirt, and cotton sweatpants pulled at his core heat and quickly dispensed it into the evening air like a truck radiator. A cold burn marked the spot where his bare maximus touched snow. Sharp pain cut at his wrists where his cuffs didn't quite reach his mittens. Now the spasm in his back—the ruptured disk swollen like a wet horsehide baseball—wouldn't allow him any more movement than to touch his nose with his fingertip like a stopped drunk driver. He missed his nose on the first try in the numbing cold and poked himself in the eye.

Full-blown night had fallen on the Hams Fork Valley. The Hale-Bopp comet loomed overhead in the northwest. So dark, so very dark, the light of the comet was brilliant—Wayne could clearly see the comet's vapor trail. To him it resembled a submerged Alka-Seltzer.

A bark in the far distance. They found him. It was Pete. Lily couldn't be far behind. "Get help!" Wayne yelled, slowly rolling his head in their direction. They had seen Wayne's truck, tailgate down, and were now both happily dancing around the bed. Wayne could just make out their furry movements in the security light of the clubhouse parking lot.

—

Wayne had obtained the dogs, curs mixed with a little Border collie, a little Norwegian elkhound, quite a little something else, when Robin's mother in Idaho had moved from the acreage to a facility in town. Wayne kept food and water for the dogs at first, but, over Robin's protests, gradually allowed them to set their own boundaries because, as a painter, he had better things to do than shovel dog shit, even though Robin did all of the scooping. "This is open-range Wyoming," he said. "Besides, fencing is inhumane."

Some days, when he walked from the IGA parking lot to his pickup, the dogs would spot him and light out for their favorite artist. Wayne would hobble, arms loaded with grocery sacks, to the truck, start the engine, and speed home, the brace of dogs in hot pursuit. At the gas station he'd call, "Lily! Pete! How in heaven are my dogs!" then spin gravel on his way to canine-free 714 Cedar Street.

Sometimes the dogs would follow him all the way home, where Robin spoiled them with hot dogs and elk jerky—Wayne's private stash—but most often they got distracted by other dogs or wild animals along the way—mice, rabbits, deer, ticks, worms. Folks in town, dog lovers, often fed them, and better than Wayne Kerr ever did with his hard off-brand kibble. The dogs had seen Wayne on his way to the golf course but a stunned mule doe ran in front of them and through the bank parking lot and Wayne was forgotten. What he saved in dog food was now costing him dearly.

—

Wayne didn't know that his core temperature had lowered to ninety-seven degrees. The muscles of his upper back, shoulders, and neck had contracted in what researchers call pre-shivering muscle tone.

He tried to meditate. His mind went to a dream state. He reminded himself that he couldn't sleep, for sleep would result in death. Death would come in the form of warmth, he knew. Wayne was cold to the bone, but cold meant he was still alive, now thankful for the excess body fat he carried. He imagined a New York gallery premiere, a showing wherein he walked, decked in black tie and tails, from painting to painting, one glorious and divine explosion of color to the next, gently spilling champagne from the crystal glass in his palm to the golden carpet, an offering to the gods of inspiration and success. Standing on the carpet were hundreds of polished dress shoes with tassels—art enthusiasts!

"So it wouldn't be lack of a model that would keep me from painting the best work of my life," Wayne mumbled through his frozen beard. *Golf. Golf will keep me from leaving my mark. And no honorable Grim Reaper—just a visit on the links from Jack Frost himself, half a mile from the IGA parking lot. This is the artistic equivalent of coitus interruptus—only to have back all that time wasted in bed!*

Why didn't I bring my cell phone? He remembered reading of a mountaineer who froze to death near the summit of Mount Everest. There was a fierce storm and the man had little hope of being rescued, but he pulled out his cell phone and called his wife and told her good night before he died. Everything was about satellites.

The cell phone sat on the seat of the Apache, now guarded by two sleeping dogs. Instead of putting the phone in the golf bag like

so many dentists and CPAs, he had slipped two Wyoming bagels—
Pabst Blue Ribbons—into the side pocket where his cell phone
wasn't: dinner.

Half the beer ran through his beard, temporarily thawing some
of the ice, then refreezing yellow hoar. Though the beer was cold,
desperate respiration had left Wayne feeling dehydrated. The
alcohol warmed him temporarily, but he knew the beer would eventually work against him, throwing a monkey wrench at his hypo-
thalamus, his thermostat gone haywire. The cold that he felt on his
skin would soon settle in his core. In the dead silence of the night,
he could hear the hard slosh of liquid down his throat, the pumping of blood in his ears. He no longer felt the pain in his back.

Wayne needed, while he still had some of his faculties, to write his
will. From his jacket pocket he produced a three-inch score pencil
that read *Eat at Luigi's* in tiny letters and two wadded dollar bills—
they would have to work. Everything to Robin. Everything. He
gripped the pencil like a chisel, the dollar bills unfolded flat against
his mittened right palm. She was good enough for his last donation.

He carefully carved the message with the pencil, concentrating
on each letter like the lines of a painting, and resting between
words:

> MAY   YOU MARRY
> SOMEONE
>   WHO APPRECIATES WHAT
> YOU   HAVE TO
> OFFER. SORRY I
> DIDN'T.   EVERYTHING
> IS YOURS.
>   LOVE
> ANYWAY,
>
> WAYNE

Wayne thought about the will for a long time. Here the artist would view his life like a mural. He had been what he thought of as happy—nothing like forced reflection and bleak prospects to show your life really isn't as great as it seems. There was the temptation to informally will something lewd, a frozen body part, to the Mormon church, the Baptists maybe, but now they were the warm ones in their glowing chapels, and what if such a gesture was the straw that kept him out of one of their heavens? Lying on his back in the snow, Wayne felt only envy toward them, no rancor. He wadded the bills and painfully shoved them back in his pocket.

Fifteen minutes later he pissed his pants.

Wayne didn't understand the physiology of what was happening. For an hour he had been in the temperature range which renders the enzymes in your brain sluggish and inefficient. To Wayne it seemed like alcohol, but without the beautiful warmth that went with it. Wayne's cerebral metabolic rate now fell 4 percent with every one-degree drop in body temperature. Amnesia would come when his core temperature dropped to ninety-three—good thing the will was finished.

Blood thick as cold olive oil. His oxygen intake had fallen off. Arrhythmic heart. Hallucinations.

One foot in the Mead Hall and Grendel is about to rip the frozen meat from my bones. Heavy breathing. The Donner Party? No. Horses. The mighty Seventh Cavalry has arrived! Corporal, get this man some blankets and build a fire. We'll break here for coffee.

Real hypothermia. Just before total loss of consciousness, Wayne felt an intense heat. The constricted blood vessels near his body's surface dilated suddenly, producing the sensation of burning skin. *Not too close to the fire, Corporal, careful!*

Wayne threw off his mittens and tore at his down coat. He unzipped it and began to unbutton his flannel shirt, but his plastic fingers were so stiff he could only rip the buttons off. Legs on fire, he tried kicking at his sweatpants, the snow, sweat, and piss frozen stiff hours ago, but his back wouldn't allow it. Burning to death, Wayne screamed a banshee scream.

Dead silence.

He watched the breath of scream rise and vaporize in the night air. Was he dreaming? Was this hell? A test before heaven? In a way, this exposure was more like painting than anything else he'd experienced. Wayne had created the situation for himself, a universe of his own making. He would suffer through this canvas of elements, then seal the experience with a signature. Years ago, when Wayne's painting had been real, paintings would sometimes take him in, shake and threaten him, but always throw him back, which was a relief—and often enough to keep him from painting again for months at a time. This time the signature would be the county coroner's.

Wayne, sure now he heard heavy breathing and footfalls, tried to muster up all his attention and focus on reality for just a few seconds. A brief period of lucidity. Yes, very real breathing and running.

The dogs drew up on top of Wayne and, taking turns standing on their master, commenced to lick the frost, frozen spittle, beer, and snot from Wayne's beard.

Pete brought a mouse and dropped it on Wayne's chin, an offering of food as genuine and generous as anything ever given to Wayne. The dogs circled and pawed the artist in his down coat, now ripped. Tiny goose feathers floated in the air. To a would-be rescuer it might have appeared the dogs had happened upon a giant pigeon.

The dogs settled in, one on each side atop their master. Wayne lay there staring out the round hole his hood made against the night sky. He could see the comet between the dogs' muzzles, Hale-Bopp, and its vapor trail. Mars was brighter than it would be for the next several centuries. Orion, virile as ever, three stars in his belt. Venus, close to the morning horizon. *I could paint her,* thought Wayne. *I could have her in my studio and paint her.* The Big Dipper might have been full of hot coffee, the Little Dipper a splash of Jim Beam.

Now a kind of numb peace eased him into sleep, remembering how Custer's dogs kept the Indian fighter warm on high plains winter nights. At times Wayne would wake, but just long enough to tell himself he was alive, beating back the black wolf of hypothermia that would have eaten a skinny man hours ago. He could feel the canine heat from both sides. If he got hungry enough he had a mouse, which he clutched like a teddy bear against his chest.

Wayne, bourbon-warm through his core, fell asleep hard and slept through the coldest hour, early morning, just before dawn. He slept through the bread trucks grinding up 189 and out of the Hams Fork Valley. He slept past the shift change at the coal mine, when a steady convoy of pickup trucks and old cars whine up and down the highway and cross the river at the bridge just below the golf course. He slept through the spring morning song of tough Wyoming robins. Eyes closed, he slept through the warming sun, his bodyguards pressed close as the subtle heat reached the three of them from ninety-two million miles away and cast a small shadow on the sand and snow behind them, behind the dogs and still-life mound of Wayne.

ABOUT THE AUTHOR

JON BILLMAN has worked as a wildland firefighter and seventh-grade teacher. He is now at work on a novel. He lives in Kemmerer, Wyoming.

ABOUT THE TYPE

This book was set in Fairfield, the first typeface from
the hand of the distinguished American artist and engraver Rudolph Ruzicka (1883–1978). Rudolph Ruzicka was born in Bohemia and came to America in
1894. He set up his own shop, devoted to wood engraving and printing, in New York in 1913 after a
varied career working as a wood engraver, in photo-
engraving and banknote printing plants, and as an art
director and freelance artist. He designed and illus-
trated many books, and was the creator of a consider-
able list of individual prints—wood engravings, line
engravings on copper, and aquatints.

Printed in the United States
by Baker & Taylor Publisher Services